Johnny Moonbeam in Cyberspace

a novel

by

Thomas Guy Kimpel

Mallard Multimedia

4216 N Verde Street
Tacoma, Washington 98407

ISBN 978-0-9885356-1-9

Printed in USA

For my wife Lee, whose tireless efforts and dedication as a child advocate and child psychiatrist has made, and continues to make, a positive difference in the lives of so many young people.

Shirley, Marc, Travis & Susannah –

One @ a time, no fighting now,

Enjoy!

P.S. - check out www.johnnymoonbeam.com

Prologue: Stormy Weather

JOHNNY MOONBEAM LOVED TORNADOES. He loved the thunderstorms that spawned them. The way a single lightning bolt lit up the whole sky, crisp, booming thunder, so close it made the house rattle, and the wind as it screamed across the landscape, plundering everything in its path, were tonic for the boy's soul. There was nothing unusual about this. And yet, in Johnny's case there was more to it. What truly captivated his heart, and what he envied beyond anything else about these atmospheric demigods was this: they were absolutely, undeniably, free. Freer even than the king of the jungle, because a lion could still be captured and caged. Like Johnny.

Even as a baby Johnny liked stormy weather. A colicky infant, he would scream for hours, inconsolably. The only thing that seemed to settle him was, as his father put it, "Give the little son-of-a-bitch a good thunderstorm, and he sleeps, well, like a baby." However, at six feet, one and a half inches tall, and one hundred and eighty pounds, Johnny Moonbeam was no baby. He was almost fifteen years old. Sleeping was no longer an issue, and he didn't scream anymore—though there were times he still wanted to.

Johnny had lived through hundreds of thunderstorms—growing-up in central Indiana as he did, they were an unavoidable part of life. And yet, as much as he still enjoyed them, he longed for something more. It was time to move on, a natural progression as far as he was concerned. Johnny Moonbeam wanted to experience a tornado. He ached to see one with his own eyes, up-close and personal. As a charter member of cyclone alley, there was no shortage of tornadoes in the Hoosier state. Watching them, however, was a bit trickier. Still, Johnny knew it could be done. He'd seen the videos on The Storm Chasers website, and figured *if they can do it, then so can I.*

*****

The sky was black and sirens screaming in Mystic Indiana, a small town just north of Indianapolis. The wind picked up, now blowing with purpose as the torrential rain came down sideways in large sheets mixed with hail the size of marbles. Save for an occasional flash of lightning, the power outage encompassing most of Central Indiana left the day darker than night.

The citizens of Mystic had long since retreated to the safety of their basements, but they were not afraid. Having lived through so many tornado warnings, they could no longer sense the danger. They did, however, continue to accept it as fact and held on to their respect for it. Some played cards or read by candlelight. Some engaged in activities such as ping-pong, or if they were lucky enough to have a table, shot a game of pool. Most just shot the shit. And when there was nothing left to say they sat in the dark silence, hypnotized, waiting for the storm to pass and return to the heavens, or move on to the next town.

The sidewalks and streets and parks and yards of Mystic were empty. Even the pets were taken inside to ride the storm out. There were no golfers on Mystic's famed and usually packed Crooked Creek Golf Course that afternoon. Even the most ardent and stubborn linksman knew it was foolish to argue with an angry Mother Nature. So they picked up their clubs and headed for cover.

The golf course, however, was not entirely empty. Atop the man-made mound of grass guarding Crooked Creek's famous fifth hole stood fourteen-year-old Johnny Abel, hands held high above his head as if victorious. Like everyone else in Mystic Johnny was waiting out the storm, anxious to see what it was going to do. Everyone in their right mind hoped the storm would pass through uneventfully, as it had so many times before. Not Johnny. He was hoping the huge storm cell racing straight towards him, and the Crooked Creek Golf Course would give birth to a tornado. This was going to be the day. In every nerve of his young body, he could feel it. As he waited there atop the grassy knoll, it occurred to him that, *Johnny Moonbeam is no ordinary storm chaser. He's a storm rider*. Johnny no longer wanted just to see a tornado. He hoped it would pick him up and carry him away, because anywhere it might drop him would be better than being in Mystic.

"YESSSSSS!" he screamed when he saw the tail of a young funnel cloud descending from the cell. It was right on track. Johnny's long unrequited lust to witness nature's most violent spectacle was about to be satisfied.

And with it, the hope of a free ride out of Mystic.

*****

On another May afternoon, when Mystic wasn't shrouded in stormy darkness, had Johnny looked up from where he stood on Crooked Creak's fifth hole, he might have seen a jet passing overhead, dipping a wing. Inside, the pilot would be waving to the golfers and pointing out the site of next year's U.S. Open to his passengers.

*****

Earlier that day . . .

The gate attendant took Lisa's ticket and paused. "You look familiar," she said. A few awkward seconds of silence followed as the two women assessed each other. "Should I . . . know who you are?"

"You must be mistaken," Lisa answered curtly.

"Hey, let's keep it moving up there," said a man from back in the line.

Reluctantly, then, the attendant scanned the ticket and handed it back. "Have a nice flight," she said, and waved Lisa on her way.

Renowned child rights advocate Lisa Johnson, Time Magazine's current Person of the Year, had braved many-a-battle on her meteoric rise to the top, smashing glass ceiling after glass ceiling in the process. But nothing in the twenty-nine-year-old attorney's life had ever been as difficult or frightening as what she was about to do. The one-hour flight from Chicago's O'Hare field would take her back home to Indianapolis—for the first time since she'd run away at the age of fourteen. The air around her turned cold and time tumbled out of control. Each step down the jetway to Flight 428 was like walking against a surging tide.

Lisa always took a window seat but just then, looking down on Indiana's checkered landscape of never-ending cornfields laid out in perfect rectangles unveiling below her, she wished she'd been in the luggage hold like a cat, drugged and oblivious to her surroundings.

The first leg of her journey, from San Francisco International to Chicago's O'Hare Field had gone well. Between working on her laptop and the in-flight movie, she was distracted enough to keep the unwanted memories at bay. Now on the second leg of her journey, O'Hare to Indianapolis International, she was reminded of everything she ever wanted to forget. A favorite song from childhood, Back Home Again in Indiana, began playing in her mind.

Back home again in Indiana
And it seems that I can sing

She could hear Jim Neighbors singing it at the Indianapolis 500 as if she were there.

The gleaming candle light still shining bright
Through the Sycamores for me

Except she couldn't turn it off.

When I dream about the moonlight on the Wabash
Then I long for my Indiana home.

The voice in her head grew louder, and took on a haunting lilt, taunting Lisa until her usually impeccable logic became a tempest, raging out of control. Inside her Library-of-Congress-like mind, room after room after floor after floor of perfectly cataloged files were ripped from their shelving. Shredded beyond repair, the unbound fragments were caught up in the firestorm, uselessly flitting about like so many pieces of dust in a whirlwind.

"Stop! Stop! Stop!" She screamed, not realizing she said this out loud until the two hundred eyes glaring at her assured her that, indeed, she had.

"Are you okay," asked several flight attendants, almost in unison?

Lisa looked at them dumbfounded. Had she been given the option of jumping out of the plane right then and there, she would've gladly seized the opportunity. Instead, all she could do was stay in her seat, humiliated and terrified at the same time. "Sorry, I'll be okay," she lied, then closed her eyes and drifted off to sleep even as her tears kept falling.

Lisa dreamt. In the Cineplex of her mind, she is watching herself star in a drama loosely based on Shakespeare's Hamlet. Terrified, she wants to get up but the fasten seat belt sign flashes blood-red, and she is forced to stay securely strapped into her seat. When she looks up at the screen, young Hamlet, pointing his poisoned rapier right at her, says:

Get thee to a nunn'ry,
Get thee to a nunn'ry now!

*****

Several hours later . . .

For two hours, rain and hail and wind came and went as Johnny stood and waited atop the man-made mound of grass behind the fifth hole. Leaning into the fray, and looking half mad, half noble, he swayed only occasionally as he fought the elements. The clouds grew darker and denser, eventually forming an anvil-shaped mass. The Supercell looked just like the pictures he'd seen, and studied so hard. "Come on, do it!" he yelled, and then, "Yes!" a couple of minutes later when he saw the first funnel drop down. It lasted a few seconds and dissipated. "Come on." Then another dropped down, and another until finally one persisted. It couldn't have been more than a mile or two away at that point, dangling from the darkness and moving fast.

Johnny watched the now well formed funnel drop to earth, twisting and turning like a rope ladder hanging in the breeze. It touched down somewhere on the other side of the seventeenth fairway, pulled and sucked and filled itself up with dirt and sod and all manners of debris. Then like a two-year-old in a tantrum, spat out what it didn't like. The sight of this tornado was beautiful and dangerous and awesome and terrible all at once as it danced its way across the fairways, swerving left and right yet staying on course for the fifth green.

And then, there it was, just across the green from where Johnny stood, roaring like a freight train. The air was full of sod and benches and yellow sticks with their green flags torn and tattered and hanging by a thread among the other debris. Golf balls twirling around in a blur at two hundred miles-per-hour trailed long tails behind them, and Johnny realized the twister was on him. There was no time to wonder what this magic funnel ride might feel like as it lifted Johnny off the ground, and swept him away.

*****

The next day . . .

Lisa had not been to confession in over fifteen years. She had the option of doing it face-to-face with the priest. *No thank-you.* Just the thought of that made her wince. When your face has been on the cover of Time magazine, anonymity is a good thing. It would be hard enough this way. She stepped up to the confessional and waited before the red curtain, heart pounding in her chest. The air felt too heavy to breathe. Running was still a viable option. No. She stepped inside. A screen separated her from Father Thomas as she knelt down and crossed herself. “Bless me, Father, for I have sinned,” she said, her voice crackly and barely audible. “It has been fifteen years since my last confession.” And then nothing.

Having detected the obvious, that this parishioner had forgotten what to say next, Father Thomas helped her, something he did on occasion. “‘Fifteen years since my last confession, and I accuse myself of the following sins’ is what we usually say next.”

“And I accuse myself of the following sins,” she said then stopped again. This was worse than she imagined. The priest waited. Lisa tried to swallow, but there was nothing. Despite her best efforts to maintain composure, she started to cry. She, Lisa Johnson, unflappable attorney, mistress of control, was coming unhinged.

“There is nothing so bad that you cannot be forgiven. You are safe here. You can tell me anything, no matter how difficult it seems. If you can confess what you need to, then you’re going to feel better. God will forgive you.”

She took in deep breath and regrouped. “I accuse myself of the following sin.” The priest waited for her to continue. She needed to say it out loud, words she had never spoken, words held captive inside of her for fourteen years. She didn’t know if she could. It seemed to take forever, and then, without permission, as if by a will of their own, the words left her mouth. She tried to pull them back but was too late. Her secret had escaped. The voice—her voice—was clear and strong and seemed totally foreign. “Father,” she said, “I threw away my baby.”

Chapter 1: The Morning After

THE VIDEO WAS VIRAL before Johnny even woke up. The footage, taken from a snack-bar security camera between Crooked Creek's fifth and sixth holes, showed the twister dancing across the golf course and then, somewhere behind the fifth green, picking up a young boy and carrying him away. In addition to a record number of hits on the internet, pictures and clips from the video appeared in newspapers and on television across the country. Within a day, who "The mystery boy from Mystic" was, became a national obsession, and then, just about as fast, the story faded from the front pages and was all but forgotten. The boy was never identified. Most people, if they thought about it at all, presumed he'd been shredded to oblivion, dead and unidentifiable. Others thought it was some kind of hoax, or optical illusion. No one thought he survived.

They were wrong.

Three-hundred-yards southeast of the Crooked Creek Golf Course, the twister adopted a no passengers policy and discharged its lone patron into the darkness. The boy ended up in the middle of a freshly poured concrete foundation filled to the brim with rolls of pink insulation. It was a soft landing to be sure, but the ride, short as it was, had been more than a little rough. By the time Johnny came to the next day, the sun was high and he felt like an NFL running back on Monday morning—with the added pleasure of having played on a field of poison ivy. The itching was dreadful. Not to mention the ten wide-eyed Pink Panthers glaring at him, tongues wagging. He tried to run, but when he stood up his brain went all fuzzy and dizzy, and he fell back into the fluff. When he woke up an hour later, the panthers had slinked away, merging back with their respective rolls of insulation, harmless as pictures. And he realized: *they are pictures,* and *I am alive.* This time he waited a few minutes before trying to get up. He took it slow and easy, looking at the ground as he gradually rose up to his full height. He waited. The dizziness was gone, so he lifted his head up and looked around. For just a beat, it felt like he was falling again, that he wasn't as steady as he thought. Then Johnny understood. This time, it wasn't him. The world was out of kilter.

Storm-felled fences lay in twisted sheets, spiraling down lot-lines like strands of DNA; trees, uprooted, and carried along for two and three hundred feet or more, had been cast aside; shingles littered the landscape like confetti. At one point, he saw a winged, pastel-colored cartoon-creature—the bottom of a child's plastic swimming pool—hanging in the broken branches of an old oak, peering out as if from some exotic bird's nest. It looked like a scene straight off the page of one of those Dr. Seuss books.

Across the street was total devastation. Instead of million-dollar estates with fancy gardens and expensive cars, were piles of rubble. In the midst of the destruction, he found the occasional oddity of something left eerily whole, such as a lone door or window frame. In one yard, a birdbath remained intact, the little stone boy still peeing water into its basin as if nothing had happened. The house, not twenty feet behind, was shredded to toothpicks save for a naked staircase rising up four stories out of the rubble. A stairway to heaven. A brand-new SUV was in its usual place in a driveway, except now it was upside down, as flat as Johnny's NASA mouse pad.

He might have kept walking and gawking indefinitely had he not heard a faint whimpering sound coming up from the rubble. He stopped. "Aroooooooo," it came again, this time a bit louder, a half-howl-half-cry. Johnny recognized the sound at once.

"Barney, where are you?"

"Arooooarooowwwarooowwwooowwoo."

"I'm coming, old boy, hang on."

Barney, a twenty-eight-year-old Bassett Hound—that's 125 dog-years—belonged to Henry Mayfield, his seventy-eight-year-old faithful human. They were one of those adorable pet-owner look-alike pairs, both with huge, floppy ears and jowls hanging down to the sidewalk, flapping in the breeze as they teetered their way through the neighborhood. Johnny and Barney were well acquainted. The boy had never actually met Henry, leastwise not in a face-to-face, how-do-you-do-kind of a way. Still, because his father, Jack Abel, and Henry were good friends, he felt like he knew the old man. Johnny often eavesdropped on their conversations. Henry was part of the world outside of 4217 Mystic Lane—a place as foreign to Johnny as Mars—and the boy liked hearing the old man talk. But the chit-chat only bored Barney, and, instead of hanging with Henry, who generally ignored him at these times, the cagey hound would sniff out the boy to play with, and the two had become fast friends.

Johnny carefully extricated the hound. "Are you okay, boy?" Barney barked his thanks then hobbled off, looking and sniffing until he found a nice puddle of water. Johnny laughed, watching, while Barney slurped the liquid with his huge hound-dog tongue.

"It's sure good to see you," said Johnny, dusting off his friend and scratching behind his huge ears. "You're the only person I know outside of home," He paused for a moment and laughed. "Even if you are just a dog." Barney, panting happily, water dripping off his shiny, wet tongue, was apparently done with the drink. "Man, I bet you're hungry too. Come on now, let's go." Johnny started walking towards Henry's house. Barney did not follow the boy. Instead, he looked up, his big, brown eyes pleading. "Oh, so you want to be carried? Well, I guess you probably are exhausted from being outside all night."

"Rark."

"Okay, here we go." Johnny, who was still plenty sore, bent down wincing and put his hands under Barney's belly, prepared to scoop him up. "Damn," he said, double clutching, "I never realized you were so big." He grunted and tried again. This time he picked the dog all the way up. "You are one heavy old hound dog."

"Rark, rark." Johnny wasn't sure if dogs could grin, but right then it looked like Barney was. The hound seemed quite pleased with himself.

As slow as Johnny was moving it was still only a five-minute walk. A note on the front door said to please go inside and give Henry a call if you had any news about Barney's whereabouts. Because the land lines were down, he'd left a cell phone on the kitchen table along with a number where he could be reached. Johnny hesitated. He wasn't used to walking into someone else's house. In fact, as far as he knew, outside of emergency room visits, he'd never been outside of 4217 Mystic Lane. Until yesterday. Even then, he'd only managed to escape by decking his father. He recalled the feel of his fist smashing into Jack's jaw. For all the countless beatings Johnny had taken in his young life, it was the first time he'd ever fought back. It felt good. *I'll have to do that more often.* Then his smile faded. When Johnny got home today there would be hell to pay. Jack would be ready for him, and Johnny was too tired and too weak to do much about it. He considered not going home at all, but then looked at himself. His clothes were torn and grungy. He had no money. *No nothing. Next time,* he thought, *I'll have to plan better,* which would be easy enough, because this time he hadn't planned anything. It had all been spontaneous. He'd only wanted to go outside, to see . . .

"Rark, rark!" Barney, who apparently had a definite and immediate plan for what he wanted to do, began pawing at the door. "Rark, rark, rark!"

"Oh, right. Sorry about that, boy. I must have drifted off. Okay, let's do this." Johnny opened the door. Barney made a bee-line for the kitchen and picked up his doggie-bowl. The boy filled it with some kibble then paused, trying to decide whether or not to have a look around. *I'm already inside,* he reasoned, and *Henry is famous*. What could it hurt? Henry "Coach" Mayfield was indeed a celebrity. Of sorts: the winningest basketball coach ever in the state of Indiana. His major claim-to-fame happened in 1963 when he led the Mystic Marvels to a state championship—quite an accomplishment with only sixteen boys in that year's senior class. Johnny tiptoed through the living room, down a short hall where he peeked in the two bedrooms, and then circled back to the kitchen. He was disappointed. The air was stuffy and a bit sour smelling. The decor looked like something off the set of a 1950's rerun. It was not what he'd envisioned a celebrity's house to look like. Johnny shook his head then picked the phone up off the table and dialed the number.

"Hello, Coach here."

"Ah, hello. I'm here in your house. I found your dog."

"Is he alright?"

"A little dusty, and hungry, but, yeah, he's fine."

"Where'd you find him?

"He was buried under a bunch of trash, so I dug him out and carried him home.

"Thank God, and thank you, too. I can't tell you how much this means to me."

"No problem, I'm just glad Barney's alright."

"You know him?"

"Ah, not until just now."

"It kind-a sounded like you might have-"

"No. Anyway, I'd better go."

"Wait a second. If you don't know him, then how'd you know his name? or where to bring him?"

Johnny hesitated, "Ah . . . a man . . ." Think quick Johnny Moonbeam. "Right, an elderly man, bald, with big bushy white eyebrows, he told me."

"Hmm. Could be Jimmy Jacobs, I guess. Well, all right then, but at least tell me who you are and where you're from.

"I'm Johnny," he said, catching himself just in time before the Abel came out, and he turned it into a throat clearing. "Excuse me. Anyway, like I was saying, my name is Johnny, and I'm from . . . Broad Ripple."

"Well thanks, Johnny from Broad Ripple. I'd like to give you some kind of reward."

"That's all right. I don't need anything."

"Why don't you just hold on young man. I'd like to thank you personally for finding my dog. Tell you what. I'll pick us up a pizza on the way home. What kind do you like?"

"Ah, that's all right," said Johnny, even though pizza sounded mighty good. "I have to be getting home."

"Oh, is someone there to pick you up already or something? I'd be glad to take you home myself when I get there."

"It's not that far, I'll just walk."

"Not far? I thought you said you was from Broad Ripple?"

Oops, think fast Johnny Moonbeam. "Ah, well, I mean it's not a far walk to the bus stop." *Anyway, I hope it's not that far*.

"Well, I guess if you got to go you got to go. But I sure would like to meet you. It may sound funny to a young boy like you, but, since the wife passed away a couple of years ago, that dog means everything to me.

Johnny wanted to tell him who he really was, that he

lived just around the corner and had lived there for nearly fifteen years. But something told him that maybe this wasn't the right time. Although Henry was Jack's friend, Johnny thought he was a good person. It would probably be all right to tell him, but still, it was something he needed to think about first.

"Oh, it's no big deal. I'm just glad you have your dog back."

"Well it sure was to me, young man. Thank you again, and would you mind writin' down your name and leavin' it on the table. If there's ever anything, and I mean anything, I can do for you, you just let me know."

"Well, bye," said Johnny, and at the bottom of Henry's note, he drew a picture of a rocket with a word balloon stemming from the cockpit. Inside the balloon, he wrote Johnny Moonbeam was here, and then headed for home—where the biggest surprise of Johnny's life awaited him.

Chapter 2: Mary Valentine

INDIANAPOLIS' J B STERLING High School was located on the south side. Because it was in part a magnet school for the arts, its students came from all over the city. Which explained why fifteen-year-old sophomore Mary Valentine, who resided in a less prosperous neighborhood on Indy's east side, could attend such an uppity school. And why she was about as welcome as a Hawaiian shirt at a funeral. No matter, the girl could hold her own. She'd just been called out of history class. Again. She took her time, daydreaming, slowly winding her way through the empty corridors, and then abruptly stopped a few feet outside the outer office of the Vice Principal. Mary pulled herself up into a ram-rod straight posture, adjusted her hair and stuck a wad of chewing gum under the fire extinguisher, then sauntered into the office holding out a pink slip as if it were a medal of honor. The receptionist plucked it from the girl's hand, pinching it between thumb and forefinger as if it might be infectious, then gestured for the girl to sit and waddled over to the main office where Ed Cunningham looked up and frowned. "Guess who?" she said, waving the slip.

"Send her in."

Mary marched in like she owned the place and, without looking, plucked the slip from the woman's plump fingers and handed it over to the vice principal. He looked at the note. "I thought I just took that thing away from you."

"No, you took my blue iPod. This one is white, see?"

"Mary," he sighed, "how does someone on both the school breakfast and lunch programs afford not just one, but two iPods?" She shrugged, as if to say, who knows? "May I see it?" She pouted. He waited. Eventually, Mary slapped the iPod onto his upturned palm. He turned it over and around, examining it. "This is interesting."

"What?"

"There appears to be a name engraved here, Andrew M. Smith. Why is that?"

"Beats me."

Ed was tired. He'd been down this road with her before and decided it wasn't worth it. "You can go now," he said, "but I don't want to see you back here again today. If I do-" Mary cut him off.

"Hey, like, it wasn't my idea to come here in the first place."

"Just go."

"What about my iPod?" He gave her a look that said don't mess with me then curled his fingers around the electronic device and pocketed it. "Like, okay, just chill."

The bell rang as Mary made her way back down the hallway. Fourth period, lunch, so she headed to the cafeteria. If not for the food, she wouldn't go there at all, but hey, a girl has to eat something. The only thing in the fridge at home was beer. She went through the line and was about to sit down when Jason Michaels, All-City middle linebacker and All-state jerk, bumped into her. On purpose. *Moron.*

"That looks yummy. What is it?"

Mary tried to ignore him and his big-as-a-house sack lunch, hoping he'd go away, but he didn't.

"Hey, how's your new stepdad? What's his name, Dave? Oh no, that was two stepdads ago, this one's Brad, right?"

"Why yo-" she said, about to let go a string of curses, when a group of cheerleaders flocked to Jason and gathered around him. Mary regrouped and flashed him a smile. "Why thanks for asking, and yes Jason, his name is Brad. He's doing fine." A brief pause for effect and then, leaning into him, she added, "Oh, and, by the way, how's your syphilis doing? Are you still contagious?" The cheerleaders' eyes grew wide, and they backed away as Jason's face turned beat-red. Mary plucked another iPod from her pocket, this one silver, and put in the ear-buds, hoping this playlist would be better than Smith's. *That dude, like, has no taste at all.*

Jason's fire-truck red face was spewing curses like water from a hydrant. Mary didn't bat an eyelash. She just dug into her garbanzo bean casserole.

Chapter 3: A Surprise for Johnny

JOHNNY'S PARENTS WERE nowhere to be found, either inside or out, at 4217 Mystic Lane. The house was disturbingly quiet. Quieter even than could be explained by the power outage. There was only one place left to look. A place Johnny had never been before. A place he wasn't keen on checking even now, and yet it seemed there was no choice. So he sighed, and gathered up the last driblets of spit from inside his mouth then snapped his head back and forced a swallow. It went down hard and painful, and he wondered why this was necessary in order to bolster one's courage. Still, it was a relief. He'd been standing outside the door so long his feet were about to grow roots. Now, with nothing left to do except move forward, he placed his right hand on the doorknob and gripped it, hard, with what he hoped was unflagging determination, yet, in truth, felt more like shaking-in-your-boots scared. Fourteen, almost fifteen, years and he'd never set foot inside his parents' bedroom. Now he was about to go in uninvited. He gave the knob a gentle twist, moving ever so slow, as if disarming a bomb instead of opening a door. Then he turned it a little more, and waited. He repeated this routine a couple of more times, and then, on the third try, the latch popped, giving way as it cleared the jam. A narrow beam of sunlight shot through the open crack, and spilled into the darkened hallway. Johnny flinched then recovered and gave the door firm push. Hinges creaked as it swung open.

Johnny froze.

He did not believe what he saw. He could not. To believe would be to hope, and hope was bad. As soon as you let it in, it crushed you. The boy understood this all too well and did not wish to repeat the experiment. Leave bad enough alone. Good things were for other people, the ones on TV or in books, not for him. Life was a game of survival, nothing more, nothing less, like being stuck in perpetual battle on World War II's Eastern front. And yet there it was, dangling before him like a worm on a hook. *How? Why?* He wondered, though only for a moment because the answer was as obvious as the belt-striped scars across his back: he was either dreaming or hallucinating. He shook his head, blinked and rubbed his eyes then blinked again and waited. Everything looked the same, so he pinched himself. It didn't hurt, not really, so he still wasn't sure. Then he let go, and his eyes fixed on two crescent-shaped marks where his nails had dug into the smooth flesh of his inner forearm. Surrounding the two dents, a patch of white-blanched skin slowly pinked, and as it did so, reality seeped into his brain. Johnny realized that what he saw was real, and with that, the mystery of the missing parents came to a rapid conclusion. Jack and Jill Abel were laying in their bed, looking as peaceful as Johnny had ever seen them. They were also, most definitely, dead.

Johnny Abel was free, for now anyway, but he knew if anyone found out it would be all over, and he'd be worse off than before. Only later, when he had time to ponder the events of that first day of a new life, did he realize that most fourteen-year-olds would have cried out in anguish, or cried for help, or just cried. He was stunned, naturally, by the sight of his parents' dead bodies, and yet, as soon as the shock wore off, Johnny only wanted to cry out in ecstasy. Many fourteen-year-olds he supposed, would have felt abandoned or broken, but Johnny experienced no such sentiments. Instead, he was overwhelmed with a sense of wonder, like the world was opening up all around him, and he would finally find out how big it was. A normal fourteen-year-old would've certainly called the police or gone to a neighbor for help. For Johnny Abel, however, normal was no more than an abstract concept, one he knew little about. He did know this much: calling the police always makes things worse.

I have to get rid of the bodies. It was the first thought that came to Johnny, once his mind had cleared. He was right, too. There was simply no way around it, for if anyone found out it would be all over. *I'd be worse off than before.* And yet, to see his parents laying there all pink and shiny and...and dead, *well, they are dead, of course,* but still, just the thought of it gave him the heebie-jeebies. To touch them was unthinkable. Then he realized it would take more than a touch. He would have to handle them, pick them up and physically move them. A chill ran straight to his bones, and Johnny quivered like a dog shaking out its coat. Then, just as a healthy panic was about to set in, the electricity kicked in and the house hummed back to life. Until then, it hadn't even occurred to him there was a power outage.

Johnny, not anxious to play the role of undertaker, did what any normal teenage boy might do. He procrastinated. He booted up his PC and logged onto *Battle for the Universe*, a new online, multiplayer game. For the most part, online games bored the boy. They weren't challenging enough. With even the most difficult games Johnny, a computer whiz of gargantuan proportions, would quickly rise to the top of the leader board, so far ahead of the other players it wasn't fun anymore. This one, however, was supposed to be infinitely difficult. Johnny hoped this was true, for he would continue to play it until he was either ranked number-one or became utterly exhausted. To his chagrin, it was not much different from the rest of the games. Two short hours later, atop the list of local rankings, was the name Johnny Moonbeam.

Rats.

Time to get to work...except...maybe I should figure out why they died first. Then he remembered all those television shows where the body was brought in for the coroner to determine the cause of death. *Guess not.*

Rats.

It was definitely time to get started. He entered a Google search for *taking care of dead bodies,* but it came up limp. *Disposing of dead bodies* yielded more information, but it was all medical/ technical/ public health babble. Not helpful. *How would a crook put it?* He typed *getting rid of dead bodies*. Bingo, 340,000 hits, page after page of detailed descriptions of how to dispose of dead bodies. One suggested putting them down the garbage disposal. It sounded good—until he read the part about first having to cut the bodies up into small parts. *No way!* There was also a warning about the bones and meat sometimes clogging up the drains. *Gee, Mr. Plumber, I had no idea it was my parents stopping up the sink. I wonder how that happened.* Another site explained how one could take the bodies out to sea in various states of preparation, such as burning them with acid or fire or chopping them up with a food processor first. *Gross! I don't have a boat, and anyway, Indiana is about as far away from the ocean as you can get.* Burying the bodies was impractical and far too risky. *Besides, someone would probably see me.* Frustration grew as Johnny realized that nearly all the otherwise potentially viable options entailed cutting the bodies up into small parts first. That, he knew, was not going to happen. Still, there had to be a way.

He did a search for preserving dead bodies and spent an hour reading about the mummification process. It wasn't practical, but it killed some time, and it was interesting. He sighed. It was eleven o'clock already. Johnny was hungry. *Maybe I should take a break and grab something to eat.* Then, without even trying, everything clicked into place. Eating meant food. Food led him to freezers. And freezers made him remember the huge deep-freeze in the garage. Jack used it for venison or when he'd buy a whole side of beef—"Cheaper that way." If it could hold a whole deer or half of a cow, why not two lousy parents? It was worth a shot.

The freezer was full, which complicated things a bit. Johnny saved what meat he could fit in the kitchen freezer and the rest he put into heavy-duty trash bags. Later, when it was dark out, he would surreptitiously dump these into the many construction bins in and around that new development next to Mystic Meadows...Laurel Highlands. Now it was time for the main course, moving the bodies to the garage. Johnny thought it was going to be awful. He was wrong.

It was worse.

His first major discovery was as un-nerving as it was surprising: dead people are not quiet. They complain. They make noises. Gross and disgusting sounds like burps, farts, grunts, and sighs. No sooner had Johnny entered the bedroom than a long, sibilant hiss, like the sound of an over-inflated balloon sputtering about, greeted him. He looked up, startled, half expecting to see one squirreling around near the ceiling. Of course, there weren't any. It was Jack. *Nice touch dad.* His parents were especially vociferous when moved. The stairs were the worst. The bodies sort of got ahead of him and went bumping down on their own in a clamoring chorus, like a rogue percussion section. BANG, THUMP, GLUB, GLUB, AHHHOOOW, WHACK, GLORP, BELCH, SCREEECHHH, POP, HISSSS, BURP, GURGLE, SHOOSH, PHFFFT, BUMP,

FART. They leaked, too, all kinds of nasty fluids. Moreover, the smell was putrid; overwhelming. Please! If he thought about these things, he would unravel, so he tried not to. Johnny willed himself to keep moving forward, slow and steady, like a bulldozer. For six long hours, he rolled and wrapped and pushed and shoved until, despite their protestations, he managed to wrap his parents up—first in sheets and blankets, and then in a tarp—and, finally, wedge them into the freezer.

Chapter 4: A Surprise for Mary

THE SILVER IPOD WAS A KEEPER, so Mary hid it where Ed Cunningham could not get his greedy paws on it—in her bra. All it cost was a little stuffing, and even if she told you where it was, you couldn't see it. It was a new model with sixteen gigabytes of music she might just as well have picked out herself. It had to be protected. As soon as school was out she ducked into the girls' room and did a reverse switch, put in the ear-buds, and cranked up the sound.

"Hey, ghetto chick," yelled Jason Michaels, fully recovered from the lunchtime debacle. "Say hi to your new daddy for me when you get home."

Mary did not hear him as she climbed onto the bus, bobbing and weaving to the music. The jeers and catcalls that routinely attended her—"Hoo-we, look at that white meat," and "Hey baby. You can sit on my lap"—also failed to make it past the sound barrier as she zigzagged her way down the aisle, slapping away would be groping hands with uncanny deftness. She took a seat, as always, in the back. Though she appeared lackadaisical and relaxed, on closer inspection one could see her eyes continually scanning the environment, always on guard. Like, a girl can't be too careful.

Mary's eternal vigilance, however, was about to fail her when she needed it most.

Though she would never admit it, especially to Jason Michaels, Mary was profoundly ashamed of where she lived. Unlike the suburban North side of Indianapolis, where Johnny hailed from and the neighborhoods had pretty names and reeked of affluence, Mary lived in a not-so-pleasant section of real estate south of the city. Her neighborhood was nameless and reeked of garbage. Drugs and drug dealers were rampant. Every third or fourth house was a meth lab or boarded up and rotting away. Gangs liked to hang out in Mary's neighborhood, and at least once a week there was some kind of shooting. The cops? If they even came at all, it was too late to be of any use. And so for Mary, who did not like to give herself away, the bus ride home became an exercise in deception and self-control, which, after years of practice, she was quite good at.

This particular day, however, was different. She didn't have to pretend to be okay, she just was. As the bus pulled into her neighborhood, a new playlist came up on her silver iPod: Ke$ha, her favorite. It distracted her from the usual torment of riding through this place she both loathed and had to live in. *I love you dude*, she thought, referring to the iPod's original owner, a tall geeky boy with greasy hair and size fifteen Converses that flapped like a pair of diving fins when he walked. *Who da thunk?*

A few minutes later, she exited the bus through its folded front door and stepped out into the sunshine. *Your Love is My Drug* began to play. "Yes!" she whispered, and, overwhelmed with delight, closed her eyes. For barely any time at all. And yet, it was too long. Brad's truck should have been parked ten miles away in Eli Lilly's employee parking lot. When he did get home, usually about five o'clock, he always parked it in the yard beside the house. On this particular day, however, the reason for which Mary would soon find out, the rules did not hold. At two-thirty, in the afternoon, Brad was home and his rusted-out-Chevy-half-ton pickup was parked, not in the side yard, but down the block across the street. She missed it. On most any other day Mary, with her constant vigilance, would have spotted it. She would have been ready. But not today.

For the most part, Mary despised the ramshackle old house on East 36th Street. When she first got home from school, however, it was almost inviting. For a couple of hours, she would have it all to herself, no yelling, no fighting, no hitting, and no wrestling on TV. It was about the only time she could truly relax and let her guard down. Mary coveted it. She smiled in anticipation of this brief respite from the chaos of her life, and then stopped a moment on the sidewalk, as she always did, to get her bearings. The concrete steps leading to the front door were in such disrepair that, out of context, it would have been difficult to guess what they were. Not a one of them even approximated level anymore. Once she was properly aligned, however, her feet took over, automatically placing themselves on the few remaining navigable regions—to the far left of the first stair, middle of the second, then left again then far right then skipping the fourth one altogether and so on. After safely traversing the last obstacle—a huge crack Mary called the Grand Canyon—she unlocked the front door and ambled inside. She was about to un-sling her backpack when Brad's voice froze her. "You ain't getting' away from me this time, you little slut." Before she could even turn her head, Brad planted a fist squarely in her gut, and she fell to the floor.

*****

Mary came to in her own bed, Brad on top of her. She screamed and fought, digging her sharp claws into the right side of his face just above the eye, and dragging them down his cheek. He grabbed her forearms and pinned them against the bed. "Goddammitall," he said, wincing in pain, "you little bitch, try anything else, and I'll rearrange that pretty face of yours." Mary spat on him and continued to fight, kicking and squirming and writhing for all she was worth.

"Get...off...of...me!"

At first, he laughed, but then Mary started to gain momentum. "Enough already."

"Get...off..." he let go of an arm and slapped her, quick and hard, then pinned her down again.

"That was a warning, little chicklet. You want to keep pushing? Go right ahead." Mary spat in his face and continued to flail. He let go again, this time making a fist and holding it squarely above her nose. She stopped. "That's a good girl."

Inside, Mary was on fire. Almost as bad is the main event was the knowledge she could do nothing about it. She was helpless. There was only one thing worse than that. Then a large teardrop formed on the outside of her right eye and that was it, the worst. Damn. She couldn't even wipe it away. It stayed there for a few agonizing seconds, a swelling meniscus of self-loathing. Then it broke loose. She felt the salty-sting as it rolled and stuttered down the side of her cheek. The real hurt, however, penetrated much deeper. She was humiliated. It would have been easy to wallow away in self-pity. She almost did, but then she rallied and reminded herself how worthless that would be. It would not save her. Willing herself to let go of everything in order to concentrate, Mary pushed down her petty emotions, pushed away the physical pain of Brad inside her, pushed away the shame, pushed away the anger . . . and then she was floating. Thinking. *There's got to be something I can do.*

Brad groaned and pulled himself off her. Mary's body tensed, ready to resume the fight, to jump up and go after him. She would have liked to at least poke an eye out or bite off an ear or something. Mary was no wimp and, armed with ten knife-like nails, a good set of teeth, and a strong right foot she could have done some real damage. Especially given how angry she was. But it only would have made things worse. And so when Brad, hitching up his pants, said, "Don't you move, little girl," she complied. Then he walked away.

She closed her eyes, trying to block him out of her mind. The zip of a zipper made Mary want to puke, but she managed to maintain composure until she heard the sound of footsteps slowly padding away from the bed. *Faster, go faster*. Finally, the door opened.

"And don't even think about tellin' nobody," he said, and then the door closed.

An overwhelming sense of relief washed over her, and Mary allowed her eyes to open again. The tears wanted to come, and so she bit her tongue. She would not break down. There were important issues to deal with. Specifically, two thoughts were spinning around her mind. First, she would never, ever, let this happen again. Second, she was going to get out of this freaking place for good. So, instead of running off half cocked and accomplishing nothing, she focused all that anger and rage, like a laser beam, on how to accomplish these goals. All she needed was a little time. It would take two weeks at least until the beer and whiskey drowned out enough of Brad's shame for him to try again. Plenty of time. Calmly then, Mary straightened her dress, got off the bed, and took the longest, hottest shower of her life.

Chapter 5: Johnny and Buzz

NARY-A-CLOUD HUNG THE SKY over central Indiana on the first full day of Johnny's new life, a life without Jack and Jill. Sitting on the kitchen table, he let his gaze stretch out through the sliding glass doors, beyond the fences and the corn fields, and out to the horizon. Everything looked fresh and exciting from this new vantage point. A nice view, he thought. For nearly 15 years the fierce gravitational pull of his father held him in such a tight orbit, he scarcely knew anything outside of 4217 Mystic Lane. Now Jack was gone and the universe seemed infinite, as it should, with endless possibilities. It was nothing special. He knew that. At least for most people it wouldn't be, but it was for Johnny. It was, in fact, what he'd always wanted: a chance to have a normal life, to be a normal boy. Though he would never have set out to do it this way, it happened and Johnny saw no reason why he shouldn't take full advantage of the situation. He would make the most of it. *Starting right now.*

Clear and focused as a five-year-old on Christmas morning, Johnny threw himself into the task of what amounted to setting up house. He knew in general what needed to be done. He had to get a system in place that would keep the household running smoothly without drawing attention to the fact that his parents were no longer the ones running it. What that involved specifically, he wasn't sure of, but he knew how to find out. With his adept searching skills and high-speed Internet connection, he soon had a list of things to do. Hacking into his father's bank accounts was a piece of cake. Jack had been a thrifty saver, and Johnny quickly figured there was more than enough money to last him at least a year. *Perfect.* Then he was on to the next task: setting up automatic bill paying for the monthly bills—home, car, insurance, gas, electric and so on. He found a yard service that he could pay online with a credit card and never have to lay eyes on. It would be like magic. *This is so cool! You can do just about anything online.* Except, he realized with some urgency, pee. *Guess I'll have to take care of that the old-fashioned way.*

Things continued going smoothly as, one-by-one,

Johnny attended to the long list of administrative tasks he'd compiled. Methodically checking off each item as he finished, Johnny was so focused he worked straight-through lunch and dinner, stopping only because he noticed the night sky outside and a spectacular full moon shining through his window. Two thoughts occurred to him at once. First, when did it get dark out? And second, I NEED FOOD.

Johnny picked up the cordless phone, called *D'Amato's Italian Bistro,* and ordered a large cheese pizza, two liters of Coke, and a pint of chocolate-chip cookie dough. While waiting for the delivery person, he clicked the remote and started surfing through the three-hundred odd channels available for his viewing pleasure. He came to the program guide and looked at some of the titles. The Josh Jargon Show, today's topic: The Oedipus complex: men who kill their father and marry their mother. *The first part I can understand, but the second part is just gross. Geez, you'd think there would be something worth watching.* He abandoned the guide and continued to surf, hoping to find something on one of the channels that would catch his interest. He did, a documentary on The History Channel called *Race to the Moon.* "Awesome," he said, feeling better already.

Twenty minutes later, Neil Armstrong was about to step out of Apollo Eleven's Lunar Module, when there was a knock at the door. As hungry as he was, Johnny did not want to miss this. "Just a minute," he yelled. Neil slowly made his way out of the landing craft and down the ladder. The knocking grew louder and more incessant and just when it seemed that he would have to miss Neil's famous, 'One small step for man. One giant leap for mankind', Johnny was saved by a commercial for ladies' undergarments. "Coming," he said, and ran to the door.

"That'll be $15.23," said the delivery girl.

Johnny counted out the exact change, twenty-three cents in coins and three five-dollar bills—money transferred from his dad's pockets—then handed it to the girl and took the food and drink. "Thanks," he said, and started to close the door.

"Whoa, chump, not so fast," said the girl as she stuck her foot in the jam and held out a hand.

"What?" he said. She was looking at him as if were some kind of alien.

"The tip man, the tip."

"Ah, how much would that be?"

She smiled. "Oh, it varies, but usually about . . . ten to fifteen bucks." Johnny gave her a twenty, and she thanked him. Fifteen minutes later, the entire pizza, one liter of Coke, and the pint of cookie dough, unbaked, was devoured. Five minutes after that, Johnny passed out, half lying, half sitting on the couch as Neil Armstrong and Buzz Aldrin reminisced about their trip to the moon.

*****

After checking the oxygen regulator on his helmet, Johnny Moonbeam closes his face mask and heads outside for a stroll on the lunar surface. Even after twenty years, he still loves walking on the moon with its low gravity, never growing tired of bounding along like a giant rabbit. Sometimes he stops to see how high he can jump or how many somersaults he can turn, but not today. A reflective and melancholy mood has seized him. This will be his last day on the moon. He is tired. Twenty years of fighting the notorious Gypsy Giants, an intergalactic gang of planet-plundering pirates, has taken its toll.

The moon's Milchius region, where Captain Moonbeam built his fortress over twenty years ago, is blessed with some of the finest scenery the moon has to offer. There is a fierce mountain range in the distance and a valley with a plethora of huge craters and other rock formations. He was just a kid then, fifteen years old, and all by himself. He would've gone crazy if not for the small handful of people—a few reclusive millionaires and some former astronauts—who, over the next several years, followed him and settled in the same beautiful valley forming a neighborhood of sorts. He pauses and smiles when he sees the home of his dear friend, Buzz Aldrin, which looks like an overgrown version of the Apollo 11 landing module.

The entrance to Buzz's home is twenty-five feet off the moon's surface and has no steps. This is not a problem. Johnny takes a small hop step, then jumps, and lands right at the front door. An electronic eye senses his presence and admits him into the equilibration chamber where, after atmospheric adjustments are complete, a green light flashes. Johnny removes his spacesuit and strolls into the main living area, where, as always, he is greeted by a tremendous bear hug. "I've got to do something," says Johnny, barley able to talk for being held so tightly, "or one of these days you're going to forget to let go and I'll die right here in your arms."

Buzz unlatches himself and slaps the boy on his shoulder. "Good to see ya, Johnny boy! It just won't be the same around here without you." They look at one another for a minute, and then Buzz says, "Can I get you a beer, kid?"

"Sure, sounds good."

"I hope it's okay, but all I have up here is," Buzz pauses for dramatic effect, "light beer," and starts laughing.

Though Johnny has heard this many times before, he laughs. After all, Buzz is pushing a hundred years old and Johnny doesn't mind cutting him some slack. "In that case, let me have the darkest light one you can round up." It's the thing he says every time and it never fails to please his friend.

"That's a good one, kid. I'll be right back." Buzz shuffles off to the kitchen, shaking his head and laughing the whole way. His memory is slipping, but otherwise Buzz is in good shape. He's been a great help to Johnny through the years, mostly with emotional support, but occasionally with technical support as well. *I'm going to miss you old man.*

Buzz hands him a dark, smoky looking ale in a glass with a top—it's almost impossible to drink anything from an open mug without getting thoroughly doused. "Cheers!" he says, and they both take a long drink.

After a couple minutes of chit-chat Johnny asks his friend, "Do you think I'm doing the right thing?"

"Referring to your plans to retire from the hero business, return to Earth, and try to have some kind of normal life?"

"Yeah."

"Hell yes!" Buzz yells, spraying a fine mist of beer throughout the room as he does. Johnny looks a bit hurt. "Oh," said Buzz, "I see. You want me to tell you that those poor earthlings won't be able to get by without you, that they need you, and that the universe will go to hell in a hand-basket if you don't continue being some kind of half-baked superhero?"

The words sting. Johnny can't believe Buzz would actually say anything so harsh. Not knowing what to do, he just sits there, stunned.

"Man, you can be one sensitive boy, you know that?"

"Yeah, well, I think I've heard that before."

"What I mean is that your job is done. You got rid of the Giants, saved the Earth, and now it's back to the way it should be. Part of that means people there need to take care of their own problems." Letting it soak in for a few seconds, Buzz adds, "Things are back to normal now. There are still problems, of course, but they can, and need, to deal with these on their own. If you keep doing it for them, they'll grow dependent on you and never learn how to take care of themselves."

Johnny sees his point. "And then they would be in even worse shape when I die, which I will do eventually, because," he adds, "after all, I'm only human myself."

"Right," says Buzz, slapping him hard on the back. "And besides, you deserve to find out what life is really all about, to enjoy all those normal, wonderful things that humans should experience, like falling in love and having a family, and watching the Yankees beat the Red Sox."

*****

Later that day Buzz walks Johnny to the Moon Cruiser and they say their good-byes. Johnny is feeling better and looks forward to a normal life on Earth. Buzz is right, Johnny deserves a shot at a more human experience with all its joys and sorrows and glories and defeats, and he is going to go for it. From the pilot's seat in the cruiser, Johnny gives the thumbs up and Buzz returns home to watch the blastoff.

Several hours later, as Buzz turns on his stove and starts to cook dinner, he wonders. *I did tell Johnny that I'd borrowed some fuel from the Cruiser, didn't I?* Everything up there runs on rocket fuel, and a few days ago Buzz ran out. He knew Johnny wouldn't mind him borrowing some fuel, but he can't remember if he actually told the boy about it. Finally he decides that he is just being paranoid. *Hell, of course I told him. I wouldn't forget something that important.*

Johnny is enjoying his last ride in the Moon Cruiser. Just like him, the cruiser will be retired after this trip. They'll probably put it in the Smithsonian he thinks, and it makes him smile. But then, as he is about to reenter the earth's atmosphere, a process that requires a fair amount of fuel, the Cruiser does not respond.

"No!" screams Johnny when he sees the fuel gauge on empty. "No, it can't be! No!"

*****

Johnny woke with a start up, sweat drenched and screaming.

Chapter 6: Scheming

Mary was a schemer and a dreamer. A do-it-yourself kind of gal, independent as a wild tomcat. Planning her escape from hell, however, was more difficult than she'd bargained for. She'd pulled off any number of shenanigans in the past, but this was different. It was serious. It had heft. It wasn't like if she failed, she could blow it off and go on to the next thing. The gravity of it started to weigh on her.

Three days and still no plan. Mary, frustrated, finished watching the latest episode of American Idol then lifted a yellow legal pad from a stack next to her mother's work satchel and went upstairs to brainstorm. She scribbled down random ideas, shuffled them into lists and rearranged them. When nothing looked right, she crossed them all out then tore off another page to start anew. She even tried free association once, accidentally writing down 'Brad' then attacking it with her #2 Ticonderoga until there was nothing left of pencil or pad. She restocked, wrote THIS SUCKS, and sighed, blowing an errant strand of hair from her eyes, trying to refocus. She doodled for a while, drawing fierce-faced-Manga-girls who, it turned out, were no smarter than she was. And then it occurred to her that maybe, just this once, it would be a good idea to get some help. But how? She had no one to confide in or even talk to. Lola, her mother, was her only family, and if she gave a hoot in the first place Mary wouldn't be running away. An inept mother was one thing, but one who didn't love you was an entirely different situation. The realization echoed through her head, gaining momentum until it was almost physical, like a dark knight galloping, closing fast with lance pointed right at her heart. Then a chink, something braking in her usually impenetrable armor, and the voice within her head started laughing. Mocking her. *You have no one. No one loves you. No one cares about you. No one. No One.* NO ONE!

"Stop, stop," she said, "stop it." By the time the voice inside her head finally faded she had passed out on the bed.

*****

The sun was high by the time Mary woke up. Mid morning she guessed, missed the bus for sure. She went downstairs. Brad and Lola were gone to work. No milk in the fridge, no nothing—except, of course, beer. Wouldn't want to run out of that. Mary found a half eaten bag of stale chips and a diet Pepsi from Lola's private stash, took them upstairs, and resumed her task. *Where was I?* She tapped her pencil on the pad of paper, thinking, and soon remembered. She wrote: Get help. Tap. Tap . . . there has to be a way . . . tap. Tap, tap . . . her eyes brightened. *The internet. That's it, you can find out anything on the internet.* Except Mary had no way to access the internet and wouldn't know what to do if she did have access. Details she thought, one thing at a time, and headed out. She knew just where to go.

About a half-mile walk from Mary's house the neighborhood morphed into a slightly better tended yet even more menacing area known, unofficially, as Ward 81. She wasn't sure what the 81 meant, but figured it had something to do with motorcycle gangs. Until then, she'd only ever passed through the small cluster of tattoo parlors and shops adorned with swastikas and skulls and cross-bones. Everywhere she looked there were Harleys and leather jackets and forearms as big as trees. Even at ten in the morning, it was a little scary. Get a grip, girl, she told herself, then shrugged it off and found what she was looking for.

It was dark in Vince's Internet Café, the air thick and hazy. Stifling. It stank of sweat and a kind of smoke that did not come from cigarettes. She looked around and, once her eyes adjusted, was relieved to see that there were, indeed, five computer stations along the far wall, of which three were occupied. That was good because she would need someone to help her. She assessed the candidates for this position. In the last, or furthest, cubicle, a young man was intensely banging away at a keyboard. He looked like he knew what he was doing. He also looked like a character from a bad horror film, his body covered with piercings and tattoos she, happily, could not identify. *If I wanted nightmares, I'd just stay at home.* Next to Godzilla-Boy was a forty-five-ish-year-old woman—at least Mary thought it was a woman—who looked like she would bite anyone who might be so bold as to approach. *No thanks.* The last customer was in the first carrel, a gaunt, ancient dude with a tremor who appeared to know even less than she did, which left only the man behind the counter. Vince. The cafe's proprietor. She knew it was him because it was tattooed across his forehead. His facial expression said BAMF. He did not look schmoozable, but what did she have to lose? She walked up to the register. "So," he growled, "whadda ya want, missy?"

She gave him her best smile and looked at the price board. "I'll have a Mocha Java."

"With or no?"

"With what?"

"Whipped cream," he said, speaking the words slowly as if she were an idiot.

"Ah, yeah. Of course."

"Anything else?"

"Well, I was hoping you'd help me look up something on one of those computers."

Vince held out his hand, fingers greedily snapping. Finally he said, "ID."

"What?"

"I gotta hold on to your ID in case you try to screw me. It's two dollars the first 30 minutes and a dollar for each 30 minutes after that." Mary didn't have either the ID or the two dollars.

"What? Aren't they like, free, when you order a drink?"

"You want free computers, go to the library."

"Really?"

"Yeah, really."

Finally, something helpful. "Okay," she said and started to leave.

"Hey, what about your drink?" he asked, the words laced with sarcasm.

Mary was slightly taken aback, but quickly recovered. "Why don't you just stick it up your ass."

"Woah," he laughed. "Uppity little bitch you are."

"Have a nice day, sewer breath," she replied, and was out the door.

Outside a police car was stopped at the intersection. Mary walked up and rapped on the window. It came down. "Ah, Officer, can you tell me where the library is?"

He looked at her, "Shouldn't you be in school?"

"I am, it's called home school."

"Right. So, what's your name?"

"Deborah Smith, now, could you, like, just answer the question?"

The officer thought about asking for her address and phone number but the light turned green and it wasn't worth it. "Go down to forty-eighth, take a left, and about ten blocks down you'll see it on your right."

"That's a long way. How 'bout a ride?" He scowled, a disdainful look, then shook his head and was gone.

Asshole.

The library was a much friendlier environment. Mary found a nice-looking, studious young man and slinked up to him. She was a beautiful young woman with a petite figure, perfect complexion, and wavy, Auburn hair that draped her shoulders like velvet curtains. It was the brown eyes however, huge and perfectly round, that seemed to hypnotize almost anyone in possession of a Y-chromosome, turning them into drooling puppy dogs, happy to be at her complete disposal. She batted her long, lacy lashes and he was under her spell.

"What do you need me to look up for you?" he asked.

Mary could have told him anything, that she was with Al Qaeda researching how to bombs and it would have made no difference. Still, for her own sake, she stuck to the plan. "I'm doing a research project on runaways."

"What aspect?"

"Say what?"

"I mean, what do you want to know about runaways?"

"Like, how to do it and survive, you know, find a good place to go, don't get caught, that sort of stuff."

The boy searched and searched, every angle, with every key word he could think of, and yet the results were always the same. Instead of supplying any useful information, ninety-nine percent of the hits extolled the virtues of not running away, or told what hotline to call, or where to get help. Mary didn't want any of that. "Jeepers, how's a modern girl supposed to know what to do?"

"I don't know," he said, wiping spittle from his chin.

After forty-five minutes, she thanked him and gave up.

Frustrated, yet undaunted, Mary marched out of the Library. *Well girl, looks like you're on your own.*

As usual.

Chapter 7: Phony Phone

SCARCELY A WEEK HAD PASSED and already the house at the end of Mystic Lane was on full autopilot, running like a well-oiled machine. Johnny was especially proud of what he considered his crowning achievement: bringing his parents back to life.

*****

Three days ago . . .

As the inevitable calls kept pouring in, flooding him with questions, Johnny realized that in order for this stay-at-home-on-his-own idea to work, he would have to find a way to make people believe that his parents were still there and in charge. It was the only piece of business that remained, but how to do it? *Maybe I could disguise myself as Jack when I need to?* But Jack was four inches shorter and several inches wider than he was, just for starters. *No, that won't work. Disguise myself as Jill?* Laughable. *There must be something I could do with computer graphics.* He thought about how realistic videogames had become and it gave him an idea.

Maybe I could make avatars of my parents, project them in 3-D, so they could move around the house. His imagination took off: Jack's avatar going out for a chat with Henry, Jill's avatar answering the phone in her mousy voice. It might really work. Henry wouldn't know the difference, but then, there was Barney to consider. He'd sense something fishy right off and go over to sniff out the situation. Johnny saw the hound's nose going right through Jack's leg and laughed at the picture. Henry would have a heart attack right there, and then I'd have to do CPR and call 911, and my cover would be blown. He sighed, *well, so much for Jack-atar. What about Jill? No. Even if I could, it would take forever. I need them here now.* Still he thought it was a great idea.

The picture of Jill answering the phone stayed with him. Maybe *if I just had their voices that would be enough.* He knew that in the gaming world, players changed voices all the time, and though he'd never seen one, it followed that there were programs designed solely for that purpose. He found several, evaluated and compared them, and decided one called *WaveMorph*, a voice altering program, was best and downloaded it from the internet. It turned out to be one of his most useful and favorite tools.

Using some Jack and Jill sound clips he had stored on his hard drive, it was easy to replicate their voice tones. It took considerably more practice to get the speech patterns just right, but he did it. In the end, he had Jack and Jill down so well that even the FBI's state-of-the-art voice analysis software couldn't tell the difference (Johnny knew this for a fact because he had hacked into the FBI and tried it out). After routing all phone calls through his computer it would be just like one big happy family again—at least as far as the outside world was concerned.

Now all he had to do was try it out.

It didn't take long.

Bdddring—Johnny picked up, or he thought with amusement, 'clicked up' then pushed 'M' on his keyboard for 'Mother' so that the person on the other end of the line would hear Jill's voice. "Ah, well, good morning. I mean, hello," he answered in a perfect rendering of Jill in her immediately-post-breakfast-with-Jack-just-backing-down-the-driveway-on-his-way-to-work-still-frazzled voice. Jill, is that you?"

Johnny didn't know who was on the other end. *Would she have known?* He had not anticipated this problem, but what could he do? "Ah, yes and who am I speaking to?"

"Oh, I'm sorry Jill. This is Larry, Jack's boss at work. I'm glad I finally got a hold of you. I was about to send someone out there to check on things. We've called several times over the past week but the only person we've been able to talk to was some kid that I don't know and, well frankly, we just need to understand what's going on."

"That's my nephew. He's been helping out since Jack's been so sick."

"That's nice," the man said, though Johnny thought it lacked sincerity. "How is Jack doing?"

"He's out of the hospital now but still needs to take it easy for a while. Strict bed rest, the doctor said. That's where he is right now: upstairs in bed, sleeping."

"My goodness, what's the matter with him? Is he going

to be all right?"

Oops, guess I should have thought of that already. But he hadn't. Jack had always been so healthy that Johnny's mind went blank. *Shoot, I'll just have to buy some time.* "Oh excuse me for a minute. My nephew is trying to tell me something. Be right back." Johnny typed most common reason for hospitalization of a forty-five-year-old male and Googled it. The answer came up immediately. "Larry, are you still there?"

"I'm here."

"Now, what was it you wanted to know?"

"We kind of need to know what happened, what's wrong with him?"

"Oh dear, I thought my nephew told you already. I'm so sorry. You see. Jack had a heart attack. It was completely of the blue, you know, just one of those things that happens," said Johnny, then gave the man one of his mother's polite laughs.

"Well, I'm sorry to hear that. Is he going to be all right?"

Johnny did a Jill sigh, "It's too early to tell, but we hope so."

Seeming somewhat impatient, Larry cut to the quick. "When can we expect him back at work?"

"Oh, well, I really couldn't say. Right now, we're just praying that he gets better. I'll let you know when I can tell you more, okay."

"Well, actually, we need some kind of estimate," and then, as if it were what he had intended to say, "or a guess, if that's all you have. It's just a formality, really."

The man sounded apologetic, which Johnny took as a good sign. Not wanting to deal with him any longer than necessary, Johnny pushed a little harder. "Well, I never," Jill's voice sounded exasperated, "Jack has never missed a day of work his entire career. I can't imagine why—"

"I'm sorry. Just have him give me a call when he's up to it, okay?"

"I'll make sure to do that. Well, good-bye now and thank you for calling."

"Good-bye," said Larry, "and take good care that husband of yours. We'd hate to lose him."

Johnny hung up the phone then jumped up, clenching and shaking his fists in victory, "Awesome! It worked. It really worked. Woo-hoo!"

He was all set now, ready to explore and enjoy his new life.

Or was he?

Chapter 8: Gone Shopping

Mary was used to disappointment. She was also used to getting over it. Within a couple of days, she regrouped her resolve and thought she was probably even better off on her own. Running away was all about deception and survival, which, if they were subjects taught in school, she would be acing. *I could, like, write the friggin' book.* Meticulous planning and preparation would be essential. She had a jump on things from last night when rather surreptitiously one big piece of the puzzle came to her on a virtual silver platter. An advertisement on TV: *Just fifteen minutes from Downtown Indianapolis exists a wonderland of luxurious estates featuring parks, manicured gardens with fountains, swimming pools and convenient shopping, and all with easy access to world-class golfing. Let yourself be pampered at Laurel Highlands. Live the life you were meant to.* It was like the dude had been talking right to her, like it was meant to be. Now that she'd figured out where to live, she would need an appropriate wardrobe to match, something she could manage quite well on her own.

Shopping, or rather shoplifting, was not a haphazard endeavor for Mary. It was an art form requiring precision and finesse. It was the kind of venture she understood, in which attention to details wasn't just important. It was everything. On her way through Ward 81 she'd picked up copies of several underground newspapers. *The Indy Anarchist*, in particular, had some illuminating and timely pieces, including one called *Shoplifting with Impunity*. Though she had no idea what impunity meant, she correctly inferred the article would be useful. It was. Apparently, Caucasian females forty-to-fifty-years-old were the lowest on the totem pole of shoplifter demographics and therefore, engendered the lowest level of suspicion. The guards paid them no mind whatsoever. Mary contemplated this. It made sense because, given the choice between a middle-aged mommy and a chic adolescent chick like her, who could blame them?

Mary went to work immediately, glad she had taken a summer theater program the year before. She'd done it mostly to get out of the house, away from Brad and Lola, but ended up actually liking it. And learning some very useful skills. It was a good program, exposing kids to all facets of theater, including makeup, an area Mary paid especially close attention to. Not to mention the nice stockpile of materials she pilfered for some future, though, at that time, unknown, purpose. Now she had a purpose. Mary figured if she could make a welve-year-old boy look like Frankenstein, she could make herself look middle-aged. It was challenging, but with good materials, a bit of training, and a God-given talent, four hours later Mary fairly resembled a forty-five-year-old woman with two-point-two kids, a wealthy ex-husband, and enough money to buy the moon. Now the hard part. She reached back and tried to recall what they'd taught her about acting, wishing she'd paid better attention. As it turned out, though, she remembered quite a bit, which both surprised and pleased her. Mary spent the next two days studying women shopping at the mall, or at the grocery store, even at school. She watched how they walked, how they talked, their mannerisms, and incorporated them into her new persona. And she practiced. By the third day, she was satisfied. She made herself up one more time, grabbed a dress from Lola's closet, and was off.

*****

"May I help you with something?" Mary was in the 'Young Miss' section of Macy's, shaking her head at the selections.

"Why, yes. I was looking for something for my 15-year-old daughter. Leave it to her and she'd come home with $500 of clothes and only one yard of material. I just can't understand how they dress these days."

"So, you need something that she'll wear, and you think is acceptable?"

Mary's eyes lit up as if she'd won the lotto. "That's it," she said, "exactly. Is there such a section?"

"Not necessarily a section, but I think I can find some compromises you'll both be able to live with."

Mary could see the dollar signs flashing in the saleslady's eyes. "Why I just can't tell you what a blessing that would be. She's a size two, a very petite girl. If you wouldn't mind picking out a few things while I shop for," Mary paused here and looked away. "Undergarments for myself," she whispered, and then continued as before. "After I'm finished," she cleared her throat, "*there*, I'll come back *here*, and see what you have." The clerk went off and started rummaging through the racks, pulling out various outfits and combinations. They were hideous. It didn't matter though, because she wasn't going to buy them anyway, wasn't even going to take them. Casually, she walked by the checkout island and grabbed a couple of large bags with the store's name on them, pulled a roll of 'PURCHASED" tape from underneath the counter, then slipped them into her cavernous purse. Instead of women's undergarments, Mary made a beeline for the new twenty-something section and loaded her bags with a preselected stack of sexy—and expensive—attire. She looked at her new watch. It was the first item she'd acquired. Fourteen minutes, time to go. Fifteen at any one store was the limit. *Don't act rushed but don't stay longer than 15 minutes*, it was one of the golden rules put forth in *The Indy Anarchist*. Mary sauntered through the store, smiling politely at the employees as she walked by and then out the door with her bargain bags full of merchandise.

There were other golden rules too, including not returning to the same store if possible and not getting too greedy. Over the next several days Mary made the rounds of several malls and several different stores until she was in possession of the best wardrobe she'd ever had—or even seen.

The most difficult and highly treasured of her acquisitions were the red, knee-high cowgirl boots with 3-inch heels and studded with real gold.

They'd been risky, but they were worth it.

Chapter 9: Talk Radio

TWO WEEKS PASSED. Outside, the sun hid behind a blanket of clouds, and the blackened sky broke loose in a deluge. Thunder boomed, windows rattled, and overwhelmed storm drains backed up. Streets ran like rivers. Inside 4217 Mystic Lane, however, a different kind of storm was brewing.

Johnny was under siege, his mind inundated with repeated acts of self-flagellation. Most of his young life had been a fight for survival, but at least he could see his nemesis. This was different: the enemy was invisible. And it was winning. Askew in his father's leather recliner, wearing the same garments he'd worn the past three days—a pair of plaid boxer shorts and what used to be a white T-shirt, both ripe with body odor and stained with sweat—the boy's mind was racing. Johnny was in a dangerous place. He needed a distraction.

He scanned the room for something, anything, to occupy his mind. At times like this, even a few seconds were a blessing. And there it was, a small pewter fairy about three-and-a-half-inches high in the form of a naked young woman perched on the coffee table in front of him. Her butterfly wings, powder blue and made of silk with delicate, pewter veins, fanned out behind her in a vee, wide as she was tall. Ever since he could crawl, the little sprite with the impish grin on her face had been taunting him, daring him to touch her.

Now, finally, he did.

Securing each wing between thumb and forefinger, he picked her up and commenced the experiment he'd so long wanted to perform: could she fly? Did her wings really move, and, if so, how far? Carefully, in tiny increments, he started moving them apart, and then back, gradually increasing the distance with every trial . . . apart and then back . . . apart and back . . . until . . . crack ... snap! About that far. Johnny plucked the remains of the fractured fairy from his lap and placed her back on the coffee table, where she had previously resided in a glorious wholeness. *Like me,* he thought.

The demons had fled, but would soon return if he couldn't find something else to do. Johnny looked around the room for another trinket to experiment with. Most of them, however—and there had been fifty or more figurines, primarily fairies and elves, at one time in the living room alone—had already been put through their own trials and were no longer in need of testing. Then, on the other side of the room, he spotted the radio. He got up and turned it on. Back-to-back commercials for two mattress chains played, each one laying claim to the lowest prices, the best selection, the best service, and the most convenient number of outlets. Impossible he thought. One of them must be lying. *Isn't it illegal to lie on the radio? Shouldn't they be arrested?* For a while, he considered calling the police. It was the most intriguing dilemma he'd faced in days. Then the show started. He made a mental note and put the mattress problem on hold.

"Good afternoon and welcome to *The Ricky Randall Show* on WKZQ. With the rash of teen suicides in the area recently, we are pleased to have Dr. Jennifer Winslow, M.D., head of child psychiatry at Indiana University, here to discuss her latest book, the highly controversial bestseller *How to Keep Your Teen Alive*. We'll be back with Dr. Winslow after this message. Don't go away."

"The following is a public service message from WKZQ. As a dad, you'll probably spend years teaching your son how to hit a baseball . . ." *Kids play baseball? Dad must have known; it was his favorite sport. I wonder why he didn't he teach me?* . . . "How to throw a tight spiral and hit a receiver . . ." *Oh, that was a fun day. Jack said I was hopeless, a sissy, and that I threw like a girl* . . . "How to hit a jump shot . . ." *What's a jump shot?* . . . "Hit the open man..." *Open where?* . . . "And maybe the most challenging of all, how to hit the books . . ." *They did give me books, and made me study. I'm thankful for that anyway, but why would anyone hit a book? That's just stupid* . . . "But the question is this: how much time will you spend teaching him what not to hit? Teach your son often and early that all violence against women is wrong."

Johnny considered this. *Sure, I guess so,* he thought, though no one ever told him as much, and he realized it wasn't something he felt in his bones. What he felt in his bones was this: hitting women and children is just part of life— technically wrong, like going sixty miles an hour when the speed limit is fifty-five— but something most people do and nobody worries about, not even the cops. Questions started flying around his head like a pinball. *What about kids?* He presumed it was all right to hit boys, but what about girls? And when, exactly, did girls become women, anyway? Was violence against men okay? It was mind-boggling. Johnny would have missed the rest of the show altogether if not for one of those emergency broadcast system tests. The test screeched and grabbed his attention as the silver ball slid between two flippers and out of his head.

For the next hour, Dr. Winslow's talk about teen suicide riveted the boy. He'd never thought about it, and, even as bad as he felt right now, he was sure he would never do it. Yet, it was interesting, especially in the *how*. After the doctor finished her spiel, listeners were encouraged to call-in with any questions. Johnny had several, but there was one in particular he was most curious about. The sixth time he dialed, he got through.

"Hello, this is The Ricky Randall Show. Could I please have your first name, where you're calling from, and what it is you want to comment on?"

"Is this Ricky Randall?"

"No, I'm the call screener. Can you give me your information?"

Johnny originally answered in his own voice, until it occurred to him that if they were to figure out he was a fourteen-year-old boy, they might worry about him. Especially given the question he had in mind. He decided it would be better if Jill made the call and hit 'J' on his keyboard, which prompted the computer to morph his voice to sound like her.

"Caller number three, are you there?"

"Yes," said Jill's voice. If the call screener was concerned that it sounded different, he didn't say anything. Probably, thought Johnny, there are so many calls he didn't even notice. "My name is Jill and I'm from Mystic. I'd like to ask about the difference in success rates for the boys and girls."

"Fine, now hold on and we'll have you on the air with Ricky in a few minutes. Thanks for calling."

Though less than fifteen minutes, it felt like forever until Ricky asked for caller number three. "Jill from Mystic, you're on the air with Ricky Randall! Now, what's your question for Dr. Winslow?"

"Ah, wow, I mean . . ."

"Don't be shy now, just ask away."

"Okay," said Jill's voice with a squeak. Johnny cleared his throat. "I was surprised to hear the statistics about how much more successful boys are when they try to, you know, do it, and I wondered if you could tell me why?"

"It's okay to say the word suicide, Jane."

"It's Jill."

"I'm sorry. I mean, Jill, because if we can't even say 'suicide' out loud, how are we going to talk to our children about it? That's part of what I'm trying to do with my book, take the mystique out of it because part of the problem is the way we treat it as such a taboo subject—"

"But what I wanted to know—"

"I didn't forget your question, Jane. It's quite simple, really. The thing is, boys use guns. Girls use other methods like pills or cutting their wrists. There is no margin for error or forgiveness or time for second thoughts with a gun. It's just, 'BANG'! And it's all over."

A surge of energy went through Johnny, and he felt almost like his old self. Jack had a whole slew of guns, all kinds, and the boy knew just where they were. He wanted to ask what kind of gun was best, and exactly how should one do it in order to obtain the best result? But he'd been disconnected. *Oh well, that information must be on the Internet.*

It was.

That night, for the first time in quite a while, Johnny fell into a sound and peaceful sleep.

Chapter 10: Last Day of Fourteen

JOHNNY FELT GREAT, TOP-'O-THE-WORLD, energy to spare, ever since the talk-radio-show with Dr. Winslow. He told himself this was coincidence, though, on some level, he knew better—honesty would have spoiled his newfound nirvana. He knew this because, after the show, he'd looked up her website and read:

> . . . many patients become energized once they make a firm decision to execute a plan for suicide . . . They feel great . . . This does not mean they are better. They are not cured. In fact, they are usually more determined than ever . . . Occasionally, especially teenage patients, might not even be aware they have committed to this...but when I see them bouncing into my office feeling great, I get very concerned.

That's just a bunch of malarkey. Johnny tried to put it out of his mind. *I'm not going to kill myself. It's crazy.* That he'd looked up on another site the best way to do it didn't mean anything. It was *interesting*. The fact that he'd uncovered Jack's stash of guns was nothing unusual for a boy to do. That he'd picked out a late model Smith & Wesson handgun, loaded it, and started carrying it around with him was purely coincidental. He was just *curious*. Besides, you never knew when you might need to defend yourself.

And yet Dr. Winslow's words lingered as they grew ever louder, looming up like vultures cropping dark shadows on his fragile existence. They were getting harder to push down. Johnny desperately needed a distraction. Finally, he found one. He'd been standing in it all along: the house. It was a royal mess. It would take days, even weeks, to clean up, but that was the whole point. For the time being, staying busy was all that really mattered. Johnny got to work immediately.

*****

Two days later, with the house cleaner than it had been in years, his energy was gone, and the doldrums were back. To make matters worse, it was his birthday. Birthdays, for Johnny, did not lend themselves to happy memories. They were better off forgotten, which, of course, meant he could not get them out of his mind. As a little kid, his mother tried a few times to throw a birthday party for Johnny. It always backfired, though, with Jack invariably turning it into a nightmare. Jill soon gave up, and Johnny's birthdays were simply ignored. This was better, but it still hurt. Johnny invariably remembered his birthdays, and though he'd never been to one, he knew that other kids had parties and celebrations and presents, and he didn't. Johnny understood, had always understood, that he was somehow different. Defective. Unwanted.

It was almost noon, and though Johnny had been awake since eight o'clock, he had yet to find a single reason to get out of bed. He might have stayed there forever, save one complication: he needed to pee. Bad. He'd needed to for some time, and yet the pain of his over distended bladder was such a comfort, he didn't want to. Until now, when he realized it was going to release its contents on its own accord, whether he wanted it to or not. Apparently, even depressed people do not relish the idea of lying in a bed full of piss. So he gave in and pulled back the covers in order to sit up and get out of bed. As soon as he moved however, the pain exploded, and he thought his bladder would burst. He could hardly breathe. Standing was even worse, and the pain of trying to walk seemed unbearable, but still, he had to move. Slowly, stooped over and holding onto the wall for support, Johnny waddled inch by inch across the hall. Each movement was like a knife through his abdomen. Halfway there he started leaking on the carpet. And that's when a not so small voice started up in his head: Jack. *You stupid boy! You idiot! You moron! Look what you've done! Why, you disgusting little piece of shit! You worthless little dumpster boy!* Despite the pain, Johnny picked up the pace and made it into the bathroom just as his bladder exploded like a fire hose. The floor and walls got a good dousing before he made it to the toilet and could appropriately direct the flow. *You're going to lick that up, boy, while I get you a diaper*.

"You just shut up! Get out of here you dead son of a bitch!" Johnny yelled aloud as he stood over the john. The rapidly shrinking bladder started to cramp, each spasm sending a fresh bolt of pain through his body. By the time he finished, tears were running down his face. He sat down on the urine soaked floor, rocking back and forth with his arms folded over his abdomen. Lost in pain and humiliation, Johnny remembered Dr. Winslow's words and knew she was right.

The pain let up after a few minutes. He went back to bed and lay down. This time, however, instead of staring blankly up at the ceiling, a whirlwind of excitement and anticipation was swirling around his mind. Concrete plans of suicide began to stew in Johnny's head as he lay there thinking how peaceful death must be. Though these thoughts were new to Johnny, still raw and fragmented, their ingredients were as old as he was. Accumulated throughout Johnny's young life and preserved in the deep freeze of his mind, chilly memories, like so many chunks of beef and vegetables destined to one day become the evening supper, had finally been taken out of the freezer and allowed to thaw.

The pain and humiliation of the previous half hour lit a fire under those ingredients. The simmering stew began sending out wonderful aromas. Johnny could almost taste it, soothing as chicken soup boiling atop the stove. He started to feel better and placed the gun on top of his caved-in belly. It was cool and refreshing, and it was powerful. *It's easy.* He remembered the doctor on the radio say, "It's so easy, just bang, and it's all over." His hollow gut seemed to reach up and leech power from that gun until it swam thick in his blood, until it could not be controlled or contained, until the concentration was too high to manage. There was no longer any choice. All that power had to be spent.

Johnny was excited, not about today, his birthday, but about tomorrow, or rather, about the lack of a tomorrow . . . and all the tomorrows thereafter.

Chapter 11: Time to Go

SHE NEEDED MORE TIME. Whatever plan Mary came up with had to be foolproof. Though anxious to be gone, she was willing to wait in order to get it right. When she got home from school, she'd thought, just another week or so, and I'll be ready. Two hours later, Brad, grinning broadly with a beer in one hand, caught her alone in the kitchen. Before Mary could negotiate her way between the table and chairs and clutter and out of the tiny room, he, for the first time since . . . since it happened, placed his other hand firmly on her ass. And squeezed. Hard.

Time was no longer an issue. She had none. Mary could no longer afford to wait until her half-baked plans were fully cooked. Though her current state of preparation lacked depth and attention to detail, *at least,* she rationalized, *I'll be heading in the right direction. Besides, I'm good at improv.*

Later, Lola said, "Mary, Brad and I are going out for a while. You can order a pizza or something for dinner if you like."

Right, like we're the Brady bunch or something. Normally, Mary would have given her mother an ear full, pointing out that, without any money, she couldn't get a pizza. And by the way, there's no food in the refrigerator, as usual. That night, however, she was just glad they were gone for a few hours. *Time to get ready.*

*****

A couple of hours of packing and last-minute planning, and Mary was ready to go. Almost. Looking at herself in the mirror, she inhaled, trying to accentuate her figure, but to no avail. She frowned. *Fifteen years old, and still with boobs as small as egg yolks.* Disgusting. Embarrassing. She was tired of looking like a kid. *Like, you can't wear a fancy bra without at least something to show off.* Tired of waiting for the real deal, Mary took matters into her own hands and grabbed a wad of tissue. Then she pulled a thin, gold box from under her mattress, untied the crimson bow, removed the top and laid open the tissue to reveal a shiny, white bra with a laced border and a little red heart in front where the straps crossed. She put it on, carefully padding it with the tissue to make up the difference between her almost A-sized breasts and the C cup brassiere. Back at the mirror, she turned right, then left, and after that straight on again. Nice she thought, that's better. When Mary procured the lingerie from Victoria's Secret, she'd almost been caught, and, for a while, wondered if it was really worth it. Now, looking at the results in the mirror, she had no doubt. *Probably a good idea not to go with the D cup.*

She'd chosen the rest of her outfit with equal care. Over the designer bra, she wore a sheer top lifted—this one, like most, had been easy—from an exotic boutique called Lovers Layers. It was soft and delicate, cottony, colored canary yellow, and embroidered with a smattering of abstract, pastel-colored poppies. Purple lace adorned a low, v-neck collar, and looked like butterflies flitting among the flowers. The skimpy shirt left a bare midriff above her new sunshine-washed Calvin Kleins. A new pair of red leather boots, cowgirl style, finished off the outfit.

Mary took her time with the new Max Factor. Makeup was artist's work. It could not be rushed. Finally finished, she lingered in front of the mirror admiring her new look, turning all which ways to get different perspectives, ultimately deciding she looked perfect from every angle. In less than three short hours, Mary transformed herself from cute kid to sexy young woman. She took in a deep breath and grabbed the bottom of her shirt–what there was of it, anyway–and pulled tautly downward. Her belly button ring was still easily visible, which was good she thought, however, the new, albeit somewhat augmented figure was the key. She was sexy, hot, and much too young. It could be dangerous growing up too fast. Mary was aware of this. However, living with Brad wasn't that safe either.

Tonight, I am like, so totally out of here. Watch out, Laurel Highlands, the unstoppable Mary Valentine is on her way! Then the front door opened and slammed shut, and Brad's drunken voice slid through the house, slurring and sloshing its way like a pint of draught slung down the length of some slimy bar. "Marr-yy, you home?"

Lola's mousy voice said something too soft to understand. Mary waited as the familiar dance of yelling and pleading played out then climaxed with the loud crack of Brad's hand against her mother's face. This one would leave a mark, maybe even a bruise. Mary could gauge these things, could tell by the sound of it. He was left-handed and so a slap to Lola's right cheek was more coordinated and fierce, giving it a crisper tone.

"Mary, where are you?"

It was time. *Come on, chick, just do it.* But she couldn't move.

"MARRY?"

The sound of her name on his tongue made her sick. It took everything Mary had to step into the hall and carry on. By focusing solely on the act of placing one foot in front of the other, she made it to the top of the stairwell then stopped, taking hold of the banister and steadying herself. Some thirty feet away, one foot still planted firmly on the living room floor, the other hanging in the air, poised, and ready to climb, was Brad, his beady little eyes looking up at her. Full of lust. Behind him, curled up on the couch, Lola buried her face in the cushions and whimpered unintelligibly. Brad smiled as his foot fell hard on the first step. Mary's plan suddenly seemed silly and foolish, but there was no time to reevaluate. There were no other options. It's now or never, she told herself, and ridiculous or not, summoned up her courage and set the plan in motion.

"Come and get me, big boy," she said, striking her best Marilyn Monroe pose, right hand high , wrist dangling, and left side on tiptoe.

"What the . . .," said Brad, tripping on the stairs. Still, he did not take his eyes off her, eyes now swimming with both lust and rage. Mary shot back into her room and locked the door.

"I'll get you, you little witch," he yelled, and the speed at which he broke through the door and entered the room took her by surprise. With no time to think, Mary lunged for the thick rope hanging from her ceiling. It was attached to an old fishing net she'd found at a weird thrift store a few blocks from their house. When pulled, the rope was supposed to release the net so it dropped to the floor. Unfortunately, she hadn't expected the latent slime factor which, when she took hold of it and squeezed, a small amount of slick, greenish material was simultaneously released from the rope's damp interior. Her hands slid. Nothing happened. Except Brad, gaining on her, so close she could smell the beer on his breath. She tightened her grip, clamping down as hard as she could until, finally, it held. The rope came with Mary as she dove out of the way. The net came down and wrapped-up Brad like a fly in a spider's web. The more he tried to free himself, the tighter it got, until he could not move at all. Mary watched, laughing, while the net paralyzed her pursuer. This was supposed to be her cue to exit, but why not have some fun? Just as she prepared to give him a parting kick in the balls, her mother appeared in the doorway. Lola screamed, dropped down on top of Brad, hugging him. He was crying. Lola, trying to comfort him, looked up at Mary, "What have you done to my baby?"

"Your baby? What is wrong with you? I'm your baby." Mary said, holding back tears, pretending the giant hole in her heart didn't bother her. Then anger took over. She re-loaded, fired and landed her boot-tip squarely in Brad's crotch and marched over to the window, leaving the note she had written for her mother stuffed in her pocket. She started crying again, cursing herself as she ran away from a life of terror and towards the unknown.

Mary ran as fast as she could, not knowing or caring which direction she was headed or where she was going. The girl never once looked back, afraid she might see Brad charging after her, foaming at the mouth, fixing her with his primitive, inhuman eyes. The threat caused panic, which, in turn, stimulated her adrenal glands to release their entire load of adrenaline. The effect was similar to that of a rocket launching from Cape Canaveral. Mary's feet and legs were moving faster than she thought possible, so fast, in fact, she wondered for a moment if she might be flying. She did not stop for intersections, did not even look.

Every cell in her body was focused on running. Nothing else mattered or even seemed to exist. She was oblivious to the sound of screeching tires, of horns honking, and of the people screaming at her. On one occasion a middle-aged man, no doubt the father of some hormonally deranged daughter of his own, tried to stop her. Standing in the middle of the sidewalk, he braced himself and tried to grab her. Mary never even slowed down, but she must have seen him because she gave him a perfect straight arm, as if she had been an NFL running back all her life, and sent him reeling onto his backside. She ran and ran, until she was spent.

Chapter 12: Michael

AFTER A WHILE, IT OCCURRED TO Mary that she could back off and take it easy; that she would be alright. She found a bus stop and waited. Several busses passed by before one of Metro's finest slowed down as it approached. It hissed to a stop. The door swung open, and one relieved Mary Valentine stepped aboard, all smiles and swagger. Then she reached for her backpack to get the fare, and the smile slid off her face. There was nothing there. Triumph turned to defeat, relief to horror. At first, she though it fell off somewhere along the way. She closed her eyes, trying to visualize where it might be. It worked. In her mind's eye, clear as a photograph on a sunny summer day, she saw it. The picture, however, was not quite what she expected: her backpack, along with everything she'd so carefully planned to use for her get away—including $350 in cash—was still sitting by the window in her former bedroom. In the emotion and chaos of leaving, she'd forgotten it.

*****

After driving a city bus for nearly fifteen years, Michael had seen about everything. So when Mary Valentine walked aboard, and her facial expression collapsed from somewhere between joy and satisfaction to terror as she reached around for a nonexistent backpack, he knew exactly what happened. For example, he knew she had no fare. He also knew she'd meant to bring it, that it was an honest mistake. "Forgot your backpack, right?"

The girl looked at him, mouth agape, and froze for a moment. Then she recovered and said, "Yeah, and that's where . . ."

"All your money is."

The girl nodded. "You some kind of mind reader?"

"No, but I ain't blind either. So, where you headed in such a hurry?"

"In a hurry?" she said, trying not to sound defensive.

He rolled his eyes. "Just take a seat and tell me where you want to go." She did, right behind him. Michael started the bus moving.

"I'm going to the north side. A place called Laurel Highlands, to . . . ah . . . visit my grandmother for a few days. I promise to get the money for you when we get there."

"Well, I'm not going that far, but I can get you to the station where you can catch a transfer. And don't worry about the cash, you can pay me some other time."

"Thanks a lot, mister, I, like, really appreciate it."

"Someone chasin' ya?"

"No, like I said, I'm on the way to my grandma's house."

"Yeah, and I'm Elvis Presley."

"What do you mean?"

"I mean you've been running, hard. You're in a big hurry to get somewhere. And don't tell me you just can't wait to see your granny." The girl flopped back into her seat and went quiet. At the next stop, after the only other two passengers exited, Michael pulled away from the curb and continued his route. After several seconds, he met her gaze in the mirror.

She understood at once the question in his eyes. "Away," she whispered.

"Away?"

"You said I was running fast to get somewhere. You were wrong."

"You're running away then?"

There was a long silence as Michael thought about his own daughter who had run away when she was thirteen-years-old—run away because of him. And for good reason. He wasn't the same person now but he still lived with that truth every day. He glanced up at the mirror again and caught the girl's eyes.

"You sure it's really that bad at home? Sometimes it ain't that good out here. You know that, don't you?"

There was a connection between them. They understood each other on some level that, while neither could define it, made sense to both. "I know," she said. "But if it's worse out here, I'd rather just die anyway, so I'm willing to take the chance."

The driver shook his head. "Okay," he said, and turned his eyes back to the road. It was hard to see through the curtain of tears welling up in his eyes, tears that then ran down his cheeks in rivulets, tears he had needed to rain for more than twenty years. Nothing else was said until they reached the downtown station.

"This is as far as I can take you." Michael pulled out a small, white pad and started to write.

"Is there a bus to Laurel Highlands?"

"In about an hour," he said without looking up, and then tore off a slip of paper and handed it to her. "Here."

"What's that?"

"An all day bus pass, take you anywhere you want to go. Just show it to the driver." Michael took a step, stopped, and then pulled a business card from his pocket, scribbled down his home number, and gave it to her. "And this is my card." He said, then he nodded and continued on his way.

Chapter 13: Ralph

MARY LOOKED AT THE CARD: Michael P. Quackenbush, Driver First Class & Chief Instructor, Indianapolis Metro Transit, then inspected the pass, running a finger over it to make sure it was real. "Gee, thanks mist . . . she started, eyes shining as she turned her gaze back to the kindly bus driver, but then stopped. The man had vanished. A little disoriented and taken aback, Mary looked around the station, but there was no sign of him. Michael was gone.

"Oh yeah, that Michael, he's a slippery one." A male voice, soft yet coarse and deep, came up behind Mary and startled her.

"Who are you?"

"You can call me Ralph. I'm a friend of Michael's, and his boss." The man tapped lightly on Mary's pass. "Did I hear you say Laurel Highlands?"

"Ah huh," she said, not quite knowing what to make of the large man in a well pressed, three-piece-suit, looking down at her with a wry smile on his face.

"Well, it just so happens that's where I'm headed. You see, I live there."

"Wow, they must pay drivers really good around here."

He chuckled, "I'm not a driver, at least not anymore. I manage Metro, and not just this station, but the whole shootin' match. So, yeah, I do alright."

Mary nodded.

"Anyway, I'd offer you a ride up there except for the fact I'm a stranger and, you know, I wouldn't want you to feel uncomfortable."

"You're a friend of Michael's?"

"You bet, served in 'Nam with him. He saved my life over there more than once."

Mary looked at the pass, debating between waiting an hour for the bus or an express ride in, what? A Cadillac? Mercedes? BMW?

"Well, young lady, you take care now," the man said and started walking away.

"Wait. Maybe it would be alright if I went with you. I mean, like, since we're both friends of Michael's and all."

"Sure it would. You just wait out front and I'll pick you up in about five minutes."

A couple minutes later, as Mary waited out front by the curb, the sound of a car alarm split the night. It lasted about five seconds before going silent, and then a couple more minutes passed before Ralph pulled up in a late model Lincoln. The passenger's door opened and Mary climbed in.

Chapter 14: Johnny's Angel

WHETHER OR NOT YOU BELIEVE in angels, this is what happened . . .

Ralph seemed like such a decent fellow back at the station. Now, after a few minutes riding in the car with him, Mary wasn't so sure. Had she made a mistake? Probably not, she decided. Still, something about him gave her the creeps. She wanted out. *Get a grip, chick, you're just being paranoid*. And it was true, he hadn't done or said anything in particular . . .

And then he did.

Ralph's meaty hand came down hard and fast, a bolt of lightning clapping against her thigh like a whip. The sound of it thundered through the car with a fury, piercing the strained silence. Mary wanted to vomit. She tried to throw it off, but he only squeezed down tighter, his huge hand nearly encompassing her leg.

"Get you filthy paw off me," she said, trying to keep her cool. "What do you think you're doing, anyway?"

An evil grin spread across the man's face. "What do you think, sugar?"

"I think you're a creep."

"Ooh, that sounds like fun."

"Look mister, you've got the wrong chick," she said, and at that moment Mary realized she did not feel afraid, which both surprised and pleased her. *Well good, because I am not going to let this piece of shit ruin my plans. No way!* Then she looked at Ralph, who was about as big as a gorilla, and almost laughed out loud at her own audacity. But that was exactly how she felt, as if she were totally unstoppable. "Let me out of this car you son of a bitch."

"And if I do?"

"I'll say a prayer for you, asshole."

"Well now, that's real sweet of you. But I don't think I'll stop, not right yet anyway. I gots to find just the right place for us."

"Let me out, you big scumbag."

"Now, don't go getting all worked up and mad, honey. We gonna have a gooood time. You'll see."

Mary tried to open her door but couldn't.

"Child safety locks, my dear, for your protection."

"You are going to be sorry, mister, I guarantee you that."

"I don't think so. I'm kind of looking forward to spending some time with you. I like feisty girls."

"So, you do this all the time then?"

"Let's just say, it's been a while."

Mary didn't answer. It was time to be quiet and think. *You're not going to out muscle this ape, chick, but you can darn well outsmart him. You're good at this stuff.* Reminding herself to stay calm, she relaxed, and less than a minute later, Mary had a plan.

And then she put it in motion.

"Copper! Copper!" she screamed, pointing out the back window.

Ralph's eyes jerked up to the mirror. He looked left, right, and everywhere until he was spinning and bouncing around like a bobble-head doll. There were no police of course, but by the time Ralph figured it out, Mary had already taken off her seatbelt and grabbed hold of the steering wheel.

"What the . . ."

Mary yanked it for all she was worth. The car veered off to the right, barely missing the ditch before Ralph pushed her away and regained control. Almost. As a parting shot, Mary reached out and dragged her well sharpened nails across his face. She wanted to poke his eyes out, but with the car jerking and Ralph shoving, was happy to feel her claws digging anywhere into his flesh.

"Aahhhh! You crazy bitch."

The resulting wounds, which would forever brand him with three long stripes across the forehead, bled profusely and immediately. Ralph's eyes filled with salty blood, stinging, and temporarily blinding him. His hands came up and Mary spun the wheel, this time the opposite direction. The car careened across the pavement, jumped a ditch on the left, then jerked and shuttered to a stop.

Ralph was still clearing out his eyes and cursing when, in one continuous motion, Mary released the child-proof locks and fled.

"Is that feisty enough for you?" she said, and then ran

off. The Lincoln came to rest against a decorative hedge, and, though Mary could not see it at the time, about two hundred feet down the road was a gated entrance that said: *Welcome to Laurel Highlands*. She ran along the hedge and listened. When she heard Ralph get out of the car and start running after her, she ducked through it: The pretty foliage was not as substantial as it looked, giving way to a tangled mass of shrubbery and undergrowth. It then fell off abruptly over a steep, wooded slope, almost a cliff, and Mary never saw it coming. She didn't care either, just tumbled along for the ride.

At the bottom of the slope, the wooded area was replaced by gravel path, the other side lined by a continuous row of fencing. It was pitch black. She listened for Ralph. He was in the woods now. Mary grabbed the first gate handle she came to and tried to open it. It was locked. She took several steps back, closed her eyes, and charged. "Ouch." Nothing happened. She heard Ralph in the woods behind her, closing fast. She backed up a little further this time, charged a little harder, and the gate shattered. Alarms went off, and floodlights lit up the night around her as she stumbled into someone's backyard. *I'm safe she thought*, knowing that Ralph would never follow her there.

Mary let her body collapse and came to rest looking at the stars, lying on a bed of petunias in someone's backyard. The ground was soft and the flowers wet with dew. There was a petal lodged in Mary's bellybutton ring. It tickled. She extracted it from the gold loop and held it up, awed by its simple beauty and velvety feel. After a few seconds, she let it go, watching as it fluttered gracefully to the ground to be among its siblings.

Nothing had gone as planned, but still she had done it—she had escaped. Exhausted, she closed her eyes. This is the end of the line for now, she thought, but that was okay because wherever she was and whatever happened next had to be an improvement. For the first time since leaving home, Mary allowed herself to relax. She was dirty, hungry, cold, wet, lost, and exhausted. *Life is good*, she thought. *Life is very good*, and a brand-new kind of smile lit up her face.

*****

Inside the house, the upstairs bathroom was aglitter

with shards of shattered mirror reflecting light from the hallway like a broken disco ball. In the middle of the floor, standing in stunned silence, was Johnny, gun still clenched in his right hand, smoking. He'd missed. *The stupid alarm ruined everything. I'm still alive.* He let go of the gun and listened as it rattled to a stop on the tiled floor. *I can't even kill myself. I can't do anything right.* He slumped to the floor and drifted off, feeling sorry for himself.

And all the time, the alarm continued to blare.

One by one, the neighborhood dogs joined the clamor. The hideous howling rose up in the night and spread through Mystic Meadows like a wave. Previously darkened bedrooms and bathrooms and patios began to flicker with light. Johnny was jolted back to the present along with the reality that, if he didn't turn the alarm off within sixty seconds, the police would be knocking at the door. He jumped to his feet in a panic and took off like a rocket for nearest control panel, which was in his parents' bedroom. When he got there, the words *intruder in zone two* flashed their ominous message in bright red letters and the countdown until the authorities would be called stood at four. *Fingers, don't let me down now.* He punched in the code just in time. The words stopped flashing and reverted to the default: *normal.* Up until then, he'd missed the whole point of it. When it finally occurred to Johnny that the alarm did not go off just to cause him grief, that there was a real intruder somewhere zone two, he felt a little shudder go through his body. He checked the hand written note taped to the panel box, zone two was the backyard. At first, Johnny was apprehensive about going downstairs to check it out then, when he realized that ridiculous that was, a mirthless smile spread across his face. *What's the worst that could happen? Someone might kill me?* Which was what he wanted in the first place. *That figures* he thought, then went downstairs as calm as if getting a glass of milk.

The backyard lights had gone out so he turned them back on. *What the? Why is a girl lying there in the petunias?* He slipped out the sliding glass door and quietly made his way across the lawn towards her. Apparently, because there was no movement or indication on her part, she hadn't seen him.

Johnny, in no hurry to get the girl's attention or wake her, crouched down a few feet from her and waited, contentedly taking it in. Not that he didn't want to meet her, to talk with her, because he did. That would happen soon enough. For the time being, just watching her there, lying on a bed of flowers, breathing slowly and staring up at the sky, felt like a religious experience and Johnny was loath to disturb it. After all, he thought, it isn't every day that a real angel comes along and saves your life. As he watched her stare off into space, Johnny contemplated what had and had not happened. What would it have been like, he wondered, if... But suddenly he couldn't even think about it, not now that life was precious, and certainly not in the presence of this girl-angel. Was what he had tried to do only a few minutes ago even real? *Maybe it was just a crazy dream*. It wasn't. The unmistakable sensation of gun barrel still lingered in his mouth and it repulsed him. Johnny spat, trying to rid himself of the taste. But he couldn't.

Sitting in the wet grass, looking at Mary lying there, Johnny could hardly believe that he had really been so close to killing himself. But he had. Johnny remembered feeling calm and peaceful at the time, something that now seemed unfathomable. Even weirder was that he had taken his time, meticulously moving the gun around in his mouth, trying to get it just right. He remembered his right index finger gradually tightening around the trigger. He had even pulled the trigger. And he heard it, the sound of the alarm hit him like thunder. For the briefest of moments he thought it was the gunshot; but in the next instant, Johnny's whole body jerked and the gun slid out of his mouth as it went off. The bullet grazed his forehead, leaving an inch-long flesh wound before going on to shatter the bathroom mirror.

Now, as he was still quietly squatting in the grass, Johnny was scared to his very core when he realized how close he had come to actually succeeding. The slight nick on his forehead was undeniable evidence that he had actually pulled the trigger, evidence that if the alarm had failed or gone off one split second later, he would have been dead. Suddenly, Johnny couldn't imagine ever wanting to kill himself. For the first time in memory, life seemed to have some value to it, like it might be worth living, like it might be worth the struggle. He was anxious to meet this girl, to find out who she was and how she ended up in his back yard.

Yes, thought Johnny Moonbeam as he watched this girl-angel, *life is good.* He grinned and whispered, "Thank you," in awe of the girl, in awe of life, in awe of everything.

Chapter 15: Just a Girl

JOHNNY WAITED, STILL AS A stone and hardly breathing, watching his angel and trying to take it all in. After twenty minutes, however, and the angel having yet to move, Johnny's legs went numb. His knees ached. He tried to change position without making any noise, but his feet were too big and his limbs wouldn't work properly. He slipped, plunking right down onto the soggy grass. On his butt. The little pop-of-a-noise that ensued, short and squeaky, resembled that of a goose honking. It rippled through the late-summer evening silence like a fizzled firecracker, soft and mild, yet definite as the night itself. The angel's body stiffened, and Johnny saw her mouth begin to move.

"Oh, shit. Where the hell am I?" she asked, and a reverence that had hitherto dominated the night disappeared like a sweet dream in the morning fog.

He walked over to her. *I guess you're not an Angel after all. You're just a girl.* "Hey," he said.

"Achhh!" Mary shrieked. It was so loud Johnny worried someone might hear and call the police. She swung her head around and looked up at him. At first glance, Johnny seemed like a giant looming over her. She started to panic. Her body tensed, preparing once again to run, or do battle.

"Quiet," he whispered.

She was just about to scream again, or kick him, or both when he came into focus. There was nothing small about this person who towered over her like a skyscraper. The boyish face, however, still puffy with the last remnants of a baby's cherubic roundness, and two sparkling, sapphire blue eyes staring down at her in wonderment, said innocent. His mouth was open in a large 'O', and he reminded her of the Pillsbury doughboy. "Hi," she said, and burst into laughter.

"You look awful, like you could have come straight out of one of my nightmares."

"Thanks," she said in a sarcastic tone, but then, after surveying the damage, "I'm sorry your nightmares are so scary. Anyway, my name is Mary Valentine."

"You have goose-bumps all over you."

"O-kay," she said, drawing the word out slow, and giving

herself time to think. *That was strange*. "And your name is?"

"Oh, my name is Johnny . . . ahh . . . Johnny Moonbeam."

Moonbrain? she thought, *oh, whatever*. "Well, it's nice to meet you." Until Johnny pointed out her gooseflesh, Mary hadn't even noticed she was uncomfortable. It wasn't exactly cold outside, and yet, for a June evening in Indiana, it was relatively cool. And for someone lying on the ground soaking wet, it did feel a bit chilly. "Burrr!" she said, and held an arm out. When Johnny pulled her up, the gentle breeze hit her wet body like a blast of Arctic air. She hugged herself and started bouncing up and down, trying to stay warm, then gave the house a longing look. "Oh Jesus," she said, "I had no idea it was so freaking cold," then turned back and looked at Johnny. She waited. But he just stood there with his mouth half open like he was about to say something, but never did. *Like, dahhh, girl shivering to death in your backyard . . . warm house thirty paces away . . . Earth to Moon, ah, Moon . . . whatever*. Still, he didn't do or say a thing. Jesus, thought Mary. "Do-do you-you th-th-think we-we might ba-ba-be able to-to ga-ga-go insi-si-side or something?"

"Oh . . . ah . . . right, of course, I'm sorry," he said, led her inside, and sat her down at the kitchen table.

Mary looked blue in the kitchen light and started shivering even harder, her teeth audibly chattering. "Ah, ah,. . ." stammered Johnny, wondering what to do and then, finally, "I'll be right back," and he took off at a full sprint.

There was a loud crashing sound, like glass breaking, and Johnny said, "Ouch."

"A-are yu-yu-you okay?" She asked.

"Yeah," he said, but his voice carried with it the strain of someone in pain. "I'm fine." A minute later he limped back into the kitchen, shirt torn, blood on his hand, carrying two of his mother's finest handmade quilts. "Here, these should warm you up."

Mary looked at the quilts then back at Johnny. "These are too nice for someone as wet and dirty as I am. Your mom will kill you."

"It's okay, really." He draped one of the quilts around her shoulders; put the other one in her lap.

Mary shrugged. "It's your ass that'll get in trouble, not

mine." She adjusted the quilts so that both of them were wrapped tight around her. "Ah, heaven," she said, then looked up at him, "thanks."

"You're welcome."

"Where are your parents anyway?"

"Well, they're, ah, ah . . . they're not here."

Mary rolled her eyes, "I guessed that much."

"Oh."

"So, you're parents are?"

Dead? In the garage? Frozen? No way, he thought, and decided it would be better to lie. "They went on a trip to," he paused, and then too quickly, added, "to Chicago."

Mary knew he was lying, *but, hey, I'm warm, dry, and safe. At least I think I'm safe.* Maybe I'd better check it out. "You're not some kind of mass murderer, are you?"

"Oh no," said Johnny, aghast.

"Well, I'm glad that's settled." She looked around and listened. Outside of them, she could not detect any other signs of life. "So, you're like, here all by yourself?"

"Yep."

"Cool," she said, and waited. Johnny didn't respond. He just sat there looking uncomfortable. "Like, what is it dude?"

"What's what?"

"It looks like something is bothering you, what is it?"

"Well, it's just that I'm not used to having friends over," he stopped and then added, "I know we're not exactly friends, but anyway, what I mean is I'm just not sure what to do." Johnny felt the heat rising in his face and knew that he was turning red as a tomato. He looked away, and put his head down.

"It's okay, dude, is that all?"

"Well, I don't want you to be upset with me. I'd really like to do a good job at whatever it is I'm supposed to be doing in this situation. So, maybe you can help me out, I mean, if that's okay."

Mary gave him a warm smile, reached across the table, and took his hand. Though she wouldn't have thought it possible, he turned about three shades darker red. She had to suppress a laugh. "You're doing just fine, but I wouldn't complain if you offered me something hot to drink. Like maybe some hot chocolate? That is, if you have some."

Now there's something I can do. Why didn't I think of it? "Hot chocolate coming right up," he said, relieved to get his hands busy doing something, especially something that would please her. Within minutes he had a mug of hot chocolate topped with mini marshmallows for each of them.

Mary took a sip, "Perfect," she said.

"You really think so?"

"Definitely," she drank some more. "This really hits the spot. Thanks."

"You're welcome," said Johnny, beaming.

Something was nagging at Mary. Something couldn't quite place. She sighed and took a few swallows of her drink. And then it hit her: she had no idea where they were. She was pretty sure it wasn't where she was supposed to end up, but, still, she had to ask. "Johnny, is this, like, Laurel Highlands?" She tried to sound hopeful, but it came out lame.

Johnny laughed.

"I guess not, then" she said.

"Well, you're close and at the same time you're far away."

Mary frowned. "What is that supposed to mean?"

"Well," said Johnny, "this is Mystic Meadows, the only houses left over from the old Mystic, before it was almost wiped out by the great Palm Sunday tornado outbreak of 1965. Of course, we weren't alive then, but I'm sure you've heard of the famous Palm Sunday tornadoes?"

Mary shook her head.

Johnny's speech took off, going faster and faster, with big, sweeping gestures of his hands and arms. "You see, there was this huge outbreak of tornadoes across Indiana and Illinois and Ohio. In all, there were forty-seven tornadoes and 271 people died. Indiana," he said with pride, "was hit the worst. Ten of the tornadoes touched down in our state, including the biggest one, the only F5 of the day." Johnny was so excited and talking so fast that even if Mary had been interested, she probably couldn't have understood much. "Of course, there were several F4's in Indiana as well. But that big one, it was in Elkhart, was this huge double tornado. I've got this really cool picture—"

"Oh, yeah," interrupted Mary, "I get the point. So you

were saying about Laurel Highlands? That it's, like, far away but also close?"

"Oh, right," said Johnny. His face slackened. "Ah, yeah, like I was saying," he pointed out the window a bit west of where she had come in, "Laurel Highlands is just over that rise. That's why it's close. It's the newest bunch of houses in Mystic, and they're all huge mansions, I guess, though I've never been there myself. Anyway, that's why I say it's far away, because everyone over there is a millionaire."

"Dude, like, no way! You mean a bunch of millionaires live practically in your backyard and you've never been there?"

Johnny looked down at the floor for a second then back up. "I mean, of course I've been over there," he lied. "What I meant was that I've never been inside any of the houses."

"Loads of millionaires, that's, like, so rad." And then, as an afterthought, "Oh, and, like, what did you say this place is called?"

"Mystic Meadows."

"Right—"

Knowing what she was about to ask, Johnny cut in. "No, there are no millionaires over here. At least I don't think so. We're not poor or anything, but I don't think anyone's what you would call rich."

Mary sighed.

"Why are you so interested in Laurel Highlands, anyway?"

"No reason," said Mary, but he knew she was lying.

As they continued to sip their cocoas, Mary kept a light conversation going. It was actually more of a monologue, which suited Johnny just fine because he didn't have to say anything except an occasional yes or no or uh-huh. She kept it light, talking about simple things such as the weather or TV shows. If she brought up a subject that Johnny knew nothing about, he just nodded in agreement. After a while, though, she stopped. Her eyes glazed over and she was staring down into her empty cup, like she was far away or in some kind of trance.

Johnny waited for a minute then asked, "Mary, are you okay?"

"Yeah, sure, I mean not really . . . oh, I don't know!" She

looked up at him and her eyes, so bright and full of life a few minutes before, were dull and red and watery. And then she was full out crying.

"What's the matter?" he asked. What did I do wrong? he wondered.

She looked up at him briefly and, as if she could read his mind, answered. "You didn't do anything wrong. It's just," she shook her head, breathed in and out a few times. "I don't know what I was thinking. I ran away from home tonight with this stupid idea that when I got somewhere, well, anyway, it was just a stupid idea. I don't know what I'm going to do now."

"It couldn't have been any stupider than what I tried to do tonight," he said, not meaning to, and wishing he hadn't. Mary gave him a questioning look. "Well, I tried to," he stopped for a moment trying to think what to say. "I tried to run away too, sort of anyway. It was a little different, but the same idea, I guess. Anyway, it didn't work out for me either."

"At least you have a bed to sleep in. I don't even have a place to stay tonight. I'm like, so FUBAR."

Johnny had no idea what FUBAR meant, but he didn't think it was good. "You can stay here if you want to."

Mary looked at him, studied his face, "That's nice of you to offer but I doubt that your parents would be too excited about it."

"I'm sure they won't mind," said Johnny "really," because I don't think dead people can mind one way or another. "But you know what?" Johnny asked. "I'm glad it didn't work out, because if it had then I wouldn't have met you." Johnny looked at her, hopeful, but then saw that she had her head down and was still crying. The reality hit him square on like a hard snowball to the face. "I'm sorry you don't feel the same," he said, suddenly ejected.

"Jesus," she said, sounding a bit angry, "it's not all about you. I'm glad I met you too, but there's a lot of crap that I'm not so happy about. So just chill already."

"Sorry."

After a bit Mary looked back up and said, "You really mean it about me staying here?"

Johnny nodded.

"Okay, thanks," she said, giving him a faint smile.

An awkward silence settled over them, and everything went still as a picture. The only sounds were of crickets chirping, in the distance. They sat for a while, just looking at each other, and then, not knowing how or why, the atmosphere gradually changed and two strangers found themselves inexplicably at ease. They no longer felt any pressure to say anything or to make small talk, like they'd known each other for years. Focusing on the present, on each other, all their extra baggage seemed to go adrift. It was a strange sort of comfort, but it was good and they grew wary of breaking the silence. It had been an overwhelming day for the both of them, and yet it already seemed distant. They had both needed a chance to empty their minds of all the chaos and try to find some kind of equilibrium. And, somehow, in each other, they had.

They both silently feared that whatever had come between them might be so fragile as to be destroyed by even the smallest movement or sound. But then Mary started shivering again, and though she tried to hide it, Johnny could tell she was uncomfortable. I have to do something. Anyway, someone has to say something sometime, don't they? "Mary," he said, with some degree of trepidation, "you've still got those wet clothes on. Let's find you something dry to wear."

Mary waited just a fraction of a second before responding, gauging, as was Johnny, the effects of his transgression. The words, though spoken softly, had shattered the silence and ripped through the stillness of the night. This was expected. This was okay. But what was important, and what they both took in with great relief was what the words did not do. They had not sublimated the serenity that had enveloped them nor had they done anything to diminish the bond that had formed between them. The relief was so palpable, so intense, they both grinned.

"That may be the best idea I've heard today," said Mary. "In fact, I'm pretty pooped. I think I'll just go to bed, if that's okay?"

Johnny bowed, and, using his best French accent, said "I vill show you to your room, Madame." Then he placed a hand on the back of her chair—as he'd seen the waiter do several times in Breakfast at Tiffany's—and pulled it out for her as she stood.

"Why thank you," said Mary, laughing.

Pushing the chair aside, he made a motion with his left arm and said, "Sis way Madame, vollow me." Still playing the part of maître d', Johnny was about to take her to the hotel's finest luxury suite on the second floor when he stood up straight and stopped in his tracks. Something was different. It took several double takes to figure it out, or maybe just to believe what he was seeing. But there it was, or rather, there it wasn't—her left breast was gone; disappeared. He knew better than to stare, but it was impossible not to. *How in the world did?* And then he noticed something hanging out from her shirt, covering her navel ring.

Mary could tell he was looking at her chest. At first she just chalked it up to the perky new look that she had installed earlier, but then she realized from his expression that something was wrong. She looked down and saw that the pad, the one that she had so carefully positioned in the left side of her new brassiere so many hours ago, was no longer there. *Jesus, this is embarrassing. It figures though, the way things have been going.* She found where the stuffing had dropped down, snatched it up with her right hand, and then put it behind her back. "Well," she said as if nothing was wrong, "what are you looking at?"

"Nothing," said Johnny, and he did an immediate about-face and led Mary up to her room.

*****

Later that night . . .

In the process of saving the lives of 5000 refugees aboard the floundering Zeldarian vessel, the Cruiser incurs critical damage to its stabilization systems. It is shaking violently then starts to break up. There is nothing Captain Moonbeam can do about it . . . .

*****

Johnny opened his eyes and there was Mary, her arms cradling his head tightly in her lap. "It's okay, it's just a dream," she kept saying over and over, "I'm Mary, remember? Everything's okay now, I'm here."

He was crying, cleansing tears that had needed to be shed for years. It felt good, but still he tried to stop. *Boys*

don't cry, right?

Chapter 16: Good Morning, Johnny Moonbeam

BY SEVEN-THIRTY, THE NEXT MORNING, Mary was wide-awake. By eight o'clock, she'd showered, dressed, and made her bed. By eight-thirty, she'd prepared batter for waffles and set the table for breakfast. By nine o'clock, she'd taken a walk outside and discreetly collected a bouquet of flowers from various neighbors' gardens. By ten o'clock, she was going flat out crazy.

I think Moonbrain needs a little help getting out of bed. There has to be a stereo around here somewhere. A thorough search, however, revealed only an old boom box next to a stack of about twenty CD's. *Welcome to the Stone Age.* Mary flipped through the CD's. Patsy Cline . . . *never heard of her* . . . toss. Johnny Cash . . . *isn't he, like, country?*. . . toss. *Lester Scruggs and Earl Flat?*. . . extra hard toss. At the last one, Beethoven's Fifth Symphony, she shrugged her shoulders, "Well Ludwig, you have just won the wake-up Moonbrain lotto." With no idea of what she, or more specifically Johnny, was about to hear, she put the disk into the dusty boom box and hauled it upstairs. She put it outside his bedroom door, and turned the volume up as high as it would go. "Wake him up, Ludwig baby!" she whispered and an earsplitting DA DA DA DAAH, accompanied by some seriously nasty speaker static, filled the house. *Well, that ought to do it.*

It did.

*****

After another successful mission, Captain J. Moonbeam is just a few light-years from his beloved lunar home, a large complex hidden within the rugged landscape of the Moon's Milchius region. Suddenly, without warning, he comes under enemy fire. The veteran space-pilot calmly, but quickly, secures his helmet and has just locked down his silver spacesuit when a deafening explosion rocks the ship. Air hisses out through a hole in the main cabin, followed by a growing stream of debris. With no time to spare, no choice, and for the first time in his glorious career, he initiates the ejection procedure. Moments after being flung from the cockpit, he watches, helpless, as his trusty Moon Cruiser comes apart, disintegrating right before his eyes. Now he is floating, freefalling through space, trying to get his bearings, when . . . whop, thud . . . his body slams into something.

*****

"Ouch. What the hell? Where am I?" Johnny blinked and looked around. *Oh, my bedroom floor. On Earth. Rats.* He'd been having a peaceful, wonderful, dream—something that virtually never happened; Johnny almost always had nightmares if he dreamt at all—when his ship had inexplicably been attacked, the explosion so real it still rang in his ears. Now that he was fully awake, Johnny realized what the sound really was. Beethoven, blaring in from the hallway, and making his head hurt. He opened his door and the volume tripled. He staggered for a second then laid into the offending boom box as hard as he could. With his bare right foot, the one that now hurt like all get-out. "Mary," he yelled, holding the rail and hobbling down the stairs.

In the kitchen, Mary arranged the flowers in one of Jill's vases and placed it on the table, the finishing touch for her masterpiece of a breakfast. She heard Johnny stumbling down the stairs and turned around to see the bedraggled boy glaring at her, clutching the walls for support. "Oh dear," she said, barley able to control her giggles. "I think I messed-up."

"You did it?" he roared, less a question than accusation. "You're the insolent bitch that turned the goddamned music up full blast?"

*****

Mary, who moments before had been in the most excellent of moods was stunned into silence; absolutely speechless, a rare phenomena indeed. It was not supposed to go like this. He was supposed to come into the kitchen, happily-appily, oowing and ahhing over her lovely breakfast. *Where did this . . . this . . . animal come from?* She'd expected him to act like a person, and now here he was, sounding like Brad. I should know better by now. After all, he is just a guy. Regaining her composure, she glared at him, eyes ablaze.

"I'm sor—" he started.

She cut him off. "Too late, asshole, I think I'll let you make your own breakfast." Mary turned and picked the large mixing bowl up off the counter then slowly walked back over to Johnny, and deliberately, carefully, poured the batter over his head, leaving the bowl atop him like a hat, and stormed off outside.

Johnny stood, looking bewildered, and watched her slam the door as batter slimed its way down his body.

*****

Halfway around the block Mary realized she was running. She stopped and leaned over, hands-on-knees, to catch her breath. And, perhaps, her reason as well. *Why do I always have to be such a hothead?* After a minute, she continued, this time at a normal pace, wondering if the boy who yelled at her so wickedly a few minutes ago was the same person who'd been so kind the night before. Of course, he was, but why such an asshole all of a sudden? She kept walking. *I did wake him up a little rudely. Not to mention, out of a dead sleep.* Then, when she first saw him standing in the archway, all red-faced with rage, dressed in a pair of too-small rocket-boy pajamas, he'd looked so goofy she'd been unable to stifle her laughter. *I guess that pushed him over the edge,* she thought, because that's when he yelled at her. It didn't seem so bad now. *I mean, I've like heard worse.* And the look on his face when she poured the waffle batter on him was priceless. It reminded her of the cowardly lion from the Wizard of Oz after Dorothy slapped him in the face, saying, "Why did you have to go and do that for?" *I guess I could give him a break.* She laughed to herself, and the world seemed right again.

Henry Mayfield, retired basketball coach and forever neighbor of the Abel's, walked out of his driveway and onto the sidewalk as Mary passed by. He was taking his ancient Basset Hound, Barney, for a walk. They both looked at her suspiciously. "Don't remember a-seein' you 'round here before. You visitin'?"

Mary turned toward the man. He bore an uncanny if not somewhat disturbing resemblance to his hound: big, fleshy jowls hanging down past his chin and lolling back and forth as he talked. "No, just out for a walk," she said sprightly, "and come to think of it, I don't remember seeing you around much either. Oh well, it sure is a nice day, don't you think?" And she continued on her way.

*****

Henry, chagrined at the girl's impertinent behavior, decided the best course of action was to forget about it. "Who cares, anyway?" he said, stroking Barney's head affectionately, and resumed their walk. When they got to 4217 Mystic Lane Barney stopped. He started sniffing around and barking, something he rarely did anymore. Henry looked at the hound, scratched behind his huge ears, and looked back up at Jack's house. Though it had been a few weeks by then, he continued to be bewildered anew every time he saw it. "Where in the hell do you think that Jack done run off to?" In reply, B arney just barked some more at the house and Henry thought about the young girl he had just seen. It made him wonder. The girl, there was something about her. And then he remembered. A man had come knocking at his door about ten o'clock the night before asking about a girl–his daughter–who had, apparently, run away. At the time, Henry didn't know anything. *But now, maybe I do.* "You see, Barney," he said, "this noggin can still put two and two together once in a while." The hound moaned and shook his head, ears flapping like flags in the cool morning breeze. Henry pulled the wallet from his trousers, took out a hand-written card that said, "Ralph Jordan, Transportation Specialist, Indianapolis Metropolitan Bus Co." and dialed the number on his cell phone.

"Hello." The man sounded grumpy, if not downright mean, which surprised Henry because he'd been so polished and polite the night before.

"Oh, I'm sorry. Didn't mean to wake ya."

"What you want?" the voice growled.

Normally, after being treated in such a harsh manner, Henry would have hung up. He was about to do just that then stopped. *He did lose a daughter, after all, maybe I should cut him some slack.* "This is Henry Mayfield. I live here in Mystic Meadows. You come-a knockin' at my door last night. Remember?"

"Oh yes, sorry to have been so rude. I extend to you my sincerest apology." Ralph said, sounding once more like Emily Post's protégé. "I'm a bit stressed as you might imagine. Thank you so much for calling." Then, after a few polite exchanges, "I can be there in about an hour, if that works for you?"

"That'd be just fine. I'll be home all day. The house number is 3746, light blue with a purple door."

"Thank you again. It was so thoughtful of you to call."

Ever since the death of his beloved wife about a year-ago Henry, for the most part, merely existed. Until now. The chance to help this nice fellow find his lost daughter exhilarated the elderly man and, for the first time in quite a while, he felt alive.

*****

Mary came back determined to give that boy a piece of her mind. Until she saw him. Right where she left him, dressed in his pajamas, and other than sitting, did not appear to have moved an inch from where she doused him with waffle batter. He'd wiped off none of it. The large, white mixing bowl still adorned his head, looking like a ceramic sailor hat with the sides down. The batter thickened, had crusted in places, and covered nearly his entire head and torso, his hair a mass of moldy dreadlocks. Sunken behind the gooey mask, his eyes looked brighter and bluer than usual. Two owl eyes peering up at her.

"Johnny," she said, barely able to talk for want of laughing, "you look ridiculous. Like, I mean, why are you just sitting there with that stupid bowl on your head?"

"Well, you're the one who put it there," said Johnny stone-faced, and it completely disarmed her.

"But why..." She trailed off, overtaken by a fierce case of the giggles.

"You ran out of here so fast you didn't even get a chance to see what I looked like. I thought you might want to, so I waited. I figured I owed you that much, because you were right. I was being an asshole."

"You're so crazy I don't even know what to say."

"Does that mean we're friends again?"

Mary put her hands on her hips and tried to look stern, but Johnny knew she was laughing inside.

"Come on, Mary, I'm really sorry. I sounded just like my dad, which, believe me, is the last thing I want to do." Johnny rose up on his knees, put his hands together, and bowed. The ceramic bowl fell off his head. "Please forgive me," he pleaded, looking even more ridiculous, if possible.

"You big goofball, go get cleaned up. I'll make breakfast."

*****

Johnny walked into the kitchen, hand-combing his wet hair and grinning. "About time, Moonbrain," said Mary. "The waffles are almost done."

"Good, I'm starved," he said, rubbing his hands together.

"Hey, before sitting your ass down, grab the strawberries out of the fridge, 'kay?"

Johnny fetched the berries and sat down. "Ah, Mary," he said, pointing to the counter behind her, "is that the way it's supposed to look?" Mary had overfilled the waffle iron. The top was rising, opening up like some giant's mouth, and spewing half-done waffle out over the counter and floor.

"Oh shit." She hustled to clean off the excess batter. "Wow, I didn't know these things, like, rose so much."

By the time everything was on the table, both were famished. They attacked the feast with the zeal of two hungry lions, destroying five large waffles and an entire carafe of OJ. More importantly, they avoided any small talk. He finished a full waffle ahead of Mary, and not used to eating in the company of anyone, let alone a girl, proceeded on with his post meal routine as a matter of habit.

That's when Johnny learned that, once a good belch had been put in motion, you couldn't do a thing about it. It was like trying to stop a bullet after pulling the trigger. Living by himself, this little ritual of producing the biggest burp possible had been rather fun. Now, sitting across from his unsuspecting guest and helpless to stop it, he was mortified. But the foul-smelling gas was already passing through his upper esophagus, and *crap, it's going to be a big one*. As it passed through his throat, knocking at the door so to speak, he tried once more to mollify the effects, but to no avail. A huge, aromatic BUURRRRRRRRP was unleashed and echoed throughout the house.

Mary waved a hand in front of her face. "Grrrrooooss!"

"Oh geez, I'm sorry," Johnny said, his face turning crimson.

*****

"You don't mind if we watch Chicago on pay-per-view, do you? I just love Richard Gere."

"Sounds good to me," Johnny said, though he'd rather see something like an old Twilight Zone episode. He set a coffee tray, complete with sugar and milk as he'd been taught, and watched Mary load up with several teaspoons of sugar and whatever milk the mug would hold.

"Great job, dude."

"Thanks." *Well, that's something I can do right, anyway.*

"Be quiet now. Here's the show."

No problem.

*****

Mary was enjoying the movie and Johnny enjoyed watching Mary enjoy the movie. Everything was great. But then, as Richard Gere was in the middle of his one solo, "Razzle Dazzle," there was a knock at the door.

"Do we have to answer that?" asked Mary.

"I never do–unless I've ordered pizza or something. Just ignore it. They'll go away."

They didn't leave.

The knocking continued incessantly, growing louder with each volley.

"Whoever they are," said Mary, "they sure are persistent, aren't they?"

"I know," he whispered and then put his index finger to his lips in a hushing motion, "come on, follow me." He took her hand and led Mary up to his bedroom where he quietly opened the window. They listened. More knocking, louder, harder, and then two men talking.

"I reckon there ain't nobody home," said a voice familiar to Johnny.

"I think there is," replied a deep, growling voice eerily familiar to Mary.

Johnny reached outside with a small mirror and positioned it so he could see who was at the front door: Henry and Barney and some big guy he didn't know. Mary came up and looked over his shoulder.

"Oh no," she gasped, her face went white, and she slid to the floor.

"What's the matter?"

"It's Ralph.

Chapter 17: Danger at the Door

Outside, Ralph gave up any pretense of proper etiquette and let his native personality take over. Barney, suspicious of the big man all along, no longer had any doubts. He hid among the bushes, hoping to dig his way to China where Ralph monsters were not allowed to run rampant in the streets. Henry, a little slower on the uptake, nevertheless, soon reached the same conclusion.

"I'm a-tellin' ya, this house has been empty fer pert near a month now."

"Shut up, dog face."

"Don't you be a-talkin' to my dog that way, even if you is bigger than the both of us put together."

"I wasn't talking to Long Ears. I was talking to you, Dog Face."

"Well, okay then," said Henry as he wrestled Barney from the bushes. "Come on, you ole hound dog, let's get on home. I've had about enough of this low-rent S O B."

Ralph carried on knocking and yelling, oblivious to Henry's departure. "Open up, I know you're in there, you little tramp!" The man pounded so hard Johnny thought he might break the door down.

"Do something Johnny," said Mary, growing more agitated by the second.

But how? Johnny felt paralyzed. He wanted to run and hide. Then she slapped him, and brought him back to life. He looked at her, and, reflected back at him in those big brown eyes he saw a younger version of himself; the same fear and desperation, and worst of all, helplessness he'd know as a young child. He wanted to scream. He could see that she was trying to be brave, but her fully dilated pupils could not mask the pure, unadulterated terror behind them. Seeing her that way was just wrong. It pissed him off and unlocked something inside of him. Without knowing why, he began spinning in place, around and around, ever faster. As he did this, something fearless and brave took hold of him, and when he stopped, everything was different. He no longer felt like Johnny Abel. He was Johnny Moonbeam again, just like when he was a kid. And Johnny Moonbeam wasn't afraid of anything. *I can do this. After all, wasn't it only yesterday that Johnny Moonbeam saved the entire planet from those despicable Gypsy Giants? If I can do that, then one measly pervert should be a piece of cake.*

"Come on." He grabbed her by the wrist, half pulling, half leading her down the hall, then slung her into his parent's bedroom. Except now, he thought, it was her room. "Prop a chair or something against the door handle to secure it," he said and slammed it shut.

Ralph carried on, knocking and yelling, as Johnny slipped into the bathroom and picked the gun from the floor, safety still off. Then he was back across the hall into his bedroom. After snatching his digital camera off the desk and snapping several pictures of the big guy, Johnny threw the camera on his bed.

Thump, thump, thump! "Open the door or I'm going to kick it in."

"Go away right now," Johnny yelled out the window, "or I'll call the cops."

"Go ahead and call the cops. They won't find me, but at least they'll be able to call an ambulance. For all the good it'll do when they find out that you're dead. Now open the goddamned door or I'm breaking it down."

"I've got a gun," said Johnny and held it out for Ralph to see. "Now go or I'll shoot you." Ralph only laughed and started kicking the door so hard Johnny was sure it was about to cave in. He thought if Ralph saw the gun, it would be enough to scare him off. He didn't intend to shoot it. *There's no time to pussyfoot around,* thought Captain Moonbeam, and he fired a warning shot into the bushes. "I'm going to count to three, and if you're not gone, I'll shoot you dead where you stand. And if I ever see you again, I'll shoot first and ask questions later. One ... two ..."

Ralph was gone.

Chapter 18: Cybersleuth

RALPH DISAPPEARED AROUND THE CORNER, and Johnny breathed a sigh of relief. He no longer felt like Johnny Moonbeam, and all the fear that had been stuffed down during his alter ego's short tenure at the helm shot back to the surface like a torpedo. He waited a couple of minutes, which seemed more like a couple of hours, for the police or some neighbor to come over because of the gunshot, but nothing. His heart started to slow down. His stomach settled. And then, floating down the hall like a shadow, came a voice.

"Is he gone?"

Johnny's head swiveled like an owl, and he nearly jumped out of his shoes before realizing who it was. He was so frightened he'd almost forgotten about her. *Geez, I hope I don't look as scared as I feel.* He went into the bathroom and looked in the mirror, then frowned and splashed some water on his face. *Better, not great, but better.*

"Johnny?" she said, and then again, her voice growing louder each time. "Johnny, where are you?"

"Coming," he yelled, and ran to her room. "I'm right here. You okay?"

She opened the door. "I'm okay," she said, sniffling and wiping away tears with a well-used tissue. "Come on in."

The sight of her there all puffy-eyed and vulnerable was just plain wrong. It shocked him, and a wave of anger threatened to take him over. "Don't worry," he said, fighting to stay in control. "Here," he took her arm, "let's sit down," then, trying to sound as reassuring as possible, "Ralph's gone." *I will get you, Ralph, for doing this to her.*

"What happened? I thought I heard a gunshot." She looked genuinely frightened.

"You did. That would've been," Johnny shuddered, gulped, and managed to squeak out, "me."

For the first time she looked up, hopeful, "You shot him?"

Well, actually, I . . ."

"Did you get him?"

"I wasn't trying to get him. I was just trying to scare him."

"Oh," she said, disappointed. "So, what did he do then?"

An expression of Jack's came to mind. "He took off faster than a turkey at Thanksgiving." It was true. However, at the same time it also meant Ralph was still out there. Nevertheless, Mary seemed to perk-up.

"So, Ralph just, like, turned tail and ran?"

"He was moving as fast as he could, I think."

"Johnny Moonbeam, you are my hero," she said then gave him a big hug and kissed him right on the lips. He blushed. She grinned and pinched his cheek. "You must have some cowboy in there somewhere."

Johnny tipped an imaginary ten-gallon hat and did his best John Wayne imitation, "Just doing my job, ma'am."

Mary laughed, but then a few seconds later her expression changed again, more serious. "Do you think someone else might have heard the shot and maybe, like, called the cops?"

Johnny thought about this for a second. "Well, if they did, they mustn't have been too worried, or we'd know about it by now."

"You're probably right, so, I guess we're okay?"

I wish I could tell you what you want to hear, that everything is okay now, that it's all over, but I can't. Though he wasn't sure why, Johnny's gut told him they had not seen the last of Ralph. He looked her in the eyes, all business now, and said, "I think we need to be ready."

Mary's smile faded. "Ready? Why, you don't think he'll come back, do you?"

"Ah, no, of course not. . . Well, I don't think so, anyway," he lied, "but just to be on the safe side I think we should be ready for anything."

"ARGGGH!" she screamed. "I'll never be able to relax until I know for sure that dirt bag is going to leave me alone!" She took a pillow off the bed. "And how is that ever going to happen?" She flung it blindly across the room. "It's not fair! Am I the only girl in Indianapolis?" She likely would have kept on ranting for some time but was interrupted by the sound of Jill's lamp crashing to the floor. "Oh shit! I'm sorry," she said, and went over to pick it up. "Your mom is going to kill us, and it's all my fault."

"Ah, it's okay. My mom will understand." Mary was getting worked up again. *I need to calm that girl down.* "Come on, let's watch some TV for a while," he said then took her by the hand and gently guided her downstairs.

After surfing through a hundred or so channels, Mary settled on one specializing in reruns from the 1950s and 1960s called The Golden Age of Television. "Oh, cool, I love all these old shows, don't you?"

Johnny nodded agreement, though he wasn't at all sure what she meant.

After watching half of an I Love Lucy episode together, Mary relaxed. Johnny, on the other hand, grew more anxious by the minute. "Hey, Mary, I need to go upstairs and check out some stuff on the computer, okay?"

"You'll leave your door open?"

"I'll leave my door open, and if you say 'boo,' I'll be down here before your heart can pump out another beat."

Mary sighed, but then smiled and said, "I'll be fine, Moonbrain. Thanks for putting up with me and my tantrums."

"No problem. Let me know if you need anything." And, with that, he was gone.

*****

Johnny went upstairs to start gathering information about Ralph, but first there was something else he needed to take care of.

It had been a slow and painful process, but over the last few years Johnny began to realize that there was no rocket ship waiting for him; no moon base to shelter and protect him; that he had no superpowers. Even that morning it was still a process in evolution, incomplete, but then Ralph changed everything. Johnny's confrontation with a live, in-the-flesh criminal made him understand what was real and what wasn't and, more important, gave him an up close and personal view of his own mortality. It wasn't until after Ralph had departed, however, that Johnny realized these things.

For a few precious minutes, he felt like a Knight of the Round Table when, with the calm demeanor of King Arthur himself, he had delivered the fair princess to the safety of her castle and then slain the evil villain—or at least chased him away. It was in the aftermath of the rescue that the valiant young hero understood he was no brave knight. He had, in fact, been scared to death. And that was when Johnny realized with absolute certainty that he was just a human being. Any notion that he might be something more sank in the icy waters of reality and plunged toward the bottom where it would forever reside, cold and broken beyond repair.

Or so he thought.

It was such a relief to give up the pressures of being a super hero and be able to live a normal life. Which, in the end, is all he'd ever wanted. It was good. He felt content, satisfied, even happy. For about ten minutes. And then Mary turned it all catawampus again. "Johnny Moonbeam, you're my hero," she'd said. I just want to be me is what he'd thought at the time, but he would not let her down. *She says I'm a hero, so there it is. I'm a hero. I'll just have to stop pretending I'm normal.* But what kind of hero was he with no superpowers? He thought about this for a while until it came to him. *Holy Moonbrain! How could I forget about Batman? Batman is mortal and so am I.* Once he got over the fact that he no longer had superpowers or rocket ships at his disposal, like when he was a kid, Johnny decided to make the best of what he did have: brains, computers, money, and most of all a dogged determination. *Not bad.* Still, he needed an identity, something unique and special.

He was having trouble imagining a new identity until he remembered something he'd overheard, of all people, Jack say. "My boy in there, Henry . . . I mean, there's this boy I know, and I'd put up against anyone—Bill Gates or whoever—when it comes to computers. I'm telling you, he's a genius with 'em. Hell, I bet he could hack a hippo out of the damn zoo if he wanted to . . ." That was it, Johnny would use his cyber-skills to define his hero self. And so it was that the mythical Johnny Moonbeam of his youth gave way to a new and quite real one of the present: Johnny Moonbeam, Cybersleuth.

Remembering his young counterpart's custom spacesuit he made a mental note. *I will need a monogrammed JM Cyber-sleuth uniform, but it will have to wait until the good Princess Valentine is safe and the scoundrel Ralph is securely behind bars where he belongs.* That's it, he thought, ready to take on the world, or at least Ralph, except he didn't feel any different. For a minute, he was frustrated, but then he understood. *I'll never be able to just casually say, 'okay, ho-hum, time to turn into a superhero*. What was missing? All he was missing was a method of transforming himself back and forth between the two personalities. It had to be something substantial, he knew, or it wouldn't work. Then he had it: standing in the center of his bedroom, Johnny spun around in place, gradually building momentum until in a single motion he vaulted over the back of his chair. His butt landed squarely, albeit somewhat less gracefully than he hoped, on the seat, his hands poised and ready to attack the keyboard . . . and then vertigo caught up with him and flung him mercilessly onto the floor. He waited a minute for his head to clear, then got back in the pilot's seat and started surfing. He felt new and powerful. Johnny Moonbeam Cyber-Sleuth was prepared to do whatever might be necessary, soberly accepting his role in the never-ending fight against evil.

A burst of laughter interrupted him and the sleuth turned crimson. Mary was standing in the doorway, doubled over. "Ah, how long have you been standing there?"

"Long enough," she finally managed to get out. "What was that?"

"What was what?"

"You know."

"Oh, nothing really. Just helps me to, ah, concentrate," which, he realized, wasn't totally a lie.

"Right," she said, but knew she didn't believe him.

Chang the subject, Moonbeam. "Ah, I need to do some stuff. What do you want?"

"Just wanted to see if you could use a coke or something."

"Thanks, but I'm okay."

Mary went back downstairs, giggling all the way, and picked up the remote. Lassie was up next, it wasn't her favorite, but, it would have to do. Mary settled down and then, before the second commercial break, fell fast asleep. But not as peaceful a sleep as she would have hoped for . . .

*****

A modern day mythological creature called a Bralph—Ralph's head on what looks like Brad's body, except with four legs and a spiked tail—is chasing Mary around the Indianapolis Motor Speedway. She's driving Team Penske's number one IndyCar entry at over 250 miles-per-hour down the backstretch, and still the beast is gaining on her. As she rounds turn number four, the monster is less than a car length behind. Then she sees him, Johnny Moonbeam, waiting for her with his Moon Cruiser, ready to blast her off to safety. If she can just make it to the finish line, everything will be alright. She looks back. There's still a half a car length between her and the creature, just enough for her to make it. Relieved, she swings her head forward again and gasps. The boy and his ship have disappeared. There's only the checkered finish line, with the Bralph standing right behind it, ready to gobble her up.

Mary starts screaming. "It's not fair. It's not fair!" Before she is fully alert, however, the nightmare pulls her back under and the chase starts anew.

*****

Mary woke up an hour later and went upstairs. "Hey Moonbrain, how's it going?" He didn't answer or even seem to notice so she just watched, amazed. He was moving so fast it was like a blur. Hands flying between keyboard and mouse, head bobbing up and down to look at the ever-changing windows opening and closing on the monitor, and every so often swiveling in his chair to rip a page from the printer, then back pecking on the keyboard. She was getting dizzy just watching it. "Hey, Moonbrain," she called out again. Still no answer. She kept calling, louder and louder until she was almost yelling, and then, finally, Johnny started and turned around.

"Oh, there you are," he said.

"Didn't you, like, hear me yelling at you?"

"Of course, why else would I have turned around?"

"I mean before that?"

"What before that?"

"Never mind."

"Well," he said, "I've got some good stuff," and motioned for her to come over.

"What good stuff?"

"About Ralph, of course, excep-"

"There is nothing good about Ralph, Moonbrain."

"I mean good information for us about Ralph, except," he said, moving his eyebrows up and down and whispering, "that's not his real name."

"It's not?"

"Nope. His real name is James Thurmond."

"How did you find that out?"

"Well, you see..."

Uh, oh, here comes Professor Moonbrain. "How about just, like, cut to the chase this time?"

Johnny looked puzzled, "What?"

"Like don't explain to me how the refrigerator works, just give me the cold Coke, all right?"

Johnny thought about it for a while before he understood. "Oh," he sighed, "you mean you don't want to know how I took several pictures of Ralph and Photoshoped them into one decent image and then hacked into a central database called WebCop and used their facial recognition program to identify him?"

"You got it."

"Okay," he said shrugging his shoulders, "Ralph's real name is James Thurmond, and he's an escaped convict from Florida, who was serving a 20-year sentence for first-degree rape. As part of a plea bargain they dropped the other case against him, which was for rape and aggravated murder. Apparently, the prosecutor didn't think they could convict him on the second case anyway."

"Jesus Christ, Moonbrain, is that all?

"No," said Johnny, apparently not noticing that Mary had turned white. "His rap sheet says he's been convicted of child molestation, armed robbery, transporting stolen goods across state lines-"

"Just shut up already!"

I guess I'll skip the description of the rape crime he thought, and then noticed she was gone. "Mary?"

Mary, not wanting to hear anything more about James Thurmond, slipped down to the kitchen. She poured a coke for herself then sighed and did the same for Johnny, who was still calling her from upstairs. *I guess I'm going to find out whether I want to or not.* "I'm downstairs in the kitchen,

Moonbrain."

Chapter 19: Videogames, Bagels and Cream Cheese

THERE YOU ARE," HE SAID, SAT DOWN, and took a long drink, "thanks for the Coke. Now, like I was saying . . . "

He was already talking too fast about things she didn't understand. Uh, oh, here comes another lecture. I seriously can't take this right now. "Johnny," she cut him off, "I'm really excited about all this stuff, but I was wondering if . . . " Mary tried to sound enthusiastic but, apparently, it hadn't worked because Johnny, who had been pumped up to the max, deflated at the sound of her voice and appeared to shrink about three sizes.

"You don't seem very excited."

She reached across the table and took his hand, giving him a faint smile, "It's just kind of hard for me, you know?"

"Well it's kind of hard on me too. I did a lot of work you know, and ..."

"Look, I know you're working hard, and I know it's important and I know that I need to listen, but, like, right now all I can see is that son-of-a bitch coming after me. So just cut me some slack, okay?"

"Slack?"

"Give me a break, chill, whatever," she huffed, then jumped out of her seat and marched out of the kitchen.

"Hey, Mary, wait," he called, following her into the living room. "I'm sorry. I just don't understand what I'm supposed to say."

Mary made an abrupt stop and turned to face him. Johnny was barely able to keep from plowing her over as they ended up nose to nose. "I don't care if you understand or not, it's probably not even possible. I think it's something genetic with guys, they never do. But if you could at least, like, just believe me when I tell you something is bothering me and then chill out about it it would be greatly appreciated. You don't have to understand every goddamned thing you know."

But I want to understand everything. "Okay," he mumbled, "I can do that."

They sat on the sofa, no one talking. Johnny was determined not to be the one to break silence and used the time to try to put himself in her shoes, to imagine what it would be like to have someone chasing you down and never be able to relax. And when he thought about it like that he almost laughed. *I know exactly how that feels. Why didn't I see it before?*

After a while, Mary sighed, put on her best pretend smile, and, with feigned enthusiasm, said, "Okay, I think I'm ready now. In fact, I'm more than ready. I can't wait to hear what you've got."

"It's okay Mary," even Johnny knew he was being placated, "you don't have to fake it. I thought about you and you-know-who, and I think I understand." He was going to stop there but then added, "At least I do a little bit. I think."

"Thanks. And I realize that I have to hear what you found out, so go on."

"If I start getting too carried away or whatever just tell me to shut up, okay?"

Her pretend smile melted, replaced by the real thing, "No problem."

"Okay, so the reason we need information on this," he paused for an instant, "on this, ah, person, is to find out what his tendencies are, what he likes to do, stuff like that. Because most people are, what do they call it...oh...creatures of habit, that's it. They tend to do the same things they've done before. So, if we know where he likes to hang out and such, then we'll be able to narrow down where to look for him, and that will give us a better shot at catching him."

"So, what did you find out?"

"Well, he's a fanatic about New York Style bagels with cream cheese."

I must be missing something here. This is supposed to help us? "So," she said squinting her eyes and talking extra slow, "We just have to find the deli with the best New York style bagels and cream cheese, and we've got him?"

Johnny smiled, "Well, actually I just put the bagels with cream cheese in there for fun. It's true, but I don't think it's going to help us too much."

"Well, that's a relief, so, like, what else did you find?"

"He likes videogames."

Mary rolled her eyes. *Oh, right, anybody can see how*

that's *going to help*. "What?"

"I know it sounds crazy, but listen for a minute . . . " He went on to explain that, with the help of WebCop, he had learned a whole lot about James Thurmond, and it was his video game playing habits that Johnny was most interested in. It turned out that the man didn't just like to play video games. He played them compulsively, almost every waking hour. "In prison they diagnosed him as a video game addict and wouldn't let him play. It really made him mad. It was only a couple of weeks later that he escaped from prison, and the therapist thinks the reason he even tried to escape was so he could play his videogames."

"That's kind of weird, don't you think?"

"Not really, it's more common than you might think. There was this one kid who was so addicted to a game that, apparently, he couldn't tell fantasy from reality. When his parents figured out he had a problem and took it away from him, he killed them. I guess he thought it was part of the game or something stupid like that."

"Wow, that's really creepy."

"It is. There are even doctors who specialize in treating Internet and videogame addictions and so on. I guess it is kind of weird, but it's real. And that's why I don't play them that much anymore, I don't want to get addicted to a stupid game." Here Johnny explained his expertise at videogames and, while he hadn't played the particular game Ralph liked, *Total Annihilation III*, he was confident he would be able to master it without difficulty.

"Okay, but still, how does that help us?"

"You know anything about these multiplayer games?" Mary shook her head. "Well they're games you can play with other people over the Internet, against them." Mary nodded. "You first start by making your own player and giving it a name. That's the player you play with pretty much forever. The thing is, as you get better your player advances in rank and has more responsibilities and is in charge of troops and so on and so forth."

"Okay, I get that, but-"

Johnny interrupted. "Once I get my character into a high-ranking position in *Total Annihilation III*, he'll notice me in the rankings. He won't be able to resist challenging me to a game."

"How will you know it's him and not someone else?'

"That's easy. His player's name is sn-" Johnny stopped and coughed. When he had looked up Snuffboy in the regular dictionary, it hadn't made much sense, so he looked in the urban dictionary online and was pretty sure he had found Ralph's meaning. *No, I don't think she really wants to know.* "Ah, I forgot."

"No you didn't. What is it?

"Trust me, you don't want to know."

"Of course I want to know," but then, when she saw the anguish on his face, she added, "you mean, like, it's really that bad?"

"It's worse."

"Right. Well then, okay, go on."

"So, I'm assuming that he will be playing at a gaming center somewhere because I don't think he has a home computer to play from at this point. I checked it out and there are only about six gaming centers in the Indianapolis area that would be suitable to play this game the way he likes to play it."

"Okay," she said, uncertain.

"You see, like I said, once my player is ranked, he'll notice and want to play me. All I have to do is keep him occupied while someone goes and finds which one of the six gaming centers he's at. Then call the cops and bingo, problem solved!"

"You're sure you can do that? Keep him playing long enough to check out all those places?"

"Oh yeah," Johnny said with a laugh. "If there's one thing I'm sure of it's my ability to play these stupid games, and I also know these people who are addicted to them. They'll keep going until they die or someone drags them away, seriously. It's Ralph's big weakness, and we're going to exploit it."

"Except for one thing, who's going to drive around and check these places?"

Johnny smiled, "That's your job."

Mary was taken aback, but not because she was daunted by the task or didn't think she could do it. *After all, it's right up my alley*. Even though, at the time, she had no clue about whom to call for this mission, it would be, like, no problem. "You're right. I'll figure it out." What surprised her was that Johnny seemed to know without any doubt or hesitation that she would be able to do this. She wasn't sure she liked anyone to know her that well, especially when we have, like, just met. And yet, at the same time, she liked the feeling of being connected to someone. It was something new, and she thought, mostly good. Even if Moonbrain is kind of weird, he's pretty nice. Not to mention cute.

"Great, I knew you would."

"But you said he's a pretty good player, what if he beats you?"

The thought of Ralph having a chance to beat him brought a mischievous grin to his face. "Don't worry," he said with an uncharacteristic air of confidence, "He's not going to beat me."

"How can you be so sure?"

"Well, since I was about 10 years old," he said, trying to sound reserved this time, "no one has."

Mary had not known him long, but she did have an incredible ability to read people with regards to whether or not they were telling the truth, and she'd known him long enough to know that the dude doesn't lie, so I guess he's right. "How did you get so good anyway?"

He wanted to say something like, *when you're locked in your room 24 hours a day, there's not much else to do*, but instead he said, "My dad says I have a natural talent for it," which was true enough except that, presently, his father wasn't saying much of anything. "We played a lot together when I was younger," he shrugged his shoulders, "now I just play enough to make sure my skills are still up, and, like I said, they pretty much are."

Mary christened the plan Operation Catch Ralph or OCR for short. It took an hour and a half, more or less, to work out the details over pizza and coke delivered from Giamatti's. For Johnny's part, he would sign on to *Total Annihilation III*, and play until he earned enough points, which he suspected were obtained by killing people or aliens or both, to make his character one of the top ten rated players on the local network. No doubt this would catch Ralph's attention, and he would have to challenge Johnny to play. Then, while Hell-Twinkie—this was what Mary named Johnny's player—was keeping Snuffboy busy, she would make a phone call.

After brief deliberation, Mary decided to enlist the help of the bus driver, *Michael, I think his name was*, to check out the gaming centers and make the call to the police. He had been sympathetic to her and said he would help her if she ever needed it, *and do I ever need it*. She found his card on the bottom of her backpack, somewhat worse for the wear after being crumpled and wet, but she could still read the name, Michael P Quackenbush, and his number. She dialed.

"Hello, Michael here."

"Oh hi Mr.," she looked at the card again, "Mr. Quackenbush. This is Mary. I was on your bus last night. Remember?"

"Yeah, of course I remember. Did you get to where you needed to go all right?"

"Well, that's kind of what I'm calling about."

"There wasn't a problem with the pass, I hope?"

"Well, I didn't exactly use it." Mary explained.

"Good night nurse! You're not kidding me are ya?"

"No sir."

"No, I guess you wouldn't kid about that. Jesus Christ, I had no idea. I am so sorry."

"It's not your fault."

"Still, I feel just awful."

It took a while for Mary to explain the exact predicament she was in. And that was the easy part—now she had to explain the plan. The plan called for someone to be on call, Mr. Q if she could get him to cooperate, until Johnny got Ralph to take the bait. Then, Mary would call Mr.Q, who would drive to each of the six gaming centers until he found the one where Ralph was and call the police, waiting to make sure Ralph was taken into custody. That way, neither Johnny nor Mary would have to deal with the police directly. Of course, Mr. Quackenbush was reluctant at first but eventually Mary won him over, and he agreed to help them.

"So, young lady, when do you think this might all come down? Any idea?"

"I have no flippin' idea," she said, "could be anytime, I guess."

"Well I'm with you. I'm going to go buy me a cell phone right now, never had one before. No one ever needed me for nothing before but to drive the bus." He laughed a little at this, "Anyway, I'll call you when I get the phone and keep that sucker charged up and on my person 24/7. You call me whenever you need me for this or anything else."

"Thanks a lot Mr. Quackenbush, I'm feeling better already. I know you'd rather have me just call the police, but I appreciate your understanding. Well, I'll talk to you soon I guess."

"I call and give you the number as soon as I get a phone. Should be pretty quick, maybe a couple of hours. Bye now."

"Bye."

Operation Catch Ralph was in full swing.

Chapter 20: Blue Mary

A WEEK WENT BY, THEN TWO SINCE the launch of OCR, each passing day slower than the one before. HellTwinkie had yet to be challenged. Though by no means forgotten, images and memories of Ralph no longer monopolized Mary's brain. As she debated between cereal and waffles for breakfast, it occurred to her that she and Johnny had fallen into a rather predictable daily routine, a realization that both comforted and distressed her.

How can I complain? I've got cable TV. We order out for dinner every night, and anything else I need I can get online, including Victoria's Secret, which is über cool. There must be something wrong with me. Like, dah, this is what I wanted. I think. I thought?

Still, Mary was bored.

So, said a little voice inside her, you want to go back to your former life?

I'd rather die.

Bored, bored, bored, said the voice.

I'm not bored. I just need . . . a little variety. Scanning the kitchen for ideas, Mary spotted a row of cookbooks lined up along the top shelf of the pantry. *Hmm, it's not much, but. . .* She pulled down one called *Authentic Southern Breakfasts,* and began perusing it for fresh and exciting dishes. The first recipe, 'Old-fashioned sausage, biscuits, and gravy,' did not sit well. *Gravy for breakfast*? To be fair, however, she read on, 'To prepare the biscuits, first take one cup of lard.' *I don't think so!* She flipped ahead a few pages, a couple more lines, and slammed the book shut. "Take your grits and shove them," she said, re-shelving it, while at the same time crossing Atlanta off her list of cool places to live. Mary proceeded down the row, running a finger down the spine of each book as she read the title, and summarily dismissed them, one-by-one, until she came to *Simple recipes for Good Eating—Cooking Basics for Beginners* and took it off the shelf. An inscription inside the front cover read, 'For Jill on Your Wedding Day, Love Mom.'

The word Mom caught her attention.

Mary had known from the get-go the story about Johnny's parents being in Chicago was bogus. Every time she asked, he'd come up with some lame reason or another not to tell her the real deal. After a while, she just forgot to ask. Not this time, and they'll be no excuses today. In less than a minute a plan started percolating in her mind. *All I need is the right recipe*. She found it and went to work...

*****

"Hey, Moonbrain, breakfast," she called and Johnny came thundering down the stairs. He pulled out a chair, threw his right leg over the back, and sat down.

"What's that?" he asked.

"French toast, dude."

"Oh," he said, disappointment registering on his face like a neon sign. "Is this all there is?"

Mary, who'd quite purposefully placed only half-a-piece on each of their plates, smiled. "I thought I'd see if you liked it first, before making up a huge batch." He shrugged, picked up the triangular piece, and was about to shove the whole thing in his mouth at once.

"No," she laughed, "not like that. Put some butter and syrup on first, like this." She showed him.

Johnny watched and did the same. "Mmm, this is good," he said. Then, before Mary could even start, "Rou rot rany rore?" She smiled, letting him stare at the empty plate, and took a bite.

That's my boy, thought Mary, knowing one piece of French toast would never satisfy an adolescent eating machine like Johnny. "How many pieces you want?"

He swallowed. "I don't know. At least, four or five, I guess." Then, quickly, he added, "And not halves, four or five, ah, make that six, whole pieces."

"No problem," she said, then pulled a huge stack of French toast out of the oven and pushed half-a-dozen pieces onto his plate. Johnny ladled the stack with butter and syrup and began the demolition process.

"Mmm-mmm, ese are oood."

Mary watched him devour the food, still amazed at how fast and how much he could eat. "You don't have anything like, really important to do this morning, do you?"

"Ope," he said then swallowed. "Nothing I can think of,

anyway. We're pretty much on cruise control at this point."

"Oh good. Since you have plenty of time, you can tell me all about your parents."

He nearly choked. "Can I finish my breakfast first?"

"Take your time."

*****

After breakfast, they retired to the living room, Johnny in the recliner, Mary on the couch. "You're on," she said, "and this time, I want you to tell me the truth." Then, before Johnny could even think about playing innocent, she leaned forward and added, "I know your parents are not in Chicago."

Johnny closed his eyes. He tried to recall exactly what happened that day four weeks ago when life took an unexpected U-turn, and realized even he didn't know the whole story. *Okay, so just tell her what you do know.* He opened his mouth to speak but no sound came out.

"So," she urged.

He swallowed and looked right at her. He blurted out the words in bits and pieces, his voice squeaking, sounding like a speaker with a bad connection. "My . . . parents . . . are . . . dead."

In truth, Mary suspected as much. Even so, to hear it voiced aloud flabbergasted her because, now, she could no longer pretend an alternative, more benign explanation existed. "You mean, you like, killed your parents?" She barely managed to get the words out as her skin turned ashen.

"No! I just found them in their bed . . . dead."

"Riiight."

"No, really, that's what happened," he said, though agreed it did sound kind of weak.

Mary felt a bit queasy. "Okay then, when?"

Johnny hesitated, cringing, then said, "About a month ago."

Just as Mary feared, things were not adding up. "So how come you're still living here all by yourself. Shouldn't you be with some relative, like an aunt or grandma?"

"Don't have anyone like that."

"But the cops wouldn't have left you here by yourself."

Johnny cleared his throat, stalling, and then in a sheepish voice, said, "Well, I haven't exactly told anyone about it."

"Haven't told anyone? But someone has to know . . . like, I mean, the bodies? Where are the bodies?"

This is not going to go over well he thought, but what else could he do? Johnny answered the question. "Here," he said, his voice clear and resigned as if giving himself up, surrendering to whatever happened next.

"Here? In this house?"

He nodded.

"Jesus Christ, you've got to be kidding. Tell me there are not two rotting corpses in this house, this very house that I am sitting in right now." She paused for a moment, holding back a wave of nausea, then continued. "Tell me something, anything but that!"

"Well . . . how 'bout I get you a soda?"

"Soda?" she said, incredulous. "Soda? Like, we're talking dead bodies, right here in this house, how is a soda going to help?"

"Ah . . . well . . . you don't look so hot. I thought it might make you feel better."

"What are you talking about?"

"My mom says, I mean used to say, soda, like ginger ale or something, settles the stomach."

"If ginger-ale makes bodies disappear, that's great. OTHERWISE, I DON'T THINK SO!"

Several uncomfortable seconds passed, and then Johnny had a revelation. "Wait," he said, "the bodies aren't actually in the house."

Mary looked doubtful.

"Really, they're out in the garage. In a freezer."

She scowled.

"It's one of those big meat freezers." Johnny then realized another piece of good news and added, "They're not rotting either. They're just fine. So, you see, there's nothing to worry about. The bodies aren't even in the house, and they're not rotting. Everything is just fine."

"Oh, well that makes all the difference," she said, her words dripping with sarcasm. "I'm like, so relieved."

"Really, they're okay."

"Okay? Like, you mean if I were to ask them how they were, they would say, 'Oh yeah, we're just fine. Don't worry about us. Everything is peachy-keen. We're just waiting for our wonderful son, Johnny, to thaw us out. What a kidder that boy is!"

"No," said Johnny, deadpan serious. "Jill probably wouldn't say anything at all, afraid she'd make Jack and get beat up." Mary shot him a look of bewilderment. Johnny, oblivious, kept talking. "She'd just breathe in, you know, kind of dramatic-like, and put a hand over her chest, like so." He took in a gasp of air and placed his right hand over his heart as if he were about to recite the pledge of allegiance. "Jack was the one who did all the talking," *and yelling, and hitting*. "He'd probably have said something like," Johnny scowled, and, in as husky and low a voice as he could muster, continued, 'You better get us out of here, you low-rent son-of-a-bitch, or you'll be sorry!'"

"Ah, like, just so I get it right, Jack is your father and Jill is your mother?"

Johnny nodded, "Right."

"You called them by their first names?"

"Well, not to their face."

Johnny sounded so innocent, so matter-of-fact it was funny. Mary relaxed, almost laughed, but only for a second. Then the smile slid off her face, and she continued her interrogation. "What I don't understand is, if you didn't do it, why are you hiding the bodies?"

"Well . . . I couldn't just leave them there. I had to do something."

She rolled her eyes, "Of course you had to do something, but why didn't you just call someone?"

"BECAUSE I DON'T HAVE ANYONE TO CALL!" Mary cringed and looked away. "Hey, I'm really sorry. It's just . . . you don't understand. You couldn't."

"Make me."

"Make you what?"

"Make me understand," she said, hugging a pillow to her chest, "or I'm out of here."

Johnny's head popped up, eyes wide, "No, don't go. Please."

"Then help me understand, explain what the hell is going on."

"What do you want me to tell you about?"

"About you, your family, whatever it takes to convince me you're not some kind of mass murderer."

"I don't know how," he said, sniffling, trying to hold back tears. "You're the only person, other than my parents, I've even talked to since," he had to think about it. "Since the last time I was in the emergency room. I was eleven years old then." Johnny, no longer able to control it, buried his head in his hands and began to sob. *Why am I crying?* he wondered, thinking about how he didn't cry even when Jack beat the crap out of him. Johnny felt like lashing out and destroying something, then tear it to pieces. He wanted to hit someone, and hurt them. When he stood up to look for a victim, however, there was only Mary. She looked so vulnerable, all curled up on the couch, and clutching a pillow to her chest. And it took him a moment to understand that it was he, Johnny, she was afraid of. *Or I'm out of here*, she'd said, and the thought of it, as unfathomable as it was overwhelming, scared him to the core. He let go of his rage and felt his body go limp, as if it actually withered down to a wisp. The part of him that remained dropped into his father's old recliner. And then the dikes broke, and all he could do was try to stay afloat, treading water in a flood of misery and grief.

And hope to be rescued.

*****

For a long time 4217 Mystic Lane was quiet as a temple. After a while, Mary's arms loosened and she released her death grip on the pillow. She placed it beside her on the couch then sat up and gave it a proper fluffing. Johnny stopped crying, wiped his face on the front of his shirt, and sat up. And then everything seemed to freeze, as if sound and movement and space, even time, ceased to exist. They were aware and unaware, conscious and unconscious, all at the same time. They did not see the window or the curtains or the television or the furniture or the pictures on the walls. They did not see each other, were unaware of postures or facial expressions or the color of the clothes they wore. They could not, in fact, see anything in the physical world.

And yet, they did see. They were, in fact, riveted to one another with their eyes locked, staring so intensely that the superficial trimmings of everyday life had peeled away and, no longer clouding their vision, allowed them to see past the normal boundaries of sight. What they saw was this: their own selves reflected back. They were more alike than different, and they were all they had.

As intense, and, in their minds timeless, as it was, the spell was short-lived. They broke eye contact, each retreating into his own world, her own thoughts, for a while. And then Mary reached out and touched him on the forearm. She was no longer angry or scared. However, there were a few things she still wanted to know." Johnny?"

Jolted from wherever he drifted off to, Johnny's head snapped up and he looked at her, his sad eyes still gleaming. "You don't know anything about my parents, or me for that matter, really, do you?"

"No. she said. "But I'd like to."

"Okay, but it's a long story. Do you really want to hear it?"

"Yes, I really do," she said and settled back into the couch.

Johnny told her about Jack. "He was, I don't know...like a slot machine. You never knew what you were going to get, but in the end the odds were pretty clear: two grapefruits and a pear came up a whole lot more often than three apples." He gave Mary a moment to digest this. She nodded. "Sometimes, he was a great dad. He loved computers and always made sure I had the best stuff. He used to play video games with me, especially when I was younger. I think when I started beating him he didn't like it so much." Johnny shrugged. "Other times, he was like this monster. For no reason he'd go off on me, mostly, but sometimes Jill, too, and beat the crap out of us for no reason at all. Or because he had a bad round of golf. It was crazy."

"Why didn't your mom do something?"

"I think she was too scared. She did try once, though." He explained. "Jack was in one of his crazy moods. I don't remember what he was mad about, but he was slapping me around pretty good. And, you see, I was only seven years-old at the time so Jill, I mean my mom, stepped in and tried to protect me. I ran away and hid while he beat the living crap out of her. Later that night she called the police and they came by. I don't know how he did it, but Jack could be real charming when he needed to. The police ended up not doing anything. And, boy, did he ever make us pay. The next two weeks were so awful I sometimes wonder how we even survived."

"You know," said Mary, "I wouldn't blame you if you did kill them."

"But I didn't!"

"I believe you, but it's different now, with Jack gone and all, I still don't understand why you didn't call the police or a neighbor or someone. Surely they'd understand."

"The only person I feel like I know at all is my neighbor, Henry, and he doesn't even know I exist." Mary still looked puzzled. "Don't you see? If I called someone, they'd just call the police anyway, and then I'd be put in some stupid home for boys or something. No way I'm going to let them do that if I can help it." Johnny waited, trying to think how to explain. "I don't really know why you ran away either, but I'm guessing things were bad at home. Right?"

"Ah, yeah," she said, sheepish.

"So, why didn't you go to the police for help?"

"Because I tried that stuff before and it never works. They never believe the kid."

"Exactly! And that's why you ran, right?"

"Okay, I get it," she said, then paused for a while, tentative.

"What?"

"The thing is, you know, someone's going to find out sooner or later. What will you do then?"

"I don't know. I guess we'll just figure that out as we go."

"We?"

"You mean, you're going somewhere?"

Mary smiled and said, "No, Johnny, I'm not going anywhere. We'll work it out."

Johnny smiled and nodded, though neither one of them had a clue as to how they might do that.

Chapter 21: How Johnny Moonbeam got his Name-Part I

MARY HELD OFF ASKING THE ONE QUESTION she was most curious about. She thought it might embarrass Johnny. There were, however, limits to her self-control, and she could no longer wait. "Like, what is this Johnny Moonbeam stuff all about anyway?" Sure enough, Johnny's face lit-up.

"It's. . . ah. . . well. . . it's just that . . ."

"Don't worry what it might sound like, because I already think you're crazy. So out with it."

Johnny looked at her with puppy eyes, "You. . . . you think I'm crazy?"

Mary sighed, "Yes, but in a good way, Johnny, in a good way."

"Oh."

"Listen, I know your parents last name is, I mean was, Abel so I assume your real name is Johnny Abel." Johnny said nothing. "And then there're all those pictures and models of spaceships around the house, especially that nice drawing on your bedroom door with the initials JM on it, so I also know you're a space geek. It all adds up to some connection with your 'name.' Even I can do that arithmetic." When Johnny still said nothing she added, sympathetically, "Whatever it is, it won't change the way I feel about you. I'm just, like, über curious."

"Über?"

Mary rolled her eyes. "It's French, I think, or maybe it's Latin. Anyway, in one of those foreign languages it means extremely, or over-the-top."

Johnny nodded, "Oh, right."

Mary tilted her head, glaring at him squinty-eyed, and fisted her hips. "No stalling."

The game was up. Johnny swallowed. "It's kind of a long story."

"Good. I've got plenty of time."

"You promise not to laugh."

"Promise."

"Okay," he said, resigned. "Well, you see. It was my

fourth birthday. Jill, my mom, had a birthday party planned for me, my first and last birthday party ever. Anyway, she seemed really nervous. I think because she sort of forgot to tell my dad."

"Sort of?"

"Yeah, though I didn't know it then. When I got a little older I realized there were some things she *accidentally* forgot to tell him because, if she had, he wouldn't have let her do it." Mary nodded. Johnny continued. "Anyway, we'd just finished lunch and out of nowhere she sets this huge cake on the table in front of me. I can still see it, it was awesome." Johnny smiled at the memory. The cake was beautiful, an outer space vista full of stars and planets and moons with a red rocket ship flying across it, trailing the words: happy 4th birthday, Johnny, and straddling the rocket and waving was a candy boy who looked just like Johnny.

Mary let him revel in the memory for a while before, finally, clearing her throat.

"Anyway, he said, blushing. "I remember Jack's eyes got huge and he said something like, 'Is that what I think it is?' and Jill said, 'It's a surprise,' and he said, 'Ooh-whee! Must've cost a fortune. Where'd you get it?' Jill told him that she made it, but even I knew she was lying. I also knew it was my job to try to distract Jack, so he wouldn't start yelling at her or worse."

"Worse?"

"Like beat her up."

"How often did he do that?"

Johnny shook his head and mumbled, "Too often to count."

"And you?"

Johnny looked up at her, nodded quickly, then continued. "Anyway, I grabbed his hand and showed him the little boy on my cake and said something like 'it's me, me, me!' and it seemed to work. Things actually went pretty well for a while, but looking back I think Jack was doing his good dad routine and making plans for a punch line all along."

"Your dad sounds like a sadistic asshole."

Johnny thought about this for a minute. "At times, yeah, he was. But there were times when he was the best father in the world, too. It was weird. The thing was, you never knew which Jack you were going to get, and it didn't matter what you did or didn't do."

"Go on."

"Right. So, I remember having no idea what to do with the presents, because," he paused and looked away. Then, softer, "I'd never had any before."

Silence, then Mary said, "Jesus, that really sucks. Even my mom had presents for me on my birthdays and Christmas."

"Anyway, Jack showed me how to open them, and I really got into it. I got a space-bunny sleeper, and some bed sheets and so forth, and then there was this one, last present. You see, I'd never had a new toy before. Occasionally Jack would bring home some beat-up old thing—I don't know where he got them—but never a new one. 'Recycled toys,' he would say, or 'dumpster toys for the dumpster boy,' and then throw something at me that looked like it had already been through seven generations of boys. So when I tore the paper off of this brand new, two foot tall, red rocket, I was amazed. Stunned, even. At first, I didn't even know what to do with it. Then Jill showed me how the pilot came out and how to take his helmet on and off. He had a dress uniform, a dress hat, and two spacesuits. It was so cool. I remember taking that rocket and zooming around . . . " Johnny was getting animated, slipping back in time. He caught himself and re-focused. "Anyway, I caught on pretty fast and was running around the house flying my new rocket all afternoon and into the night. I was so happy I couldn't believe it." The smile faded from Johnny's face. He slumped back into the chair, and put his head down. "Then it was time for bed."

After a while, Mary said, "And that's when Jack did something nasty?"

Johnny sighed, "It's okay. The memory is nothing new. It's like a movie in my mind and always has been. The weird thing now is that I've never talked about it out loud before. It's kind of different in that way."

"You don't have to tell me about it if you don't want to. I'll understand."

"No, I want to. So, anyway, I was always really good

about going to bed, but that night I kept saying, 'No bed, no bed.' I wanted to play with my rocket forever, and never go to bed again." Johnny smiled at the memory, then, as quick as it came, it faded.

"So, how'd they get you in bed that night?" Mary prompted.

"My dad tricked me. He said there was one last present after I got in bed. So of course I was under the covers in no time flat." Johnny paused again, trying to compose himself, then looked at Mary. "You have to understand, when I was a kid, I was terrified of the dark." Mary nodded. Johnny took a deep breath. "The thing is, I always slept with a nightlight. He knew how important that was to me. Anyway, I asked if I could have my present. Jack said, 'sure,' and told me I was a big boy now. Then he ripped my nightlight out of the wall. The room went to pitch black, and I started crying and begging him to put it back. He said, 'Night lights are for babies. I thought you were a big boy.' Then I really lost it, of course, started crying like crazy and ordering him to put it back, and so he did what he always did."

Mary gave him a questioning look.

"Jack hit me and locked me in my room."

"That's awful. You sure you want to go on?"

For the first time in a while Johnny grinned at her, "Oh yeah, I do. The good part is coming up.

Chapter 22: How Johnny Moonbeam got his Name-Part II

JOHNNY WAS NOT THE ONLY ONE having a bad time of it that night. Two hundred and fifty thousand miles above him, Moon was in a most foul mood.

Damn clouds! thought Moon. *How am I supposed to have any fun if I can't see?* It never ceased to amaze him that most people still didn't believe he could do anything other than shift the tides. *The tides? What a joke! Earth people think their scientists are so smart, but the truth is they're dumber than Pluto.* Still, they were fun to play with. *Where are you, you stupid little scientists? Come out, come out, wherever you are!*

It was unusual for the whole continent to be covered with an impenetrable layer of clouds, but there it was. He flat out could not see anything over North America. Exhausted from straining to find an opening, Moon nearly gave up, about to close his eyes, and wait until next month. Then he saw something. It wasn't much, but as he took a closer look, he saw a little hole open up. Excitement rose in him like it did every time Haley's comet passed through.

When he looked down he saw that the hole was right over central Indiana. *Great. Cornfields, pig farms, and more cornfields.* The hole was getting smaller, but had also moved a bit, and he could now see a little green house.

There were no lights on inside, but Moon could tell someone was in there. Awake. He listened carefully and heard a drip-drip-dripping sound: tears, rolling off a young child's face and onto a pillowcase. *This isn't going to be any fun* he thought. But, having nothing else to do, he went to investigate. Looking through the window of the too-small bedroom, he saw a little wisp of a boy with blonde curly hair and huge blue eyes, wide-open with fear and bloodshot from crying and rubbing them too hard. He knew immediately what the problem was: *the little boy is afraid of the dark*. Moon felt sorry for the boy, but the hole was closing fast. He had to act quickly.

Concentrating for all he was worth, Moon redirected his moonlight through the window and into the bedroom.

Johnny squinted a moment before his eyes adjusted. It was as if a thousand-watt light bulb had just been turned on. This might have frightened or startled an adult, but it was just what Johnny needed. He closed his eyes and soon fell fast asleep. Moon smiled. I have to go. Before leaving, however, Moon tucked in a piece of moonlight next to the boy's heart, so he'd never to be afraid of the dark again. *Sweet dreams*, thought Moon, and he disappeared. The boy drifted off into a deep and dreamy sleep.

Once again, clouds filled the skies and Moon could see nothing. All the same, he felt oddly content and pleased with himself.

Most of the time when Johnny dreamt, they were nightmares. That particular night, however, was different. Perhaps the moonbeam . . .

*****

Sitting at the helm of his red and yellow Moon Cruiser, an interplanetary spaceship advanced beyond the imagination of even the most brilliant NASA scientists, and wearing his equally sophisticated red and silver monogrammed Johnny Moonbeam spacesuit, the young space pilot secures his seat belt and prepares for takeoff. A final check of the instrument panel reveals all systems are 'go', and so he pulls the windowed visor of his silver space helmet down and seals it shut. 5 ... 4 ... 3 ... 2... 1 ... then pushes a small green button ... blastoff! The bright-red cruiser explodes upward, slicing through the dungeon walls like so much butter. In no time, he is in the earth's outer atmosphere, and then there is black, the beautiful blackness of space. Johnny laughs, thinking how ironic it is trading one kind of darkness for another. This is better, though, so much better.

Earth had been taken over by the Gypsy Giants long before Johnny was born. The notorious Giants were scavengers, going from planet to planet, destroying and devouring everything in sight and then moving on, leaving a trail of dead planets in their wake. Earth had nearly run out of hope when Johnny Moonbeam arrived. No one knew where he came from, only that he appeared in the trashcan of a poor accountant's family, who then raised him as their own.

Johnny, however, was no ordinary boy. He had superpowers and vowed to save Earth from the Giants. By the time he was four years old, his legend was known throughout the entire world, and hope was on the rise. Jack and Jill, King and Queen of the Space Giants, also heard the legend. They feared if the young Moonbeam were allowed to grow up, he might pose a genuine threat. So Jack wasted no time in locking him up in his deepest, darkest dungeon, four miles below the earth's surface. And there, the young superhero would spend the next ten years of his life.

Jack, however, underestimated the young superhero's resilience. Johnny spends every waking hour of his captivity working on the Moon Cruiser and, finally, it is finished. As he breaks into the free vastness of space, he knows he will one day go back and defeat the Giants, and free the Earth. He would love to see the look on Jack's face when the giant king learns of the escape, but that will have to wait.

He turns the ship to the right, bringing the moon into full view. This will be his new home. He has provisions enough to last for over a year, and supplies with which to build a mighty fortress that will be his base. Once that is completed, Johnny Moonbeam will be able to start his missions back to Earth, where he will wreak havoc on Jack and Jill, and all the other Giants, saving the human children from horrors such as he endured growing up.

Activating the telescopic lens portion of his face shield, Johnny scans the lunar surface for a suitable place to land. I need to find a spot where the stupid Giants won't be able to find me. He continues searching. At first, all he sees is a fairly flat surface with shallow craters, so the cagey pilot expands the search radius, and a few minutes later sees what look like mountains. That's it, he thinks, but just then the cruiser lurches and Johnny knows something is wrong.

The ship is suddenly shaking violently, and Johnny can no longer control it. He reaches for the latch above his head, ready to abandon ship when . . .

*****

"Wake up, Johnny, wake up!" a gruff voice called out.

Johnny opened his eyes, horrified to see King Jack standing over him with his giant fist ready to strike. *What is he doing here?* But there was no time to think. "Let me go, you evil tyrant, or I'll waporize you right here and now!" Johnny reached for his vaporizing gun, but grabbed a handful of air instead.There was no gun. Slowly, it began to sink in that Johnny wasn't on the moon anymore, and that he was not a superhero. He was just little Johnny Abel.

Jack shook him harder, "Wake up, you petulant little thing, wake up!" he screamed.

The last remnants of sleep finally deserted him, depositing Johnny back smack in the middle of his dismal reality. Jack was yelling at him but Johnny just ignored him and closed his eyes. He wanted to remember. *I have to remember.* He could see Johnny Moonbeam decked out in his shiny spacesuit as clearly as if he were standing right in front of him, as if he were real. *I am real,* he thought, but the rest of the dream was vague and elusive.

"What the hell was that all about? Vaporize who?" Jack shouted.

"Shut up," said Johnny, absentmindedly, because he couldn't afford to have his concentration broken. He squinched his eyes together even tighter, focusing all of his mind's energy on trying to recall the details of his dream. It took a few seconds, but he found them—all of them—intact, right there in his own memory. *I knew it wasn't a dream.* In Johnny's experience, dreams—the good ones anyway—always faded fast and then were gone forever. This adventure with Johnny Moonbeam, however, seemed to be gaining strength, coming back to him in vivid color, just like on TV.

"Look at me when I'm talking to you, boy!" roared Jack while at the same time giving his son a slap across the face. This, finally, did bring Johnny back to the present.

"I'm not a-scared of you, Dad, not a-scared of nobody."

"What do you mean? You're not scared of me? You better be scared of me, boy."

Remembering the dream, Johnny looked defiantly at Jack and said, "Johnny Moonbeam will wapowize you."

Jack threw Johnny back down on his bed, cleared his throat, and spat on his face—a horrible, early-morning phlegm glob—and said, "That was just a dream, you little piece of shit! Now get your puny ass out of bed and get ready for breakfast."

Shit? thought Johnny, why did Daddy say that? *Doesn't he know that's a bad word? Daddy should say 'poop' instead, like me and Mommy do, because 'poop' is a good word.* He was about to educate his father on this finer point of etiquette, but fortunately for the boy, Jack stalked out of the room.

There was a bigger issue at hand than proper etiquette. *Daddy said I was a piece of poop, and Daddy doesn't lie. But how can I be poop if I'm a boy? At least, I think I'm a boy.* The idea that maybe, somehow, Jack was right scared him, so he tore off his covers and jumped out of bed to check it out. *I still look like a boy.* He ran his hands over his face and head, over his arms, legs, and torso. *I still feel like a boy.* Somewhat relieved, but still uneasy about the situation, Johnny continued to ponder the problem.

For a four-year-old boy, he was quite good at problem solving. He had to be. It didn't take long. Though he'd already done the poop experiment, he decided to double-check. Johnny sniffed his arms and feet and legs. I don't smell like poop. And then he licked his arms and fingers and knees and, with great relief, concluded, and I don't taste like poop either. *I am a boy!*

Thoroughly satisfied it was Jack who was mistaken—an idea he found somewhat disquieting—he relaxed. For just a second, and then he remembered, *Oops, I'm supposed to be hurrying my puny ass and getting ready for breakfast.* With that in mind, Johnny darted across the hall and into the bathroom.

As he sat on his big boy potty, he remembered his dream, his Johnny Moonbeam dream. *Remember, remember, remember,* he thought, willing his mind to burn the dream into his memory, while at the same time, he pounded both sides of his head with the palms of his hands. *I gotta remember. I gotta remember, because it's me.* When Johnny was fully satisfied he could play the dream back any time he wanted to, just like a movie, he got up and was about to go downstairs. And then he had another idea, one with more immediate ramifications, a revelation that would make Jack proud of his big boy. Johnny could hardly wait to get downstairs and show his father.

Johnny turned on the faucet, passing his hands through

the water for the pretense of having washed them, and then hurried out of the bathroom. As he ran down the stairs, his father shouted up. "What's taking so long? Haul your little butt down here, right now!"

"I'm coming, Dad. I'm coming!

Johnny hustled downstairs, not only because it seemed to be what "haul your little butt down there" meant, but also because he had something important to show his dad—something that, surely, Jack would want to know. *Daddy is going to be proud of his big boy* thought Johnny as he fkew into the kitchen holding his right hand out for Jack to see.

"What the hell is that?" asked his father, bemused.

"Look, Daddy. See?" said Johnny, not noticing that his father's eyes had gone icy, and he was getting up from the table. "This is poop," he pointed to the sample in his right hand, and then he pointed to his body, "and this is a boy. It's me—" And those were the last words Johnny would speak for quite a while.

Jack smacked his son's hand from below, and the shit went flying. It landed with a splat on the wall directly behind his mother, who had just managed to duck out of the way in time. Jill could see the rage rising in her husband, about to take him over. "Jack," she said, trying to reason with him, "he's only four years old. He doesn't under—"

"Shut up!"

Johnny looked up to where Jack had been but, instead of his father, he saw a volcano. And it was about to erupt. Fortunately, the boy knew all of the volcano evacuation routes by heart, and he instinctively ran to the closest one which, in this case, was the pantry.

Jill watched her son stealthily slip away and hide behind the canned goods as her husband erupted in front of her. She knew it was pointless to do anything; she'd been through this enough times to know that. But she couldn't help herself. "Jack," she said frantically, "Jack, listen to me. I'll clean it up. I'll take care of it. You go on to work and get something to eat on the way. Johnny just didn't understand. He thought you meant that he really was—"

Jack cut her off. "Oh no, dear, you're wrong," he said in a mockingly sweet tone. "That's exactly what I think he is." Now he was yelling, "A piece of shit. Shit, shit, shit, shit, shit! And I'm starting to wonder about you, too." He kicked his chair and knocked it over, then yanked the tablecloth off the table, sending the morning's breakfast flying. The dishes crashing on the tiled floor in a sea of milk and orange juice seemed to bring Jack's wild eyes back into focus, and he looked at what he had just done as if he couldn't believe it.

Jill knew by his eyes that it was over and watched, relieved, as the volcano morphed into a timid and repenting husband. It's the way things always ended when Jack had these tirades, when he returned from hell's jungles or wherever it was he went off to. The danger was over. Jill could relax. Except on this particular day she never got the chance. As Jack retreated from the table, he did not see the felled chair lying directly behind him and stumbled over it. He lost his balance and when he put down his right hand to break the fall, he inadvertently impaled it with a large shard of china, which effectively threw him back into a rage.

"Now look what you've done!" he yelled, and grabbed a plate from the floor—it was the only piece of china that wasn't already broken—and flung it hard, like a Frisbee, right at Jill, who hardly had time to blink let alone get out of the way. The plate ricocheted off her forehead and hit the wall, shattering into a hundred pieces.

When he saw the large gash, profusely bleeding over Jill's right eye, Jack was transported back to reality. *Oh my God,* he thought, *what did I do?* "I'm, I'm so sorry. I don't know—"

Jill looked up at him through the blood and tears and, knowing full well that he was now harmless, said, "Just go away, you son of a bitch. Leave us alone. Go!" she screamed. Jack hung his head, skulked over to the door, and went into the garage.

*****

Meanwhile, Johnny had repositioned himself in the back of the pantry, scared to death as he watched the action from behind a can of chow mein noodles, and thought how nice it would be if he were somewhere else. So he closed his eyes as tightly as he could and wished that he was on another planet, or in another solar system—anywhere but where he was. After holding them closed for several seconds, he opened them and . . . chow mein noodles.

Rats.

But Johnny, who was nothing if not persistent, would not give up. He decided that if he couldn't be some*where* else, then maybe he could be some*one* else. He closed his eyes again, and wished with all his little heart to be Johnny Moonbeam. He waited. He wished some more. He waited some more and then, very slowly he opened . . .

WOW! I did it! He ran his hands down the smooth, shiny spacesuit and found the JM monogram stitched over the left breast, right where it should be. He was sitting in the space cruiser, and everything was just like he thought it would be. The viewing screen revealed that he was orbiting around the moon. He'd never noticed before how the moon resembled the globe-shaped kitchen light that hung from the ceiling above the table. *That's weird,* he thought.

Instinctively knowing how to pilot the ship, Johnny proceeded to check out the rest of his surroundings. He saw it all: the terrible quake that unearthed the whole town and sent it crashing to the floor; Jack the Giant launching a flying saucer at Jill, splitting open his mother's forehead; his mother yelling at his father. *I'm sure glad I'm up here.*

I wonder why everything, referring to his parents and the rest of the world below him, is moving in slow motion*? I better fly down and investigate.* Johnny took himself out of orbit by doing the spaceship equivalent of a barrel roll. *Wheee, that was fun!* And then he put The Cruiser into a straight-out dive before stopping dead in front of his mother's face. He couldn't make out what she was saying or, better put, what she was yelling at his father because her mouth was moving so slowly.

"Hey, Mom," he yelled into the viewing screen, "I'm okay! You don't have to worry about me anymore." Johnny waited for Jill to respond, but she didn't. *I guess you can't hear me down there. Oh well,* he thought, then sighed and shrugged it off. Finding the controls for the viewing screen, Johnny decided to test it out. He zoomed in on his mother's face until her eyes, nose, and mouth took up the entire picture. The exaggerated, turtle-slow movements of her mouth made Jill look ridiculous, like a cartoon character, and Johnny couldn't help but laugh. Oops. Sorry, Mom, he thought, and then remembered something else he needed to check on and set a course for the pantry.

The Cruiser zoomed over to the pantry's open door then slowed down because, as every good space pilot knows, it is a dangerous, meteorite infested region of deep space. Only the best space pilots could navigate through its canned goods, bottled waters, and the various other strange obstacles that were always coming and going, never seeming to be in the same place twice. After a close call with an errant bag of flour, Johnny made it to the back of the pantry and there it was: little Johnny Abel's body, hiding behind the canned goods. But instead of being all tensed up and shaking, it looked calm and relaxed. Less experienced pilots might have thought it was too limp—almost lifeless—but not Johnny Moonbeam. He knew that the boy was okay, that he wasn't scared anymore, which was all that really mattered. And just how did the space pilot know the little boy was okay, that he wasn't scared anymore? *That's easy,* thought Johnny Moonbeam, *it's because he's up here with me now; he is me!*

After a minute, he turned around and navigated his way back out of the pantry. Jack was skulking towards the kitchen door, the one that led to the garage; and his mother was sitting at the table holding a bloodied towel over her right eye. As soon as he could be sure everything was safe, that the little boy in the pantry wouldn't be scared anymore, he would return and once again become little Johnny Abel.

That was okay because he now knew this: anytime he needed to, he could escape from his body, from the pain, and from his father.

*****

When Johnny finished, Mary remained silent for a while, thinking about and processing the story. When she did speak, all she could think to say was, "Wow."

"Yeah," he said, agreeing. "And from then on, every time life looked like trouble, which was quite often, I simply left my human body behind and flew off to some other universe until it was all over."

"You mean, like, pretending."

"No, like for real. Maybe not real like the coffee table here," Johnny knocked on the glass tabletop, "but real to me."

Mary thought about when she had floated above the scene as Brad raped her. She nodded. "Right, I totally understand.

Chapter 23: Laurel Highlands

MARY'S CABIN FEVER WAS ABOUT to boil over. As a part of OCR, she and Johnny agreed that, except for necessary functions like putting the trash out, collecting mail, and such—even these tasks were to be done furtively, under the cover of darkness—they would not venture outside of 4217 Mystic Lane until Ralph was securely behind bars. Another twenty-four hours came and went uneventfully. Boor-ingg. Outside, flowers bloomed full under a deep-blue summer sky.

"Where is Laurel Highlands, anyway?" she asked, gazing longingly at the backyard and wanting to open the gate to see what else was happening in the world.

"Straight ahead," answered Johnny, matter-of-fact.

"Like, where ahead?"

"Go out through the back gate and turn left on the gravel path. About a hundred yards down, on the right, there's a dirt trail. It's not much, just a little opening where the grass is trampled down. If you get to a big curve, you'll know you've gone too far. Anyway, follow that trail up the hill and through the woods. When you emerge from that, bingo, you're there."

"Oh."

"Why?"

"I don't know."

Johnny looked at her. "Yeah, I think you do."

"Okay, I just want to get out. You know, maybe do a little . . . exploring."

"Remember, we made a deal that we wouldn't go outside until you-know-who is caught."

"Yeah, but I didn't know it would last forever. I'm going crazy in here. I mean, like, what if he never turns up? Are we going to stay in here the rest of our lives?"

"I guess not."

"So, I think now would be a good time to put an end to that restriction."

Johnny did not like the idea. On the other hand, he couldn't think of a compelling reason to disagree with her. *And besides, she's going to go there anyway.* "Okay, but I'm going to stay here and listen out for Ralph."

Mary looked at him with those big eyes and asked, "Won't you at least show me where the path is?"

It was pointless for Johnny even to think about denying her. "Follow me." After a pause he asked, "Why do you want to go there, anyway?" Mary followed him through the kitchen, out of the backdoor, and into the yard. "What's there to explore in Laurel Highlands? It's just a bunch of rich folks and big houses."

"Exactly," said Mary. "Laurel Highlands is where I was supposed to end up when I ran away."

"You mean," said Johnny, pointing to a certain patch of petunias slowly recovering from a particularly vicious and random act of squashing, "you didn't plan to end up on your back right there?"

"Not really."

"Still, what's so great about Laurel Highlands?"

"Jesus, Johnny, I'm just curious. I like had this scheme planned for weeks, you know, and it didn't quite work out the way it was supposed to. So I just want to see what it looks like." She took a breath and calmed herself. "I had this idea that I could go there and find some way to fit in. Like, maybe I'd meet this old lady, who, of course, would have tons of money, and, like, her own kids would be already grown up. She'd live in this huge house, and she would be, like, soooo lonely." *Did I really think that would work?* Mary wondered, because, at this point, it sounded pretty lame.

Johnny finished for her. "She'd take you in off the street, and it would work out great for everyone. She definitely wouldn't be lonely anymore, and you would have a big house and money and all that stuff."

"Something like that," said Mary sheepishly.

Johnny watched Mary intently as she spoke, as he always did. She looked just the littlest bit embarrassed – something that probably only Johnny would have picked up on. He had a pretty good idea what she was thinking. "Yeah, it sounds kinda dreamy now. But I guess in order to run away, you have to have someplace to go. You have to have some plan, even if it is a bit, ah, unrealistic."

Mary looked up at Johnny and thanked him with her eyes. Though she would never say it aloud, Mary knew that

Johnny understood as clearly as if she had. He always seemed to understand her. *How does he do that?*

Johnny opened the back gate. "Works pretty good, considering. Don't you think?"

"Considering what?"

"Considering how a couple of weeks ago it was shattered beyond recognition by some charging rhino."

"Not to mention a sensitive rhino." Mary put her hands together and pointed them out from her forehead. Then, uttering something halfway between a screech and a moan, she bent down and charged him, knocking Johnny squarely back on his butt.

Mary stood over him, hands-on hips, pretending to look angry. But all she could do was laugh. She helped him to his feet, and they walked down to the end of the gravel path that butted up against the steep incline of trees, a greenbelt between Mystic Meadows and Laurel Highlands, until they came to a small footpath leading up the hill. Johnny pointed to it.

"There it is, when you get to the top, you'll be in Oz."

"Oz?"

"Yeah, it will be like you've been beamed onto a new planet." He paused and then said, "Did I mention they don't like people from down here?"

"What do you mean they don't like people from down here?"

"It's a long story. Down here, where we are, is Mystic Meadows. They," he said as he pointed to the top of the hill, "call it Mystic Mistake."

"Mistake? Why?"

"The developers who built Laurel Highlands promised a golf course down here, and as you can see, that didn't happen."

"How were they going to build a golf course here, anyway?"

"Well, almost everyone in the neighborhood agreed to sell out to the developers, who were offering a pretty good price for the homes. They figured it was just a matter of time before the few remaining people left joined their neighbors and sold out. They were so close they just assumed it would happen. But there was one person that they couldn't convince to leave no matter what they offered. Want to guess who?"

"The old dude and his dog," she said, laughing.

"You got it. Henry would not budge, not even for $2 million. At least, that's what I've been told." *Well, actually, no one tells me anything, so it was something I overheard. But, close enough.*

"To them, our houses are pathetic looking shacks in the middle of millionaire land, not to mention the fact that the golf course had to be built up the road a bit. They resent the hell out of us because we're like this big, ugly scar." Johnny smiled as he said this and then added, "I've always thought it was pretty funny myself."

"You sure you don't want to come?"

"Yeah, I'm sure," and then, trying to sound pathetic, "I'll be back at the house, all by myself, waiting."

Mary rolled her eyes and ran up the hill. "Okay, Eeyore, see ya in a little while."

And she disappeared into the trees.

*****

A giant hedge surrounded Laurel Highlands and its pristine estates, sheltering the residents from the cruel and ugly realities of the outside world. Mary had not been able to see Johnny for quite some time when she finally arrived at the top of the hill. The climb had been much more difficult than Mary had anticipated. She stopped for a couple of minutes in order to catch her breath and preen as best she could, given the circumstances. She pushed through the Hedge and was on the other side and gasped. *Wow, it really does look like Oz. I wonder where the munchkins are?*

She couldn't decide whether to go left or right, so she let Eeny, Meany, Miney, and Mo decide. They said left. The houses were all enormous and custom-made based on neoclassical old world architecture, with huge white columns and swimming pools. None had less than a three-car garage, and they sat on spacious, flawlessly manicured lots well back from the street, necessitating long, winding driveways. Mary was taking it all in, hardly able to believe that people actually lived here. It all looked so wonderful, like a fairy tale. There were huge flower gardens everywhere. Some of the homes had a greenhouse. *I didn't even know that was legal.*

She walked by several people—mothers pushing babies in strollers, retired couples out for a walk, and a couple of teenage girls that passed right by Mary without acknowledging her greeting. As if she were invisible. *I know you heard me when I said 'hi,' you stuck up little bitches.* She covertly gave them the finger as they walked by. *Air heads.* An older man, probably about fifty, wearing a thousand-dollar suit, got out of his car. He acknowledged her, doing several double takes and ogling her. *Like, aren't you married dude? Aren't you a little old for me?* Having a bit of fun, she led him on with a smile, a wink, and a tilt of her head. Then she scowled, and gave him the finger too. He slammed the door to his Mercedes 900 series sedan and scurried into his mammoth house. Mary laughed. *Asshole!*

Mary turned a corner and saw two kids yelling at each other. A bit closer she saw that one of them was a guy, maybe seventeen or eighteen and the other a girl, a few years younger. *Hot dude.* They had to be related, she thought, because there was, like, no other excuse for the girl to be screaming at him, and, of all things, running away. He was about six feet four, muscular build, blonde hair, and blue eyes. The girl was almost a foot shorter and appeared to be quite a nerd. She would probably look pretty decent if she didn't work so hard at being homely. *A real goody-two-shoes, that one. Probably studies all the time and gets straight A's – whoop-tee-do.* Her blond, almost white hair was done up in pigtails that hung down just past shoulder length on either side. A pair of round, wire-rimmed glasses were perched on her rather prominent nose. It was the same nose the guy had, but it looked great on him. Her clothes were the worst. *I didn't even know they sold that crap anymore – yuck!* The girl was wearing a plaid jumpsuit, white knee-high stockings, and—Mary did a double take on this—saddle shoes.

The girl, who had shoved her apparent brother in the chest and almost knocked him over, was now steaming down the sidewalk, huffing and puffing, right towards Mary. Someone forgot to tell this chick that she lives in fairy tale land. Mary could not fathom how anyone living here could be unhappy. The girl didn't see Mary and ran straight into her before Mary had a chance to get out of the way. "Sorry," said the girl, though she didn't really look it.

Mary saw this as an opportunity to get some info on her hot brother. To do this, she would have to engage the girl, subtly at first. Asking her straight out about this guy would only piss her off more.

"That's okay. Hey," said Mary, "I'm new around here. What's your name?"

"Susan Goodenough, and the asshole over there is my brother, Stephen."

"What happened?" Mary asked, trying her best to sound sympathetic.

"It's a long story, and I don't have time now."

"Well, maybe we could talk later, and like get to know each other."

Susan looked at her and frowned. "You mean, you'd like to get to know my brother."

The chick is not dumb. "No, really, maybe we could get together tomorrow."

"Yeah, right, and maybe you'll win the Nobel Prize tomorrow." With that, Susan was off.

Mary watched Stephen Goodenough throw his hands up and head inside the house. It was relatively small for the neighborhood, but by most other standards, especially Mary's, still pretty big. Like the rest of the houses in the neighborhood, it looked, well, just about perfect, beautiful but not overdone. The lot was idyllic with a stream running through the yard and beautiful flower gardens and slate lined paths weaving in and out. The house had a wraparound porch with a swing on every side and a gazebo out back. She thought about Susan and then her brother. Poor guy, to have such a pain-in-the-ass little sister.

Mary could not have had things more backward.

Chapter 24: Battle for the Universe

MARY WAS QUITE SATISFIED, pleased with her little outing. Until she read the note. Waiting for her on the sliding glass doors, it read: The battle for the universe is underway—for real.

Shoot! Johnny was right. I shouldn't have gone out. Before she had time to ruminate any further, however, Mary flew up the stairs, and then stopped in the doorway. Watching. The computer monitor was filled with strange space monsters and spaceships and explosions. Even Johnny looked alien. He was wearing a huge half headset, half helmet contraption with an antenna sticking out of one side. Instead of using a keyboard, he was using some weird console, not like a car, but one a spaceship might have. There were joysticks and dials and knobs and lights all over it, and his hands were, as usual, moving at warp speed over the controls. He didn't see her. *How could he with all that going on?* She walked in and grabbed a scrap of paper off the desk. She wrote: Sorry. I'm home now. I'm calling Michael. Then she placed the note in front of Johnny. Without missing a beat he nodded, and continued blowing up Ralph monsters.

*****

In downtown Indianapolis, at a bus stop on Tenthth Avenue between Maryland and Vermont streets, the doors of Michael's bus opened. Several passengers exited and several more started to board. "Dum-dum, Dum-dum, Dum-dum," theme music from the movie Jaws, blared out from . . . *My pocket?* Then he remembered: his new cell phone. There was only one reason for it to go off, and the thought of it sent an anxious shiver through his body. He tried to swallow but couldn't.

"Hello?" he answered, his voice hushed and raspy, mouth as dry as the Mohave Desert.

"Mr. Quackenbush?"

"Yeah, it's me, what's up?"

"It's the real McCoy. Johnny's got him online right now."

"Okay, I'm on it. I'll call you when I find him. Let me know if anything happens on your end."

"Okay, good luck, and thanks."

It was a busy lunch crowd that afternoon. The seats and aisles were overflowing with people packed in like sardines, hanging on the metal poles all the way up and down the bus. Damn! He took a deep breath. Okay. He grabbed the handheld microphone and reopened both sets of doors. Michael tried to sound calm as he made the following, bogus announcement. "I'm going to have to ask everyone to step off the bus at once. The bus' emissions indicator light just came on and the new regulations from both the US DOT and the Indiana DOT require that we evaluate the bus ASAP. A backup bus will be called and should be here within minutes. Thank you for your cooperation." *I'm gonna get fired for this.* The passengers grumbled and complained but nonetheless, did as they were told. Michael called for backup and was off to the races. He'd done all the test runs with a Honda Civic, and wondered now if the bus could make it through some of the alleyways and one-way streets on his planned route. *Well, we're about to find out.* Then he gave the dashboard an affectionate pat and was off.

*****

No sooner did Mary hang up the phone than she heard Johnny calling from upstairs. "I'm coming," she said, and took off running. "What's the matter?" she asked when she got there.

"HellTwinkie and half his fleet were creamed by a barrage of raisin bagels."

"Say what?"

"They were just regular raisin bagels," he explained, unable to keep the panic from his voice. "But instead of strawberry cream cheese, they were spread with some strange alien compound that explodes like a nuclear warhead. I should've seen it coming, but I wasn't quick enough. It just looked like a paper bag, you know? Like Ralph was just littering up the universe. And stupid me, I just looked at it, and then it opened up and all these bagels fell out, and it was too late."

"I'm sure you can, like, regroup, or something," she said, trying to sound reassuring, "can't you?"

"No, I can't. Over half of my army has been crippled. I need a new player."

"Do we have time for that?"

"We do if we buy one," said Johnny.

"You can do that?"

"Yep."

"But isn't that, like cheating?"

"*You're* worried about cheating?" She started to say something, but he cut her off, "Besides. This is WAR."

"Alright already."

"We need the laptop." Mary hesitated but Johnny shot her a look that said, *go get it NOW!* And she was off. Johnny was glad he'd insisted Mary learn how to use computers and gladder yet that she'd trained on the very notebook she was now going after. He didn't think they'd need it for this purpose—it never crossed his mind he could lose a character at any time, let alone this early in the game. *That was a stupid mistake, you moron. How many times have I told you that bombs could come in all sizes and flavors, you idiot?* Distracted by the 'Jack talk' going on in his head, Johnny lost three more ships. *Wow, nice explosions! Of course, a blind turtle could have hit them. Why'd you just leave them out there like sitting ducks?*

Johnny threw off his headset, stood up, and started cursing his father, using every word Jack had ever taught him. Then he closed his eyes and twirled around a few times before sitting back down. It worked. He was feeling better and Jack had gone into hiding again, but HellTwinkie's fleet had taken another serious hit. His army had been reduced to a small, wounded fleet while Ralph was salivating somewhere, waiting to move in for the final kill. All Johnny could do was limp through space and try to hide behind whatever he could find—a meteor, a space station, or the back side of a Moon—and hope he could hold on until the new player arrived.

"Thank God," he said when Mary burst back into the room with the laptop. *She's already got it booting up. Way to go!*

"Now what?" Mary asked, all business.

"Log on to the Internet and let me know as soon as the page opens up."

"I don't know if I can do this. You know, I've, like, never done it by myself."

"Well, we don't have a choice. If I leave Twinkie out

here by himself, he's going to get massacred. Besides, you'll do fine."

"Oh, look, I did it!"

"Good. Now, find the address bar."

"The what?"

"The one at the top of the page that says www.indianapolis_actuaries.org/home/."

"There it is. Okay, now I'm ready. What do I type?"

"www.warmongers.com/games/online/totalannihilationIIIbattleforuniverse/. Remember, no spaces between the words and slashes."

'Oops, forgot about that. Okay, now what?"

"After the last slash, put: buy/players."

"Nothing's happening. The stupid computer is just sitting here."

"Try hitting the enter button."

"Oh, I guess that might help. How's it going there in outer space?"

"I'm hanging on by a thread, but at least it looks like Ralph is going to keep playing until he totally destroys me, which is what I expected. I just have to—"

"Oh, here we are. There's a whole bunch of really weird-looking dudes here."

"It doesn't matter what they look like, only what their rank—"

"Maybe it matters to me."

"Whatever, just find one with the rank of general. I don't care how many stars. Any general will do."

"But won't we need more than just one? I mean, it looks like you've lost hundreds of soldiers."

"Thousands, actually, but that doesn't matter. A general comes with his whole army so that's what we need. Now find one." Mary looked a bit hurt and Johnny realized that he'd raised his voice. "Please?" he said sweetly, and she perked up immediately.

"Okay. Let me see . . . lieutenant, lieutenant, captain . . . oh, here's a lieutenant general. Does that count?"

"Keep looking. If we don't find anything else, it will have to do."

"Oh good, here's a three-star general. But, gross! It looks

just like Ralph. No way we're getting this one."

"That's exactly the one we're going to get. Ralph probably made it. He probably makes money selling them."

"Okay, if you say so. But I'd rather get the lieutenant general. He's actually kind of cute."

"Hit the 'Purchase' button . . . please."

"Just kidding, I already did. It says," and she paused to read for a second. "It says we need to make a bid. What do you want to do?"

"We definitely don't have time to bid on it, but they usually have a guaranteed bid amount. Do you see it?"

It took a couple of seconds, but she found it. "Got it, 500 bucks. Isn't that, like, robbery?"

"Pretty much so, but we've got no choice. Just hit the PayPal option and say 'yes' to all the little boxes that come up, and we should be all right."

It only took a few minutes to get the new player into the game and under Johnny's control. He put a smiley face on it and gave it a pair of cowgirl boots like Mary's. Then he renamed it Twinkie's Revenge, and went to work. First, he moved Hell Twinkie to a new pseudo-hiding place, one he was sure Ralph would spot. As Johnny expected, Ralph had all his attention focused on Hell Twinkie and failed to notice a new player enter the game. As Ralph zeroed in on the kill, Twinkie's Revenge settled stealthily into position. Even though HellTwinkie's forces were quickly annihilated, Snuffboy kept firing away. Just like Johnny thought he would. This overkill was Ralph's way of savoring his victory, something Johnny had learned from his research, and he was ready to take full advantage of it.

Twinkie's Revenge settled over Ralph's army of vessels, which were still blasting away at the defenseless HellTwinkie. Johnny caught Mary's eye and grinned. "Watch this," he said as a box of Twinkies fell from the bay of Twinkie's Revenge's main ship. A second later, the box opened and twelve nuclear-cream-filled Twinkies sought out their targets and destroyed over half of Ralph's army.

"Wow!" said Mary, "that was cool."

"We're good now. I could've wiped old Snuffboy completely out of the game right then, but we need to drag it out until Michael finds him," said Johnny, beaming. "We've got him right where we want him, for as long as we need him." They could almost hear Ralph seething in the background.

"Were those Twinkies you threw at him?"

"Yes, they were," he said, "very special Twinkies."

*****

Thirty minutes later, the phone rang. "That must be Michael," said Mary, and jumped up to go downstairs and answer it.

Johnny was barely able to grab her arm before she was out of reach. "Whoa, Nelly, we've got a phone right here." Johnny pecked a couple more keys on the keyboard and a number flashed up on the screen, superimposed over the battle. "Is this Michael's number."

Mary looked, "Yes! That's it," she said, jumping up and down with excitement. Then, when she couldn't locate a receiver, "Where's the phone, Moonbrain?"

"Hello, is that you Mary?" it was Michael's voice, but she had no idea where it came from. She looked at Johnny and saw a big smirk on his face. He pointed to the computer and then to her mouth and made animated talking motions with his fingers.

"Hey, Mary, are you there?"

Not knowing where to aim her voice, Mary finally said, "Michael?" loud enough to be heard in three counties.

"Whoa," said Johnny pointing to the computer's microphone, "just talk normal."

She gave him a dirty look then continued, this time in her normal voice. "Michael, it's me, Mary. Have you found him?"

"Oh yeah," said Michael with a chuckle in his voice. "I wish you could see this! It's hilarious. Three police officers are trying to disengage the brute from his videogame, and he's still holding on to the controls. And that's not even the funny part." Johnny tapped the screen. Mary turned her eyes just as a giant Twinkie descended upon Ralph's army and, in one byte, devoured the last remaining vessel of his fleet. After a loud burp, the Twinkie exploded in a firework-like display of color. The words, 'Enemy Defeated,' started flashing, superimposed over the fireworks. "The funny part," continued Michael, "is seeing this huge crazed beast crying and mumbling something about Twinkies. It's a riot!"

*****

As soon as darkness fell over Mystic Meadows, Johnny and Mary slinked out the back gate and walked about a mile to a predetermined bus stop and waited for Michael to pick them up—in his Honda. He was taking them all out for a celebration dinner. He arrived right on schedule. "Where do you guys want to go?"

Johnny shrugged his shoulders and deferred to Mary. "*Salsa Sally's Acapulco Paradise*," she said without hesitation.

"Salsa Sally's it is then." And they were off.

"What is it?" whispered Johnny.

"It's, like, this huge Mexican restaurant with a zillion things on the menu and great food and real Mexican waiters and all these fancy decorations everywhere, and they even have people playing actual Mexican music on guitars strolling around from table to table."

"So," said Michael, "sounds like you've been there before."

"Well, not really, but I've seen the commercials on TV, and it looks awesome." They all laughed.

It was a slow night, and so the restaurant workers didn't mind that they stayed on well past the time they'd finished their dinners, drinking sodas and telling stories—especially Michael, who had some wild tales to tell of his drinking days. "But you do realize, kids, that while these stories may sound funny now, and some may have even been fun at the time, the price I paid was high. For every one of them, I've got 100 horror stories I could tell you." There was a brief period of silence, and then Michael took a slug of his root beer and smiled. "Probably more, because I can't remember most of them."

Mary smiled and said, "So, what was it that, like, finally made you quit?"

Michael shook his head. "You wouldn't believe it if I told you."

"Give us a try," said Mary.

"Sometimes it's even hard for me to believe anymore,

but here's what happened. At least what I can remember. I'd drifted down to where I was on a constant drunk, and started having frequent blackouts. Sometimes, I lost track of two or three days at a time. I didn't care about anything or anyone, including myself, and would have died before long. I actually welcomed death. But then one morning everything changed. I found my humanity again. I had been ashamed of my life, but I suddenly realized there was still time to turn it around and do something good, something worthwhile. I decided that I wanted to live again, and that, of course, meant I had to quit drinking."

"So, like, what was it that changed everything?"

"Well, I was in the middle of one of my blackouts, I guess, when I woke up one morning to find myself in a dumpster." Michael shook his head. "I still have no idea how I got there."

"Ooh, gross," said Mary.

"A dumpster," mumbled Johnny to no one in particular.

"Yeah, I was sound asleep in a dumpster and then someone woke me up. And here's the part you won't believe: guess who it was?"

"I have no flipping idea," said Mary.

Somewhere inside Johnny's head a tape of Jack started playing. "Dumpster boy, dumpster boy . . . "

"It was a little baby boy, no more than an hour old, who woke me up." Mary gave him a hairy eyeball. Michael threw his hands up. "Hey, it's the God's honest truth. I swear."

"That's impossible," said Mary.

"See, I knew you wouldn't believe me," said Michael, smiling. Mary looked at him, her eyes burning, imploring him to tell the whole story. "Okay, okay, it goes like this. Someone, I don't know who 'cause I never saw, I mean, how could I see them? I was in the dumpster." He shook his head. "Anyway, whoever it was threw the baby away – can you believe someone could do that? – right into the dumpster; and it landed on toppa' me, right on my stomach, and man, did I wake up!" He laughed. "So there I am awake as a five-year-old on Christmas morning, and I hear a baby cryin'. Thought I was hallucinatin' at first, but there he was. Swear to God."

Mary was about to say something, but Johnny spoke

first. "The baby," he whispered.

"What?"

"What did you do with the baby?" he said, his voice shaky. Michael and Mary looked at him, confused. The boy didn't look well.

"Hey, you all right, kid?"

"Johnny, are you okay?"

"Just . . . tell . . . me," he managed.

"Well, I . . ." Michael wasn't sure what to do or say. "I, well, I sure as hell knew that I couldn't do anything for a newborn, so when I saw this lady in the parking lot, I just gave it to her, figuring that she'd know what to do. Her name was Jill. I remember that much, but that's all. Everything else is a blank. I never did find out what happened to the little boy, but I think he was okay when I handed him off."

"I think," said Johnny, "I know what happened." And he started to push his way past Mary. "Excuse me," he said as he made his way out of the booth. The bile was already rising in his throat, and he only made it a couple of steps before collapsing on the floor and passing out in a pool of vomit.

My dad used to call me dumpster boy. She remembered him telling her one day.

"What the hell is going on?" said Michael.

I don't know why he did that, but he did, and I hated it. "Oh my God," whispered Mary, suddenly suffused with a terrible anger and an even more terrible sadness. Never in her life had she been so outraged. Almost before Johnny hit the floor, she was there on her knees beside him. She'd picked him up, vomit and all, and held him tight to her breast, rocked him, and wept for him. He was only out for thirty or forty seconds and yet, already it seemed like half the restaurant, including the manager and Michael, had their cell phones out calling for the funcionarios to come. She squeezed Johnny harder as if that would protect him. She understood that, physically anyway, he would be fine, and he wouldn't want to be carried away in any ambulance and have to deal with the barrage of questions and investigations that would eventually precipitate. She looked up at Michael. "Stop, stop!" she said, frantically pleading. "Don't call! No ambulance. No police. Please. And tell everyone else to put their phones away, too."

Michael stopped punching in numbers, but otherwise took no action. He looked paralyzed . . .

*****

Indianapolis Indiana, June 16, 1996 . . .

A rusty hinge moans. Light seeps in through a new-made crack as the dumpster's dented lid opens, teeters at the, then tips over, bouncing several times before coming to rest against the graffitied bricks of a worn-out warehouse. Metallic echoes shoot up and down the alley, reverberating in Michael's skull as the naked sunshine pours in, piercing his eyelids like laser beams. His head is pounding. The air stinks of garbage. Needle-like pricks flitter across his abdomen then disappear. Rodent claws. He listens to the creature scuttle away.

And that isn't the worst of it.

Before he has time to appreciate the full scope of his misery something hits him square in the gut. Michael groans, pulls his knees to his chest. Rancid bile billows up and spills out the sides of his mouth. *Oh Lord, just take me now. Enough of this.* Then, as if on cue, the lid comes crashing down. A wave of putrid, garbage-laced air presses in on him, suffocating. Inside his head, some son of a bitch is playing Tarzan. Michael musters whatever strength he has left and pushes up, hard. Once again, the lid bounces off the bricks then settles against the wall.

He hears something and stills himself, waits and listens. Hears it again.

No, it can't be. And yet, there it is, as unmistakable as the stink he sits in. A baby's cry. Blinking and squinting, trying to clear his milky vision, Michael scans the garbage. Desperate, hoping to find something other than what, in his heart of hearts, he already knows it is, Michael convinces himself it's just a kitten. Then he sees it. Less than an arm's length away a small bundle wiggles and writhes. Wrapped in an orange cloth decorated with peace signs, it cries again. Human cries. *Dear God, why me?* He wants to die, to put an end to his useless life. But he knows it's not going to happen. He's not going to be that lucky. It's just not that sort of day. He also understands that, unless he does something quick, the baby may not survive. The realization washes over him like a tidal wave and rinses the drunken grogginess from his head.

He reaches for the bundle, a slow, herky-jerky motion, wishing his hands would stop shaking. The slick, silk-like material nearly slips through his fingers. He firms his grip, sweat pouring off his brow, and tries again. He manages, barely, to bring the child to his chest, then secures it with one hand and pulls back the cloth. It's a boy. "Oh Jesus of Mary, they didn't even clean you up. You poor thing," he says, covering it back up. At that moment, Michael is transformed. His self-imposed exile—living like an animal—is over. He will stop drinking and do something useful with his life. These are not the empty promises he's made a hundred times before. He doesn't even think about it in any specific sort of way because there is no time to think. He simply knows it to be true. His old life has come to an end. This miracle baby has catapulted him back into humanity. Michael flies out of the dumpster and takes off running.

I'll take good care of you he thinks, and then, realizing how ridiculous it sounds, looks for help. There's a convenience store a few blocks away with its lights on. That'll do.

As Michael approaches the store, he sees a lady step out of a van. She sees him, too, and freezes. He runs up, holding the bundle out to her. "It's a healthy baby boy, just been born. Someone threw him in the dumpster, can you believe it? I didn't see who it was." The lady, apparently too stunned to say anything, just opens her mouth. "Please take him," Michael begs. He uncovers the baby, and the infant cooperates by wiggling its arms and legs and making cooing sounds. "Please take him. Look at me . . . I can't do anything for him. You can . . . please."

She takes the baby and adjusts the makeshift blanket.

"Thank you, thank you so much, Miss . . ."

"Abel," the woman finishes for him. "Jill Abel."

Michael sees the woman smile as she holds the child. "Thank you again, Jill. I can see he's in good hands."

When she looks up, Michael is gone.

*****

"Michael," Mary hissed for the third time, this time

accompanied by a not so mild head butt to his thigh. Finally, he looked at her. "Don't you understand what's going on?" she asked.

He shook his head, still looking a bit dazed, and let go a meek, "I don't know."

"This is the boy."

"What boy?"

"The baby boy in the dumpster." Mary saw the proverbial light bulb go off in Michael's head. "Right. Now tell them to back off. It's not that kind of injury, you know? You understand now? It's not that kind of injury. Ambulances and police won't help. They'll just screw it up."

"Oh my God," said Michael. He looked at the manager and said, "It's okay. He'll be all right. I'm," he hesitated for a second, "I'm his grandfather. I'll take responsibility. Have everyone put their phones away. Just give us a few minutes." The manager was reluctant at first, but, in the end, he acquiesced.

"Mary?"

She could just make out the muffled sound of Johnny's voice. "Johnny? Thank goodness. Are you all right?"

"Well, I'd be better if you could loosen your grip just a little." She did. "Thanks, that's better. Now, can we go home?"

Chapter 25: Sweet Dreams

MARY, WORRIED ABOUT JOHNNY, insisted they sleep in the same room that night. She wanted him to sleep in the bed, but he wouldn't have it. So they dragged a mattress into her room and he slept on the floor. In the end, it didn't seem to matter. After an all day emotional roller-coaster ride, they were both exhausted and passed out almost as soon as they hit the pillow.

*****

Mary is back at the Mexican restaurant, laughing and having a good time. But something is wrong. Instead of seeing the brightly-colored decorations, the place looks like a dump. She takes a whiff. *Kind of smells like one too*. Keystone cop waiters dressed in blue, brass-buttoned uniforms and Bobby hats, with their billy clubs at the ready, are chasing around a bunch of raggedy Mexican boys. The boys, tall, skinny, and shirtless, stagger from table to table with the weight of huge metal garbage cans slung across their backs. *The bussing staff*, she realizes. Harassed by flailing billy clubs, the busboys are working as hard as they can to clear the tables. Every time they remove some trash, however, double the amount reappears in its place, and they never make any progress – except in regard to the trash overflowing their garbage cans.

In front of her, the table is littered with empty margarita glasses and Corona Extra beer bottles, their lonely little lime wedges all crumpled and sitting on the bottom. Across from her is Michael, but he doesn't look like the bus driver Michael that she knows. He looks like a bum. After releasing a loud, disgusting smelling belch, he says, "Excuse me," and starts laughing a pathetic, drunken laugh.

She turns to Johnny for comfort or an explanation or something – anything to let her know that everything is going to be alright. To her horror, she sees that the boy sitting next to her has turned into a giant Twinkie.

"Excuse me," says the Twinkie, looking ill as it slides out past her. Except it doesn't go past her, it goes right through her.

*****

Johnny, who knows a nightmare when he hears one, heard Mary screaming and got up to wake her, talking softly at first then shaking her lightly and calling out, "Wake-up Mary, wake-up."

"Go away," she yelled, pounding Johnny with her fists, and flailing under the sheets. He grabbed her by the arms and pinned her down.

"Mary, it's me, Johnny. It's just a dream. Wake up. It's just a bad dream. "

"Go away, go away," she screamed again. Then she stopped, blinked a few times, and caught her breath. "Johnny, is that you?"

"Yeah, it's me. You okay now?"

"I don't know," she said shaking her head and looking around the room. "I think so."

"That must've been some kind of nightmare."

Mary looked at him, squinting, "How do you know?"

"Let me see," he said, counting with his fingers, "you were screaming, talking in your sleep—I couldn't understand much of it, but it didn't sound good—and, oh yes, thrashing and kicking your covers all over the place. Kind of reminded me of that movie, *The Exorcist*, you made me watch last week."

"Oh God, no," she said, reaching up and ptting her arms around her neck.

"No, no, no. Not the head rotating like a gyroscope part, but you sure were, let's just say , vocal."

"You mean I was like, really talking in my sleep?" Johnny nodded.

"Talking, screaming, cursing, that sort of thing."

Mary narrowed her eyes, her voice meek. "Could you understand anything I said?"

"Well, several expletives came through quite nicely." She stuck her tongue out at him. Johnny continued, "And I'm pretty sure you said something about Twinkie boy." He looked at her, questioning, then shrugged his shoulders. "But that's about it."

"Good," she said.

Johnny frowned, "What do you mean?"

"For Christ's sake, Moonbrain, it's, like, embarrassing

to have people hear you talking in your sleep." She sighed, "I'm glad you were here, though. Did I wake you up?"

"Naw, I couldn't sleep either. Nightmares."

"You too, really?"

"Yeah," he said then paused. She had that look of curiosity about her. "But I don't really remember much about it," he lied. Johnny rolled up on his side and looked up at her. His old friend Moon, who was out in full force, set Mary's face aglow, the whites of her eyes sparkling down at him. "What was yours about?"

"You really want to know?" *I hope not, because I'm not about to tell you.*

"I really want to know."

Well, chick, time to make up a dream on the fly. "Okay buster, you asked for it, so here it goes. But I'm warnin' ya, it's not pretty."

"Anything has got to be better than thinking about my stupid nightmare," Johnny mumbled, "so please, go on."

"Okay, so we're at the Mexican restaurant just like last night. Everything is great. Then everything starts changing, you know, like it does in dreams, like without being aware of it you're all of a sudden on a new planet, or with somebody else, or you've turned into a turtle or whatever, and even though you can see you're a turtle, you don't know when it happened, and in your dream it, like doesn't even seem weird. You know?" He nodded. "Well, there was this guy sitting next to me, except all of a sudden he wasn't a guy anymore. He turned into a big Twinkie..."

Johnny laughed, "Oh no, not Twinkie-Boy."

"Be quiet, Moonbrain. You're the one who wanted to hear it. I know it sounds weird now, but in the dream it seemed, well, normal. So anyway, they brought my dinner, but it was just a huge pile of tortillas, hundreds of them. 'This isn't what I ordered,' I said, and started yelling and screaming at the waiter."

"That part sounds pretty realistic."

"Wiseguy," she said and threw a pillow at him.

"Ouch."

"So, what happened next?"

"What do you think happened? I woke up. *That's* what

happened."

"Well," said Johnny, his tone suggesting that his jovial mood had turned somber. "I suppose you'll want to hear my dream now, right?"

Of course I do, she wanted to blurt out, but managed to restrain herself. *I'd better think about this. His nightmare probably had dumpsters in it like mine did – probably even worse – so I can understand why he doesn't want to talk about it.* "That's okay, and anyway, I, like, don't need any more fuel for my own fires."

"Thanks, Mary," he said, his voice sounding perkier. "Oh, and hey, did you really dream about a giant Twinkie?"

"I most certainly did." *I just didn't tell you what really happened to him.* "And come to think of it, he was pretty worthless. What happened to things like chivalry, saving the maiden in distress and so forth, anyway?"

"I'll try to do better next nightmare," said Johnny.

They talked and joked and laughed for the next half-hour and then fell asleep without any more complications. It would, however, be the last time either one of them would laugh for quite a while.

Chapter 26: Stepping Out

After a successful OCR, Mary had expected life at 4217 Mystic Lane to improve, to be good even. Instead, it deteriorated, plummeting at times to depths she'd never imagined. She could barely keep her own head above water. Johnny, obsessed by the dumpster story, became lost in a storm of emotions. He alternated between episodes of intense rage and deep despair, and was consumed by feelings of emptiness, worthlessness, and self-hatred. Mary, to her credit, did not abandon him. Instead, she devoted herself to the task of keeping him afloat, working hard and long to distract him from his morbid thoughts while at the same time trying to nurse his confidence and self-esteem back to where he could function. It was twenty-four-hour-a-day and thankless work to boot because all Johnny wanted to do was sleep or rage. After two weeks with no sign of improvement, however, and despite giving it her best Florence Nightingale, the effort involved in trying to keep him up was wearing her down.

Finally, he started doing better. The extreme fits of rage and despair had, for the most part, leveled out. She could even occasionally engage him in an activity such as a game or watching a movie. Most of the time, however, he was still down. *I've got to get this boy's mind off the frigging dumpster.*

"Naw, you go ahead," Johnny mumbled, after she'd asked him to go out for a walk with her, as she always did. She didn't expect anything positive from him. And yet, as she thought about it, Mary realized this was better than usual. His normal response was a terse grunt. Wow, like, this is a major improvement. *There's still hope for the boy.* Mary vowed that she would not leave Johnny alone until she was sure he was doing better. *And like, you don't have to be a freaking shrink to see he's not well enough to be left by himself.* Ever since the incident at *Salsa Sally's*, Johnny had refused to leave the house, and Mary, afraid to leave him, was at the end of her rope and going stir-crazy. *Well, Moonbrain, all that is about to change. We're going out today, whether you want to or not.*

"Aww, come on Johnny. The fresh air will do ya good." She wanted to take Johnny on a walk with her through Laurel Highlands. Ever since the day she first poked her head through the hedge and into the Land of Oz, she'd been dying to go back. She was enchanted by the beauty of it and imagined that the people who lived in the elegant houses were as perfect as their lawns and gardens. It was, indeed, like walking into a fairy tale. At least, that's how Mary felt. She looked at Johnny and tilted her head a bit as if to say, well?

"Maybe some other time," he said. "I just don't feel like it right now."

Oh my God, two sentences in a row. I better check my pulse. It was time to push a little.

"You never feel like it, Johnny, but it's, like, one of those Catch-22 thingies." *I think it is, anyway.* It was her new favorite term and one she had just learned a few days ago when, in a moment of desperation, she pulled Joseph Heller's classic down from the shelf and actually started reading it. *And yes, you better believe things are desperate when I start reading books.*

"One of those what?"

"A Catch-22 is like this. Say you don't feel like going out for a walk. The thing is, I know damn well if you'd just give it a try, it would make you feel better. So then, if you did, you'd be happy that you were. Like, once you get out there, you'd feel like doing it. But here's the problem: if you wait until you feel like going on a walk before you actually do it, you're never going to get out of this frigging house. So that's, like, a Catch-22. See?"

Johnny didn't see. However, if he had to listen to her explain it again, he thought he might kill her, so he said, "Yeah, I can see that."

"Good, so let's go."

"No. You need to get this. I'm not going to get up and go on a walk today unless you physically drag me, okay?"

"Not okay," she said and then, with both hands, grabbed him, yanked him out of the chair and started pulling him towards the back door. At first, he resisted. Then she shot him a look and said, "Moonbrain. I'm about to go crazy sitting inside all day, and only one of us is allowed to be crazy at a time, get it? We're going, non negotiable."

Johnny acquiesced at once. Not because of her words so much as what he'd seen in her eyes. They pierced right through him with a raw desperation he'd not noticed before. At first, it just surprised him, then, as his brain woke up, he felt guilty. And then a different emotion emerged: fear. The look in her eyes was scary. It was like he could see inside of her that something was about to break, and that if he didn't get better soon, it would be too late. And so for the first time in two weeks, all thoughts of himself and his own difficulties vanished. His entire focus was on her.

"Okay, okay, I'm coming," he said, and then *he* took the lead and pulled *her* outside.

Mary stumbled along behind him, laughing. "What happened to you?"

When they were outside, Johnny slammed the sliding door shut and took off for the back gate. "Come on, slowpoke. I'll race you to the path." Sprinting full speed ahead, he beat her by a landslide. As he put his hands on his knees to catch his breath, he realized that he did feel better. He felt a lot better.

"Jesus Christ, Moonbrain, my legs are, like, only half as long as yours. Give me a freaking break, would you?" She gave him a quick hug, and he hugged her back, and then she shoved him backwards as hard as she could and took off up the path. "Race you to the top of the hill, slowpoke." She needn't have bothered to handicap him however, because the rocky terrain, the overgrown bushes, the overhanging trees, and the steepness of the incline meant that, on this track anyway, being short was an advantage. Johnny fell twice to his knees as he lumbered up behind her and arrived with his hair full of twigs and leaves and dirt.

"You look like a tree, Moonbrain. Here, let me brush the leaves out of your hair."

"Is this where the Entwives are?" he said in his best tree sounding voice.

"Sorry, Treebeard, I think you've got the wrong neighborhood. The Oak sisters are still somewhere down there in Middle Earth." She brushed the last of the leaves from his shoulders.

"Too bad. I thought the Entwives might really be here. Oh well, just have to keep on looking."

"There you are, all human again. Let's go," she said, and disappeared through the hedge. Johnny came out right behind her. She smiled at him. "It's almost unreal, don't you think?"

"Like I said, the land of OZ."

"Well then," she said, and, hooking her elbow in his, began skipping down the sidewalk. "Let me show you around."

As they strolled through the neighborhood, Mary pointed out which houses she especially liked and made up stories about the people who lived there. "See that one?" Mary indicated a boxy shaped mansion with huge white columns and a rounded entranceway full of lavish statues. Two semi-circular staircases, one on either side, led to a twenty-foot-high arched doorway. A white stone driveway circled in front with a large reflecting pool and fountain just inside of it.

"It looks like a castle."

"It's one of my favorites. A real queen lives there. Her husband, the king, is still alive and rules a small European country. She ran away from him twenty years ago because he beat her and was cruel to his subjects."

"Really," said Johnny, playing along.

"Yes. She had to sell her twenty-five-carat diamond necklace to get the money to live on, because her jerk of a husband—"

"The king?"

"Right, the bastard wouldn't give her a cent when she left."

"I didn't know there was such a thing as a 25-carat diamond. Do those even exist? How much is it worth?"

"I don't know . . . a lot," she replied, and then continued. "She didn't know that she was pregnant when she got to America, but eight months later the prince was born. He's twenty years old now and heir to the kingdom. So, when the king dies, which they all hope will be soon, he is going back to make his rightful claim to the throne and be a benevolent ruler." She sighed. "Such a noble prince, and very handsome too, so I'm told."

"And I suppose you will go back as his princess or queen?"

"That possibility has crossed my mind, and, like, you never know."

"But wouldn't you miss me?"

"No. You'd be our court jester." At this they both laughed and continued on. Mary pointed out several other mansions that she liked and had different stories for them all. Finally, they arrived at one of the smaller houses in the neighborhood. Mary sighed and gave it a plaintive look. "This one," she said, "I know the real story. At least some of it."

"Oh really, how's that?"

Mary whispered in his ear, "I talked to one of the kids. Her name is Susan Goodenough, and, man, is she ever a piece of work."

"Piece of work?"

Mary rolled her eyes. "A real snotty kid; a bitch."

"Right."

"You know what she called me?"

"No Idea."

"She called me a slut. Can you believe that?"

"I guess so," answered Johnny, which earned him a backhand to the solar plexus. "Ouch!"

"You're supposed to say something like, 'no way, what a little brat.'"

"Got it."

"Good. Anyway . . . "

"How old is she?"

"Thirteen."

"Right."

"Would you just shut-up and listen?" He nodded. "Like I said, she's a little snit. It's her brother that's interesting. He's major hot." The look on Mary's face told Johnny everything he needed to know about what 'hot' meant in this circumstance.

"Yeah, I get that."

"Great. Anyway, what I've been trying to tell you is there's something dark going on in that house, in the Goodenough family. The girl is a little know-it-all who wears weird glasses and has pigtails. I tried to talk to her, asked her what's wrong, but she wouldn't answer, just called me a-"

"Slut, right?" Johnny thought he was showing attentive listening—he'd looked up on the internet about what girls want out of boys, and that was a biggie. He smiled, expecting to get some kind of praise. Instead, he got another backhand.

"Shut-up, Moonbrain. Now, where was I? Oh yeah, the parents. I've never seen the mother, but I did see the dad. He got out of the car and went inside, totally expressionless, like a robot. The girl, Susan, grabbed his arm and tugged on it trying to get his attention, begging him to listen to her about something. And you know what he did?"

Tired of getting slapped, Johnny played this one close to the best and nodded agreement.

"He just kept on, like she wasn't even there. She yelled at him that he was worthless, and he didn't even turn around. Just kept walking," here Mary imitated a stiff robot-walk, "went inside and closed the door behind him. Weird, huh?"

In response, Johnny, who was distracted by something, put up his hand to signal quiet. "Do you hear that?"

Mary listened. The house was well back from the road, so she couldn't be sure, but she thought she heard something too. "Sounds like people arguing, like they're yelling," she said. Johnny nodded. Mary put a finger to her lips and started creeping around the back of the house, urging Johnny with her other hand to follow. He gave her a weary look, but she just scowled and waved him on more vigorously.

They positioned themselves under an open window in back of the house.

Where they could hear everything.

Chapter 27: Mashed Potatoes

DINNER WITH THE GOODENOUGH FAMILY was usually a quiet affair. That night was different. The tension around the kitchen table was thick, like it might take a backhoe to cut through it. But Susan was determined. About halfway through dinner, she patted the sides of her mouth with her napkin, cleared her throat and stood up. She assumed this would get their attention. It didn't. She cleared her throat again. Nothing. Twits, she thought, and then called out in a firm, but respectful, voice, "Pay attention people." No one said a thing but, at least, for the moment, they turned their heads in her general direction. *I guess this is as good as it gets*. She sighed and proceeded with the well rehearsed 10-minute lecture she prepared.

"Ladies and gentlemen, mothers and fathers, brothers and sisters, I am here tonight to remove the blinders of denial from your eyes. To see the . . . "

Stephen flicked a pea at her with his finger, "Put a sock in it, Sis."

Without looking up from the financials, Richard said, "Stephen," in a tone intended to sound like warning but instead just sounded tired.

Susan knew exactly what was coming next and was not disappointed when her mother said, "Would everyone please just be nice and enjoy their supper. I worked all afternoon preparing it, you know."

Susan looked at the people seated around her, bewildered, thinking that surely the stork had made a mistake and delivered her to the wrong family. She made a production of clearing her throat and then continued. "Like I was saying, there is a pink elephant in this house, and I want you to see it. Actually," she said, "I want you," pointing at her father, "to deal with it."

"Deal with what, dear?" asked Richard.

"Him!" said Susan, now pointing at her brother.

"Is there some kind of problem, Stephen?" Richard asked without bothering to look up.

"The only problem I have is a nosy little sister who won't leave me alone."

"Well," said June, "I'm glad that's all taking care of."

"Right," said Richard. "Now, let's all get back to dinner."

Susan was off script now, all pretense of control and presentation gone. "I don't know what it is, my brother has been taken over by some foreign creature. There's something very wrong with him. All his teachers see it. His friends see it. Why can't you see it? Please, do something."

Richard, finally looking up at his daughter, said, "Susan. Your brother says he doesn't have a problem. He looks fine to me. We're all going to finish your dinner now in silence. End of discussion."

Susan Goodenough was a precocious child with an uncanny ability to observe life as it happened around her, ferret out the hidden meanings, and actually make sense of it. One day she would write a book called Mashed Potatoes: Family Therapy for Dinner, whose seeds were sown every evening at the Goodenough kitchen table. Susan would turn the psychiatric world on its ear. Her book would eventually save and heal more lives and families than Freud's theories had destroyed. (Although, due to the sheer numbers, that part would not happen within her lifetime.)

The problem for Susan now was that she was only twelve years old. Despite the fact that she was a true genius, no one listened to her, let alone believed her. This is nuts, she thought, and resolved to sort it out. Now. She sought out each member of her family, one by one, her keen blue eyes glaring, and made sure she caught and held each of their respective gazes before moving on to the next. This was done slowly, in a deliberate and methodical fashion, like a scientist titrating compounds for a delicate experiment, and all the time squinting her eyes and frowning.

Mother was first to feel the heat of Susan's piercing gaze. June, taken by surprise for a split-second, revealed an alarmed and desperate look but then, as if nothing had happened, replaced it just as quickly with a half-baked smile, one that was supposed to reassure Susan that everything was OK. Didn't work.

Next was her father, Richard. If the look in Susan's eyes surprised or concerned him at all, no one would have known. He paused for just the briefest moment, his loaded fork suspended in midair. She sensed that he was taking it in, evaluating, but his face never changed, and before the mashed potatoes had even lost their momentum, they resumed their journey mouthword. Susan wondered if he really had paused, or was it just her imagination.

Next was Stephen. Susan could barely look him in the eyes, and when she did it was he who looked away. She was totally bewildered at the metamorphosis of this person, her brother, her former best friend and confidant. This new Stephen that she was looking at was someone she did not recognize, the old Stephen would've understood her and given her comfort. He would have known what she was thinking as easily as if he could read her mind, and, more than that, he would know what to do. That was before he had abandoned her. Stephen did not return her gaze. He just continued eating as if nothing was going on, shoveling mashed potatoes—mashed potatoes that Susan had painstakingly made herself—into his greedy mouth as fast as he could. It was the mashed potatoes that betrayed him.

Mashed potatoes were a religion with Stephen. He would eat them slowly and with reverence, paying attention to the smallest of details, just as Susan imagined the Gallo Brothers, Ernest and Julio, might sample fine wines. He could detect even the subtlest of nuances about them. He could tell, for example, what type of potato and been used. Yukon Golds were the best for mashing, according to Stephen anyway, and it was tantamount to sacrilege to pour gravy on them or to eat them in the same mouthful with your meat or peas. White potatoes were a close second and also had to be eaten in their purest form, without the stain of gravy upon them. If someone had the nerve to use an ordinary Idaho baking potato, however, Stephen, because he was always polite and well mannered, would frown ever so slightly and look for the gravy to disguise the foul taste. He could tell precisely the ratio of butter to milk to potato that was used, he could tell whether or not the potatoes had been overcooked or undercooked before being mashed, he could tell if the potatoes were fresh, or if they had been out of ground too long and had started getting soft, if there was too much or too little salt, and of course, he could tell if someone had had the nerve to put something else in them, like garlic or cheese.

Foolishly hoping that she could win her brother's heart back, she made the mashed potatoes herself that night. She'd gone to the market herself and picked out the best Yukon Golds she could find. Then she came home and carefully peeled, cooked, and whipped them to perfection. She got them just right, something that was not all that easy to do. Normally, Stephen would've savored them and given high and extravagant praises to whoever prepared them. All she could do now was to stare watch him shovel them down as if they were dog food, It was obscene, irreverent, and just plain ugly. Whatever doubts and hopes she still had were removed. This was not her brother, but some strange alien who'd invaded his body. There was nothing she could do.

Susan stood up so fast it knocked her chair over. Pointing a finger at Stephen, she said, "you are not my brother, you are a jerk," then, pointing at her father, "you are worthless," and at last to her mother she said, "and you are a lying, stupid bitch." Still no one said anything, they just stared at her with their mouths open, frozen. Susan hoisted herself up atop the table. With her arms arched overhead like a ballerina, she started turning around and around, slowly, right in the middle of the table, droning out a variety of phrases, like "This is Susan and this is my family around me. How come they don't know me?" Or, "This is Susan. Susan would like to request a transfer to another planet." Or, "Can Susan's parents tell that Susan is upset? What will they do to help Susan?" And when the silence continued she answered for them, "Not a goddamned thing." Food and china went crashing and splattering everywhere as Susan jumped off the table. She ran up to her room, slamming the door behind her.

Stephen, June, and Richard slowly emerged from their respective states of suspended animation. Richard was the first to speak, "Well. I was just about done anyway." He started making his way towards the family room, casually brushing away the larger portions of food that he was now wearing.

"I'll just bring the dessert into the family room tonight," June chimed in, "Some hot apple pie and ice cream will make us all feel better. I'm sure."

Stephen said nothing; he just kicked Susan's chair, sending it halfway across the kitchen, and skulked off to his room.

Susan cried herself to sleep, praying to God for the strength to never have to feel this way again.

Chapter 28: The Kindness of a Stranger

In the Goodenough's back yard, the drama seemed to be over. "Don't you think we should be getting back now?" whispered Johnny, but the look on Mary's face told him she had other plans. She was scheming, and that was always dangerous.

Mary smiled, "You go ahead. I'm going to talk to Susan. She could use a friend about now. Her family is, like, so totally screwed up."

Johnny looked at her, incredulous, "And how exactly are you going to arrange that? She doesn't even like you."

She looked at him with those eyes, eyebrows moving up and down as she talked, "Oh, I think she'll come around. You just wait and see. I'll be back in a while."

"So you're just going to barge right in or something?"

"Of course not, I'll knock first."

He started to argue with her, but knew it was useless. "Okay, but if you're not home in a couple of hours I'm going to come back here and check on you."

"Okay. See ya later."

They walked around to the front together. Johnny hid behind a tree and waited while Mary marched right up to the front door and knocked. *She is totally crazy.*

The door opened and a normal appearing woman inquired, "Oh, what can I do for you young lady?" June sounded as calm and cheerful as if she were selling Girl Scout cookies.

Even Mary was somewhat taken aback, especially when she saw Richard sitting in his recliner chair watching the news and reading his paper as if nothing had happened. "I'm, um, well, a friend of Susan's. I need to talk to her, is she home?"

June smiled and opened the door, waving Mary inside and thinking it must be some kind of homework issue because, unless someone was having homework difficulties, Susan had no friends. "Susan is upstairs in her bedroom, the last one on the left." June pointed to the stairs.

Richard, without even looking up from his paper, asked his wife, "Who was that, June dear?"

"One of Susan's little friends," replied June as she thought, I have no idea. Have I ever even seen her before?

That's strange, thought Richard.

Mary walked down to the end of the hall and was about to knock on the door when she heard Susan. It sounded like the girl was crying and throwing various objects around the room. Mary knocked lightly at first, and when there was no reply, knocked louder. "Go away!" wailed Susan.

Mary knocked again with the same response and then try to crack the door open, but it was locked. "Hey, it's me Mary, your new friend."

"Who?"

"Mary," she replied. When there was no response, in a louder and somewhat exasperated tone, she added, "your slutty knew friend."

"Oh, you." Nothing happened for a minute, and Mary thought that Susan was going to ignore her, but just as she was about to walk away the door opened, and Susan motioned her in.

"Thanks."

"What are you doing here?"

"It sounded like you needed someone to talk to."

"How would you know," Susan said angrily.

"We could, like, hear everything from the sidewalk." It was just a little lie, thought Mary.

"We?"

"Yeah, me and the boy I'm living with over in Mystic Meadows. We were just out for a bit of fresh air."

"You're living with a boy? You really are slut, aren't you?"

Mary laughed, "No. It's not that way at all. Let me explain." And she did. She told her about running away from home, about the bus driver, and about finding Johnny. Everything, except she didn't tell Susan about the dead bodies. It just didn't seem like the right time.

Susan did need someone to talk to and she in turn told everything to Mary. About what was going on at her family, how she was so disgusted with them and how they never listen to her and how her brother had a serious problem, and her parents were doing anything about it.

That was all easy stuff to tell, relatively anyway, but

Mary could see there was something more Susan needed to spit out. “So now, tell me what’s really bothering you.”

For a second Susan looked offended but then sighed, “You’re right. You see, Stephen, my brother, was my best friend. What the hell, he was my only friend, and now he won’t even look at me. I never realized it before, but Stephen and I have essentially raised ourselves. Our parents are totally worthless. As long as we get good grades in school, which we both do, they could not care less what goes on with us. They’re totally clueless. I hate them. I hate them.” She started crying again, and Mary wrapped Susan up in her arms and gently rocked her. Susan could not understand this girl at all, what she was doing here or who she was. But it felt good to be held, and to have someone to talk to who actually listened. For now that was good enough. It was better than good. And, it was all she had.

In a couple of minutes, Susan looked up and gave Mary a smile. “Thank you, thank you very much.”

Mary beamed; there was more to this girl than she thought. She had spunk, and she was smart. Mary found a piece of paper and scrawled Johnny’s phone number and address on it. She handed it to Susan, “Any time,” she said, “anytime you need anything you just let me know.” And then Mary showed herself out of the house, smiling, and waving at June and Richard as she walked by. Worthless bastards.

And in her bedroom Susan was smiling and a funny thought came to her. I’ve become dependent upon the kindness of strangers.

And she laughed.

Chapter 29: Stephen

DAD, DID YOU TALK TO Stephen yet?" asked Susan.

Richard, didn't answer. It had been a couple of weeks since the infamous dinner episode and, eventually, Richard had agreed, again, to talk to Stephen.

"Dad, you promised," she scolded.

"Yes, and I will take care of it," he answered, and, knowing what Susan was going to say next, added, "when the time is right."

"And that will be when, dad? When you're dead?" Susan was really angry now, "Or Stephen?"

"That is quite enough young lady, to your room now." Richard pushed her towards the hallway.

She knew he was just blowing her off again, that he was not going to talk to Stephen, and decided to try herself. One more time. Susan mimed exaggerated pushing motions here and there, first left and then right, as she zigzagged through the living room on her way to the stairs.

"Can you see these Pink elephants?" Susan grunted and pushed against the stubborn pachyderm, "Can you Dad?"

Richard ignored her. He sat back down on the couch and started reading his newspaper, picking up where he left off before he was interrupted. Susan stomped up the stairs as loud as she could.

She heard her mother June down the hall pounding on Stephen's door, pleading with him to open up. Susan stopped. By the looks of it her mother had been there for while and was just now starting to get hysterical, frantically twisting the doorknob back-and-forth, but it was locked. And then June, quite uncharacteristically, took charge. She backed up two steps and then ran forward, ramming her shoulder into the door as hard as she could. It sprung open and June fell into her son's bedroom.

Susan crept down the hall on hands and knees, trying to be as inconspicuous as possible. She almost reached the now open door to Stephen's room when her mother let loose a bloodcurdling scream. The harrowing sound stopped Susan dead in her tracks. June lunged out of the room, slamming the door behind her. She almost tripped over Susan, who, until then, could not fathom being any more frightened than she already was. She was wrong. Looming over her, instead of June, she saw something that resembled Godzilla or Frankenstein more than anything else. Susan was frozen, but June recovered and when she realized who was there, bent down and scooped Susan off the floor, gobbling her up in her mommy arms as effortlessly as if she were picking up one of Susan's stuffed bears, and carried her down the stairs. When Susan realized that she had been captured, she tried to escape. But the usually dainty and meek June seemed suddenly powerful and would not let go. Susan struggled to get free as her mother just kept saying, "No, no. I won't let you see it. You can't see it. Oh my God, oh my God!" By this time, Richard was standing, looking in their direction. And, as much as he may have wished to, not even he could deny that something was amiss.

June gave her husband a piercing, haunted look, a look he had never seen from her. He hesitated for just a moment, unconsciously trying to figure out some way to escape the situation, to pretend nothing was happening, but it couldn't be done. Not this time. He marched over to the stairs and pushed past his wife and daughter. When he came to Stephen's once again closed door, he paused and waited. Perhaps it was a last ditch effort to avoid what he knew in his bones would happen when he opened it. Stephen was dead, June's scream had told him that much already, but that was just the tip of the iceberg. Oh my God what have I done? He couldn't breathe. He didn't want to go into that room because, he now realized, that when he did, it would be the end. Not just of Stephen, but everything he, the former Father Richard McCleary, had ever been or wanted to be; tried or not tried to be; all his successes and all of his failures; everything he had ever known or not known, believed or not believed would vanish into nothing. All gone. And that wasn't even the worst of it. Richard had based his entire life on one immutable, indestructible truth, and now that, too was a lie. There would be no salvation, because there was no God.

When Richard stepped into his son's room, he was greeted by the most horrific sight he had ever seen. Worse than unimaginable. And he knew then that he would be carrying that image around with him forever, as vivid and as heavy as a cross nailed into the flesh of his bleeding back. Stephen's blue tinged body hung from the ceiling, naked, at the end of a thick, black, nylon rope fashioned into a noose. The blue plastic bag covering his head was tucked in beneath the noose and now clung to his face in a vacuum. The room was littered with pornographic images. Richard knew what this was, and it was no suicide. It was worse. Stephen had been experimenting with a sexual behavior, or fetish, called autoerotic asphyxiation, a form of autoeroticism involving partial asphyxiation. It was supposed to heighten the sexual high. But it's not supposed to kill you. He was right about that, but he also knew how dangerous it was and that occasionally someone would lose control, not be able to relieve whatever it was they were using to asphyxiate themselves, and then, it could turn lethal. Richard knew this from his days in the priesthood—dealing with kids in counseling and occasionally even in the confessional it had come up on several occasions. It unnerved him so much at the time that he checked into it and found out that it was not only real, but more common than he would have liked to believe. But then it had only been of academic interest to him. Now it had destroyed him. Richard knew all this to be true and he also knew that even experienced investigators often mistook it for suicide. A panic came over him at the thought of anyone else ever finding out. I won't let them, and he decided to make sure that no one ever would. Susan had been right. Stephen did have a serious problem. She will never see this. No one will see this. No one will know this. And then he shut the door and started to clean up what he needed to in order to make it look like it was 'just' a suicide.

As he worked to rid his son's room of the truth, Richards's own life started to come into focus. It was not something he wanted to look at. He had successfully avoided memories of his previous life for so long that he had almost come to believe it didn't exist, that it wasn't real. That was all over. Now the memories came rushing through the barriers he had built as easily as water through a broken levee, flooding and forever changing the landscape of his life. Richard himself felt as though he were under water, unable to breathe. When he at last came out of son's room and closed the door behind him, Richard was exhausted and defeated. And though he no longer understood God, or even believed in His existence, Richard did the only thing he could think of or knew how to do. He sank to his knees, bowed his head, and began to pray.

When, finally, Susan heard her father come out of Stephen's room, she bolted over to him, intending to go right around him into Stephen's room to see for herself what had happened. But when she got there she stopped. The man who was kneeling on the floor in front of her brother's door bore little resemblance to her father. He looked up at her and she knew that she was never going to get through him and she would never know what happened. She slapped him as hard as she could across his face and it was like hitting a mannequin. Too numb to say anything or even to scream, Susan ran down the hall to her own room. Just as she was just about to shut the door she heard her father chanting something.

She turned to look and saw that he was crossing himself. She knew he was speaking Latin but could not understand what he was saying. "In nomine Patris," he said as he touched his forehead, and then, "et Filii," as he touched his breast, "et Spiritus Sancti," and finally, touching first his left and then his right shoulder, "Amen." She found it both strange and eerie that he sounded like, even looked like, a priest, because they never even went to church.

Susan ducked into her room, shut, and then locked the door behind her.

She did not pray.

Chapter 30: Pizza, Phones, and Plans

Johnny continued to improve as he and Mary fell into a comfortable routine. It was the end of a particularly rewarding, albeit long, day, and they were starving. When the doorbell finally rang, they jumped up, and, nearly in unison, yelled, "Pizza!" Johnny got to the door first, and the delivery girl handed him the pizza.

"Give me the goods Moonbrain," said Mary as she snatched the extra large half cheese, half supreme, pizza out of Johnny's hands, "so you can pay the chick. And don't forget the tip this time, okay?"

"Got it mom," said Johnny.

The pizza girl held her hand out and droned, "Twenty-three dollars and fifty-six cents, please."

Johnny handed her two twenties. "Here, and ah... keep the change."

"Thanks," said the delivery girl, rather flatly, as Johnny handed her the money. When the fifteen dollar tip registered, however, her voice turned enthusiastic. "Hey man, like thanks a lot." Johnny closed the door behind her, and went over in front of the TV where Mary had opened the box and started to chow.

"Wow, wis is willy goog," Mary said with her mouth full, chomping as if she hadn't eaten for weeks.

"Wi wold woo wo," said Johnny, mocking her.

Mary swallowed and said, "Here," and flung a piece from the cheese side at him.

"Wanks," he said, scraping the cheese and sauce from his shirt onto a paper plate. Johnny then wadded the wreckage up into a ball and ate it like it was an apple. Mary looked at him as if he were crazy. "You started it," he said.

In no time, the pizza was nearly gone. Only two pieces of supreme remained. Mary could not have eaten another bite if her life depended on it. Johnny, however, was still salivating.

"Ahh, gee Mary, you don't really want those, do you?"

"Hmm, I don't know," she picked an olive off one of the pieces and placed it rather seductively into her mouth. "It is good. Maybe I'll save them for later."

Johnny looked as if he might cry.

"It is my piece, isn't it?"

"Okay, that's cool," he said, his voice slightly higher pitched than usual.

"Here Moonbrain, go ahead. I was just kidding."

"Really?"

"Yes, really."

Johnny slapped the two pieces together like a sandwich, and then disposed of it in three bites. He was still chewing when the phone began to ring. "Woo webber . . ."

Mary cut him off. "Right. I'll get the phone. You chew." Johnny nodded appreciatively.

"Hello? Yeah, it's me... What... Shit, are you kidding... Judas Priest, that's terrible." Mary, who had been standing, slid down to the floor as the phone fell out of her hand. Her eyes went wide and misty. Her face was white, and she tried to say something but her mouth just hung open, quivering, and quiet.

Johnny rushed over but Mary just stared straight ahead as if she didn't even see him. He heard someone at the other end of the line, screaming, "Are you still there? Don't go away. Please."

Johnny picked up the phone and shouted into it, "Just wait a minute." Then he looked at Mary. "What's the matter? Are you OK? You want me to hang up?"

Mary shook her head and looked at Johnny, alert now. She took the phone, "I'm okay."

"You don't look okay."

Mary covered up the mouth and the phone and looked at Johnny crossly, "Shhh! I'll tell you later."

"But-"

"Shhh! Later." And then into the phone, "I'm back, you still there Susan? Yeah, sorry, but, like, just sort of blew me away, you know?"

On the floor next to her, Johnny was trying to be patient, but could hardly stand the suspense. "Who is it?" He asked again in a loud whisper.

"Chill dude, this is important!"

"Who is it?"

"Suzie. Now shut up!"

Who is Suzie? Johnny wondered, but held his tongue.

"Sorry. Sure we can help. What? I understand . . . Just come on over whenever . . . You what . . . why do you need help . . . " A long pause ensued and Mary's face went slack. "Oh." Another pause.

Johnny heard Suzie on the other end of the phone, pleading with Mary. He started to get up, but Mary shot him a look, and he stopped.

And then, back into the phone, Mary said, "Jesus Christ, your parents are nuts. Okay, okay just a second. Call us back later tonight or tomorrow. We'll help, but we need to figure out how . . . Later. You're going to be okay. I don't know. We'll think of something."

Mary turned the phone off and looked at Johnny with the same expression she had after seeing Ralph outside the front door. "What's going on? And who is Suzie anyway?" he asked, but she was starting to turn some sort of yellow green. Johnny figured he'd better back off. "Come on," he said, walking her into the living room and sitting her on the couch. "I'll be right back." Johnny pulled a Coke out of the fridge and gave it to her. She drank half of it straight down.

Her eyes were glistening as Mary fought to fight back the tears. But it was no use. Finally, she let herself relax and fell into Johnny, holding him as tight as she could, and burying her face in his neck.

A few minutes later she pulled her soggy, reddened face off of his shoulder, and thanked him.

Johnny was confused. *Thank me for what*, he wondered? *The Coke?* "No big deal," he said. "It looked like you needed something to drink."

Mary rolled her eyes and smiled. "Not the Coke you dope."

"Oh."

"It's okay." Mary took a couple of deep breaths, found some Kleenex, wiped her eyes and blew her nose. When she looked at him, her eyes were different. He couldn't quite describe what it was about them, but they looked sad and afraid. "We have to help Suzie."

"You mean the little brainiac girl from Laurel Highlands?"

Mary nodded.

"The one who calls you a slut?"

"Called me a slut, we're past that now."

"Great. So what is going on?"

"Well," she paused, not knowing exactly what to say. Nothing came to her, so she just blurted out, "Her brother, Stephen, he, he like, he's dead."

"What?"

"He killed himself."

"Holy crap!" Johnny shivered remembering the metal taste of the gun when he nearly killed himself. Why *did I get saved, and he didn't? I wish someone could have saved him.* "How?"

"They won't tell her. She knew something was wrong with him, he tried to tell her parents, but they wouldn't listen. And now he's dead."

Tell them what? Johnny wondered but now was not the time to press for more information. *Even I can see that.*"Okay, we'll help her. Just tell me what kind of help she needs."

"I don't know exactly, but her parents are all messed up. She wants to come live with us, at least for a while."

"Okay, that's fine. We've got plenty of room, so, sure tell her to come on over."

"It's not that easy. She's already tried to run away by herself, but they keep catching her. They're watching her like a hawk." Johnny nodded and Mary continued, "Anyway . . . you see . . . they like, hired a freaking bodyguard or some bullshit, some goon that's supposed to keep an eye on her, like, 24/7. So she's asking us to help her, like, escape I guess."

"Are you up for it?" Johnny asked, wondering if he was.

"I think so. I mean, except. . . "

"What?"

"I'm scared, Johnny, really scared."

"Maybe we should just call the police? You know, an anonymous tip or something."

"No, she doesn't want us to do that. She thinks that it will just make things worse by freaking her parents out even more than they already are. She thinks they might, like, put her in a freaking cage or something." She looked at Johnny and added, "Can you believe that?"

Oh yeah, I can believe it. "Well, okay then, no police. But we need to get going. When is she going to call back?"

Mary shrugged, "When she can."

Johnny closed his eyes and searched for the calm reasoning of his inner Cybersleuth and, somewhat to his surprise, found him. "Do we need to go get her right away or do we have some time?"

"I'm not sure, but the sooner the better. How about tomorrow?"

"Tomorrow is perfect. You chill until she calls back, hopefully soon, and set a time for tomorrow night." Johnny stopped for second and then added, "It needs to be dark out, like maybe sometime after nine o'clock." Mary looked pale and almost expressionless; Johnny had never seen her look like this before. "Are you sure you're okay?"

"I'm sure I'm not okay, but what can I do about it? I'll be fine, what's going to happen?"

"I don't know yet, but I'll come up with something. I promise."

"You really think we can help her?"

"I know we can."

Coming from anyone else, the promise that he will come up with something would not have been very reassuring, but, somehow, coming from Johnny, it was. Mary felt her anxiety receding. The color returned to her cheeks, and she smiled. "So, Johnny, is it okay if she stays here as long as she needs to?"

"It's okay with me."

Mary's nerves were soon under control, and her brain started acting normal again. An idea came to her, one she couldn't hold back. And, giving Johnny one of her mischievous smiles, she asked, "You don't think your parents will mind, do you?"

Johnny grinned. "I'll ask them.

Chapter 31: Susan's Rescue-Part I

EVER SINCE SUSAN'S TELEPHONE call about five hours ago, Johnny was up in his room working on . . . something. Mary yawned. She was tired of not having anyone to talk to, tired of watching TV, and, she realized, just plain pooped. *Time to go to bed.* On the way to her room, she poked her head inside Johnny's and rapped lightly on the wall. "Hey, I'm going to bed. You need me to do anything?"

"Nope," said Johnny, flatly, and without looking up then caught himself and turned to face her. "I mean, no thanks. I'm going to do the same in just a bit." Then, with a quick flick of his head indicating the general direction of his desk, he added, "As soon as I'm done with this."

Mary stepped into the room and craned her neck to see what he was up to. "What *is* all that stuff?" she asked, pointing to a computer screen filled with hundreds of multicolored lines, boxes, squiggles, and other symbols.

"Hang on." Johnny highlighted a particular blue and red line in the middle of the screen. "There," he said. "It's a diagram of the underground electrical wiring for Susan's neighborhood." He pointed to a particular set of squiggles. "See, this is her house and this is the main box that leads to it."

"If you say so," said Mary, not even trying to feign interest, "Does this mean you have a plan?"

A mischievous smile spread across Johnny's face. "Think you could manage to talk your way into Susan's house through the front door, and then cause a distraction to get the adults, both parents and the security guard, out into the living room for about five minutes?"

"Distraction is my middle name, sir," she said, straightening up like a soldier and giving Johnny a small salute.

"Then we've got a plan."

*****

The next day . . .

Attempting in vain to pass the time without going crazy while he waited for Mary, Johnny went over the plan one more time even though he already knew it cold. Still, his anxiety was ratcheting up. *What is she doing up there?* He tried to calm himself. She'll be down in a minute. *Everything will be okay. Stay calm.* But as the seconds ticked by Johnny just couldn't stand it. *We're supposed to be there at 9:30 and its 9:27 already. We'll never make it!* "Mar-ry," yelled Johnny up the stairs, "where are you? It's getting late!"

"Chill Moonbrain, I'm right here," she said, closing the bedroom door behind her. "It's not even nine-thirty."

"But it's at least a ten minute walk and it's already," he checked his watch again, "nine-twenty-eight."

"Take a chill pill, dude. I said we'd be there *about 9:30*, not exactly." Johnny did not seem reassured. "Okay, okay, let's go."

Once outside, Johnny relaxed enough to see Mary wasn't herself either. They were both nervous. "You okay?"

"I don't know. I'm just kind of, well-"

"Kind of what?"

Mary stopped walking and turned towards Johnny, who did the same. "I'm scared shitless is what. God, I hate that."

"I'm scared too."

"You don't look scared."

After living fourteen years in a combat zone, you kind of get used to it. "Trust me, I'm scared. I think I've just had more practice at not showing it." He looked at her for a second or two, trying to gauge what she wanted. "We don't have to do it this, you know."

"Yes, we do. I'm okay now. Let's go." Johnny nodded, and they were off.

It was dark as they walked down the gravel path to the edge of the greenbelt where they would cut through to Laurel Highlands. "See," said Johnny, pleased with himself, "nice and dark, no moon." Dark was part of Johnny's plan.

"Great," said Mary as she rolled her eyes. I guess. "That's why they give you the big bucks."

"What?"

"Never mind."

Shining his small but powerful penlight, Johnny led the way up the hill and through the trees. They pushed through the hedge at the top and came out in lush Laurel Highlands. Which was lit up like a Christmas tree.

"Well, Moonbrain," said Mary, taking in what looked like a million street lights. "So much for darkness."

Johnny smiled. “Just wait. You’ll see.” He pushed ahead and motioned for Mary to follow. They walked several blocks until they were across the street, and several houses down from the Goodenough residence. Johnny kneeled down on the sidewalk and dug up a little clump of grass next to one of the streetlamps. “You ready?”

“For what?”

“To do your part.”

“Well, yeah, except that it’s about as light as day out here.” Johnny didn’t answer. He just handed her a penlight like his. “I don’t think I’m going to need—”

“Just take it.”

“Okay, okay,” she said, and took it. *Like, what do I need this worthless thing for?* She was about to say something to that effect but before she could get the words out, the whole neighborhood went black. “Sheee-it!” she gasped then, whispering, added, “Wow, how’d you do that?”

“Later,” answered Johnny, unable to hide his grin even in the darkness. “We have exactly ten minutes. Go!”

Mary turned on her now quite useful penlight and let it guide her across the street and up to the Goodenough’s front door. She turned it off. *Wise guy*, she thought as she looked over her shoulder just in time to see Johnny and his light disappear around the corner of the house. She knocked on the door, giving it two loud raps. “Coming,” she heard someone say from within. There were footsteps, and then a thwack and a crash, and then, “Ouch, damn-it!” The door opened a crack and there behind it was Richard Goodenough, Susan’s father. “Yes, may I help you?”

“Excuse me,” said Mary, grunting as she shoved the door open the rest of the way and blew right by him into the living room.

“Now wait just a minute,” he said, but there was nothing Richard could do. He slammed the door shut and chased after her

Mary skittered about the living room, shining her light as if she were looking for something, while at the same time relocating anything that was in her way. She pushed furniture randomly this way and that, tipping over a chair and two lamps in the process. She flung cushions and pillows about the room as if they were Frisbees while all the time screaming and ranting at Richard. "Where is he? I refuse to believe he's dead! What did you do with him? You better tell me, where is he? Where is he?"

In the middle of her tirade, Mary glanced over at Richard. He just stood there, apparently stunned, watching. *Jesus Christ, are you, like, dead or what? I'd better get serious.* Mary started yelling even louder and picked up a stack of magazines and launched them over her head. They smacked the ceiling and then fluttered down to the carpet, landing in disarray.

Finally realizing that he had to do something, Richard ran over to Mary and tried to calm her down. "Now, just relax. What is this all about? I don't even know who you are." Mary upped the ante again by getting even wilder and louder until he grabbed her, grabbed her tight and held on. He was angry now. "What the hell do you think you're doing?"

Before he could say anything else, Mary drowned him out with a new mantra. "Get your nasty hands off me, you filthy old man! Don't touch me! Let me go!" she screamed, all the time scratching him hard right through his clothes, leaving long gouges on his back, arms, and face. In response, he squeezed her even harder. "Oh, you dirty old man! You slimebag . . . "

In the master bedroom June Goodenough, who had been holed up there ever since her son had died, jumped out of bed. She grabbed the security guard by the arm and led him away from Susan's room.

"But ma'am," said the guard, and he looked between Mrs. Goodenough and Susan's bedroom door where he had been standing guard. "Your husband gave strict orders that this room was never to be left unguarded—under any circumstances."

"I know what he said, but can't you hear?"

"Yes ma'am, I can."

"I don't think whatever the hell is going on in the living room right now was taken into consideration. So shut up and do as you're told."

"Yes ma'am," said the guard.

Meanwhile, Richard was rapidly losing whatever

restraint he might have had and started yelling back at Mary, holding onto her as tight as he could to keep her from scratching and hitting. Their plan was moving along without a hitch. *Now it's time for the Misses and the goon to enter, stage right.* And just like that, June Goodenough and the security guard emerged from the hallway, right on cue. *Okay, Johnny, your turn.* Mary smiled smugly inside herself at how well everything was going. 'Was' being the operative word, because everything was about to go haywire.

Chapter 32: Susan's Rescue-Part II

MARY RECOGNIZED THE EXPLOSION immediately. The sound of Johnny's 357 Magnum had been forever etched into her brain the last time it went off. As to why in the world he had the gun with him in the first place, she was clueless. *Not that it makes much difference now,* she thought, as the shot rang through the house like a cannon shot. All the positive energy she'd accumulated over the past twenty-four hours drained out of her at once. Mary felt herself sinking, her body limp and useless as a wet tissue, while inside, she was rigid with fear. Time froze, and, like the calm before the storm, an eerie silence followed. An endless split second later, Susan's bloodcurdling scream restarted the clocks and brought everyone back to life with an additional effect that of sprinkling something akin to miracle grow on the panic of an already hysterical scene. Their escape plan, which seconds ago seemed to be going along perfectly, shattered like a piece of crystal. Mary felt as if she was supposed to be on *The Wheel of Fortune* but instead found herself in *The Twilight Zone*. Chaos was now in charge.

*****

Meanwhile, Johnny had schlepped a large picnic table from the middle of the backyard over to, and up against the house, right under Susan's open bedroom window. He then climbed on top of it, perched himself there, and waited for Susan to give him the prearranged all-clear signal to indicate the guard had left his post. Timing was critical. From the moment he'd turned the power off, they had exactly ten minutes to get Susan not only out of the house, but completely out of Laurel Highlands. When three minutes passed and still not a peep from Susan, Johnny began to get anxious. As far as he could determine, Mary seemed to be on track, making quite a ruckus in the front part of the house. *What in the world is taking her so long? Could it be that the guard didn't leave his post? Is he still in Susan's room with her?* Four minutes and still no signal. Mary won't be able to keep it up much longer. Five minutes. *What is going on?* But it no longer mattered, because waiting was no longer an option. *I have to do something*. If he could have just aborted the whole operation, that would have been his first choice. But Mary was already in up to her eyeballs. He would have to force the issue. Just suck it in and dive through the window, see what was going on, and hope for the best.

Johnny pulled himself up, slipped his head through the window, and there was Susan, on her bed jumping up and down trying to get a huge suitcase full of to close. There was no one else in the room. What is she doing? “Susan, we’ve got to go now. There’s no time to pack.”

“But I’ve got to have my books,” whimpered Susan, who seemed to Johnny much younger than Mary had described. “Just help me get this stupid thing shut.” Then she sat down on the suitcase trying in vain to close the latch.

Six minutes. Johnny could see that Susan was not to be reasoned with. She was completely out of it. He pulled himself the rest of the way through the window and pried her off of the suitcase. “Come on, there’s no time to waste. It’s got to be now!”

“I won’t go without my books.”

Johnny looked at the suitcase. It was huge—the big Mama suitcase of one of those sets of five that come stacked inside of one another like Russian dolls. Susan broke loose of Johnny’s grip. “For crying out loud, even if we could get that thing shut, I couldn’t lift it off the bed, let alone carry it! It probably weighs 200 pounds!”

“If you won’t help me, then just go away. I’ll do it myself.”

Oh, how I would like to go away. But he couldn’t, because of Mary. He took a deep breath. Okay, here I go: Johnny Moonbeam, kidnapper. He picked Susan up and started pushing her out the window. She kicked and screamed and bit. “Geez, Susan, cut it out,” said Johnny. And that’s when the 357 Magnum, which he’d tucked into his front jeans pocket ‘just to be safe,’ discharged and they fell to the floor, Susan atop Johnny.

Susan’s hands frantically groped her own body and face as she chanted, “Oh my God, oh my God. Am I alive? Am I still here?”

“Yes,” said Johnny, as much in answer to his own worst fear as to her question, “you’re alive.”

Susan found a hole in her shoe. “I’m hit, I’m hit! I’m

afraid to look. How bad is it? Is my foot still there? How bad is the bleeding? Oh God, please let me live."

Johnny, who'd taken the gun from his pocket, set it down so he could check out Susan's injury. "I'm sorry. I'm so sorry," he said, peeling the shoe off. But there was no blood, no injury. The sock wasn't even torn. There was only a hole in the toe of her shoe. Everything else was fine. "Just your shoe was hit, not you. You're fine."

*****

The security guard and June locked eyes for an instant when they first heard the shot, and then rushed to Susan's bedroom. Richard seemed unable to do anything except hang on to Mary. "Let me go, let me go!" She tried to break loose but his grip tightened. "Can't you see? We have to go and help them. Let me go, you idiot!"

June and the security guard arrived at the bedroom simultaneously, wedging themselves in the door jam. "Get out of my way," June grunted. She shoved the guard aside and went straight to Susan, pulled her away from Johnny, and wrapped her daughter up in a tight embrace. The guard stumbled and had to catch hold of the door frame in order to regain his balance. Then, just as the guard had about righted himself, Richard ran through the door and clipped hin, and the guard went sprawling to the floor. Richard went and down sat on the bed next to his wife and daughter.

The guard grunted and cursed something under his breath as he hit the floor. Then, seeing Johnny's gun lying right beside his outstretched hand, he smiled then picked it up, pointed it at the boy, and stood up. "Okay, kid, the game's up. Now, lay down on the floor with your hands behind your head."

"But-"

"But nothing. Just do what I say and shut up!"

"Okay, okay," said Johnny. As he obediently laid himself down, he noticed Mary standing in the hallway clutching a heavy ceramic lamp. She was back from the doorway far enough to be out of view of the others, but still able to see Johnny—and for him to see her. She started gesturing wildly for him to do . . . *what?* Something was about to go down and he was supposed to help.

Don't abandon me now, Sleuth. Our time is upon us. I don't know exactly what it is that we're going to have to do. All I know is this: whatever it is, it will come to us just in time and all we will need to do is act. Oh, for goodness sakes, what kind of hero are you, anyway? A scared one, I see. Well, dah, I'm scared too. Of course, modern day heroes, especially real ones like us, are allowed to be scared. Yes, I'm sure. Because I looked it up in The Superhero's Companion: Since 1947 the Most Trusted Guide to Being a Superhero—*now, would you just shut up and pay attention so we don't miss our cue? All right, it's not the 1947 edition, it's the latest one, the 2000 edition. Never mind when I bought it, just pay attention.* And then, all of his anxieties, self-doubts, and other negative thoughts melted away, and in their place was the cool thinking, hyper focused, logical, and dogged determination of his inner Cybersleuth. (Of course, the huge shot of adrenaline kicked in by his adrenal glands might also have played a role in this transformation.)

Mary was frantic, motioning with her free hand and trying to tell him something, but he couldn't make out what it was. "I said get down, kid, NOW!" the guard yelled. Johnny did as he was told, but slowly and carefully, because at the same time he was trying to keep an eye on Mary without giving her away. It wasn't easy, but he managed, for the most part, to keep her in his peripheral vision and not stare as he put his hands behind his head and lay down. Once on the floor he could see her better again. A heightened sense of urgency was now apparent in Mary's gestures as she bent over, held the lamp high above her head and then brought it down. He got it. Standing up, the guard was too tall for her, so she wanted Johnny to get the man to bend over.

With an almost imperceptible nod of his head, Johnny acknowledged that he understood the task. She looked relieved, but only because he failed to communicate the part about not having a clue how to get the job done. Then an idea popped into his head. It wasn't great, but it might work—and, because he couldn't think of anything else, it would definitely have to do. *Oh well, here it goes.* Lying face down on the carpet, Johnny let loose a screech and said, "Oh no, I hate spiders! Please, sir, can I move? Oh God, it's coming closer!"

He sounded absolutely pathetic.

"Let me see," said the guard, disgusted, and bent down to look. Mary crept up behind him and held the lamp up high. "I don't see noth-" Mary brought the lamp down hard, right on the back of his head. THWACK! He was out like a light.

Johnny Moonbeam, Cybersleuth, took control of the situation. He snatched up the gun and, keeping it in his hand but not pointing it at anyone, looked to June and said, "Let go of Susan." When June didn't do anything right away, Johnny started to raise the gun and said, "Now."

June let go and Susan ran over and nearly tackled Mary. "It's all right, Susan, but we've got to go now."

Johnny threw Susan's backpack to Mary. "You two get out of here and I'll meet you at-" He paused, not wanting to give away where they were going, and said, "At the appointed place."

"I thought we were going to your house?" said Susan.

Mary rolled her eyes at Johnny. To Susan, she said, "Let's go," and pulled her out the door.

"My books!"

"No books!" said Johnny. "You two go ahead. I'll wait here a minute then catch up."

"Okay," said Mary, "we're out of here."

Eight minutes gone.

Johnny looked around and, being an expert at locks, noted that Mr. Goodenough had applied an outside lock to Susan's bedroom door, just like Jack had done to his. Well, I'll be. Making sure the guard was still passed out, he turned his attention to June and Richard. "You two stay right on that bed and don't move for at least ten minutes," he said then backed out of the room, shut the door, locked it, and ran.

He caught up with the two girls just as they were about to cross over into the greenbelt that led down into Mystic Meadows. As the three delinquents disappeared into the hedge, Laurel Highlands lit up and the sound of sirens could already be heard in the distance.

Chapter 33: In the Kitchen

NO SOONER HAD THEY MADE IT through the hedge, relieved to be walking down the dark and well-worn path to Mystic Meadows, than they heard voices. Susan started to say something, but Mary clamped a hand over her mouth and hushed her. *How did Susan's parents get out so fast?* Johnny wondered. But there was no time. The voices were too close to risk staying on the path. "Over here," he whispered, and proceeded to lead Susan and Mary through the thickest part of the greenbelt until they were directly behind his house. Mary, seeing where they were, started moving towards the back gate, but Johnny stopped her. "I need to check the path first," he whispered. As soon as he stuck his head out to check, Johnny pulled it right back, and in a single motion he wrapped Mary in one arm and Susan in the other and made them all lie flat on the forest floor. A couple of seconds later, a group of ten people walked by flashing their flash-lights. The beams grazed the tops of the trio's heads, but they were not spotted. They waited a few minutes, and then Johnny checked again. "All clear," he said, and they sprinted across the path and into the backyard and made it safely into the house.

The three teens were sitting around the kitchen table, quiet and uneasy. Johnny's hands were shaking so hard, he was sitting on them, hoping to hide how scared he was. Unfortunately, he was not able to sit on his legs, which were audibly bouncing up and down on the kitchen floor. His head and eyes were darting around the room. It seemed to Johnny he was using more energy just trying to stay in his chair than if he had been in boot camp doing calisthenics. *What is wrong with me? If Jack were here, he wouldn't be scared. He'd be laughing at me. Come on, Johnny, find the cyber hero inside of you.*

Johnny imagined that Jack was the enemy, not Susan's parents, or the people looking for them, or the police. *Don't be afraid of him. You're not afraid of him anymore.* Johnny's fear melted into a controlled anger and his body stilled. Until then, he had avoided looking straight at the girls for fear of giving himself away.

Now, he looked at Mary. Her fingernails were gnawed down to the quick and she was working hard on the hangnails, stopping only occasionally to twirl a lock of her hair around her index finger and then stick it in her mouth. The ends of locks of her hair were wet and frayed, chewed hard. Mary didn't even notice Johnny, her eyes darting around the room like his were.

Susan, on the other hand, was looking back and forth between them. When Johnny made eye contact, she started to cry. Bending over the table to get closer to him, she whispered, "What's going on? I'm scared. I can't take the silence anymore." In the background the blaring of police sirens grew louder.

Mary whipped her head around. Now they were all leaning over the table, whispering. "I'm scared too," said Mary. "Johnny, why are there so many cop cars around here? Why aren't they in Laurel Highlands?"

"I don't know," he answered, slow and calm-like.

"What should we do? What can we do?" asked Susan, a bit louder, beginning to sound hysterical. "Maybe we should just tell the police what happened. I'm sure they'll understand. I don't want to die." She put her head down on the table.

"No," Johnny and Mary said emphatically and in unison. Mary looked at Johnny as if asking him to speak.

"We're not going to call the police. None of us wants to go back to where we were, do we? We call the police and I go straight to some stupid home for wayward boys, Mary goes back to asshole Brad, and you go back home." Johnny saw that the girls were looking at him with anticipation, waiting for guidance or protection, or something else he couldn't give them. *But I've got to try. That's my job.* He closed his eyes. *I'm Johnny Moonbeam, Cybersleuth; fearless, in control, smart. I can deal with this. I can deal with this.*

After what seemed like a long time, but was probably only five or ten seconds, Johnny opened his eyes. His mind was clear and focused.

"Johnny, what the—" said Mary.

"Just be quiet for a minute," he said irritably, "I need to think." And then after a few seconds, he added, "Come on, we need to get upstairs. Stay low and follow me, and be quiet."

After leading them up the stairs and into his bedroom, he motioned for Susan and Mary to have a seat. They sat down, Indian style, on the floor. Johnny grabbed the mirror by his window and held it up so he could see the street. And he watched.

"What do you see?" asked Mary.

After another 'shush' and about thirty seconds, Johnny put the mirror down. He didn't say anything.

"Oh no, what's wrong? asked Susan.

Johnny sighed. "The police are going door to door, questioning people. They'll be here any time." He looked at Mary. "We need a plan."

Mary scrunched her forehead and frowned at him. "Why are you looking at me?"

Oh no, she's scared out of her wits. I need her wits—we need her wits. Then he remembered something she'd once done to help him get back in the game when Ralph was lurking outside. And, it had worked. He didn't want to do it but felt he had no choice. *Oh God, I hope this works.* It took Johnny every bit of willpower he had to reach out and slap Mary briskly across the face. "We don't have time to be scared," he said. "We need to do something."

Mary reached up and touched her reddened cheek. "You asshole, see how you like it!" she said, and started to take a swing at him.

Johnny grabbed her wrists and held firmly, shaking her slightly. He wanted to say he was sorry, but there was no time for that either. "You can hit me all you want to later; right now we need a plan." Mary seemed to wake up. Her expression changed and she looked like herself again. *I think it worked. I hope it worked. I never want to do that again—never. Come on, keep yourself together.*

"Okay, Moonbrain," said Mary. "So, tell me why they're over here?"

"Who?"

"Dah! The police. What are they looking for?"

"Probably the same thing they're looking for over there," answered Susan sheepishly. "One missing child and the two kidnappers."

"Exactly," said Johnny.

"Oh, Jesus," said Mary, and then, "but they don't know we're here, in Mystic Meadows, I mean, not for sure, do they?"

"Maybe they do and maybe they don't," said Johnny. "We know they're out there, so maybe they saw us too."

"But," Susan injected hopefully, "if they knew exactly where we were, they would have come to this house first, right?"

"You're right, but," Mary continued confidently, "they'll have a pretty good idea that someone is here, which means that we'll need to answer the door or they'll be suspicious."

"But," added Susan somberly, "they'll probably have good enough description you two, and a picture of me, of course, so that, if we do open the door, we'll just give ourselves away." Susan started crying.

"Quiet," Johnny scolded Susan, and she obeyed. "Mary needs to think."

A few seconds later, Mary's eyes came to life and she smiled that coy, mischievous smile Johnny was beginning to recognize. It meant that Mary had an idea. Not necessarily a good one, but she did have one. Johnny had learned this much about her: they would soon find out by practical experience whether or not it was a good idea or a bad idea because, sure as anything, she was going to see it through. Once Mary had her mind made up, there was no stopping her. "So, don't keep us waiting," he said.

"How do you know she's got a plan?" asked Susan.

"Just do." Johnny gave Mary a mischievous look of his own and added, "I can read her like a book. Am I right, Mary?"

"Not if I didn't want you to," she assured him.

"Just get on with it, would you?" said Susan. "You guys are driving me nuts."

"Well," said Mary, "here it is. It's easy, really. We'll just have someone else open the door for us."

"Well, that would be just great if there were someone else here," huffed Susan.

"I think," started Mary, ignoring Susan, "that a babysitter would be a good choice. She would, like, open the door and just tell the police that she's babysitting. No, house-sitting. Yes, that's better, because Johnny's parents are on vacation, right, Johnny?" She looked at Johnny, who nodded conspiratorially. "And so, like, this babysitter, I mean, house sitter, will just tell the police that she's here all by herself house-sitting and that's that. They're gone."

"But we don't have a house sitter, in case you didn't notice," said Susan a bit sarcastically.

"We will soon," said Johnny.

"It'll just take a minute for me to change into one bratty, home-alone, house-sitting teenage girl." And with that, Mary got up and started towards her bedroom. "Come on, guys, this is what I'm good at." Johnny and Susan looked at each other and, because it was a reasonable idea and because they didn't have a better one, followed her.

Susan, who was now on Mary's heels, said, "They'll still want to know where the parents are."

"That's easy, they went to Chicago for a couple days. Right, Johnny?"

"Right."

Mary was now in charge, much to Johnny's relief. "Johnny, I need some blue magic markers. Permanent ones are better, but I'll take anything you can find. Suzie, I need a bathrobe, some dorky slippers, and a bra. You should be able to find everything in the closet over there. When you've got the stuff, throw it in here," Mary said as she disappeared into the bathroom.

Johnny found a bonanza of blue Sharpies in a kitchen drawer, and, just as Mary had said, Susan found everything she needed in the walk-in closet. They threw the supplies into the bathroom where Mary was frantically undressing and applying makeup to her face. Mary grabbed Susan's arm and dragged her into the bathroom. "I need you, kid." Mary handed Susan the markers and said, "Get to work." While Susan stood there with markers in hand looking dumbfounded, Mary said, "The hair, I need blue hair. Now!"

"Yes, sir," said Susan obediently, and she immediately started the process of 'bluing' Mary's hair.

In less than five minutes' time, Susan walked out of the bathroom with a stranger. The stranger looked like a goofy teenager who used way too much makeup and dyed her hair blue. Johnny noticed that she had breasts. Mary saw

Johnny looking at her chest and smiled. “Don’t say a word, Moonbrain.”

“Now what do we do?” asked Susan.

“Now,” Mary and Johnny said in unison, “we wait.”

Chapter 34: A Knock at the Door

A TIRED AND GRUMPY MARY WANTED to get rid of the makeup she'd over applied, and that now felt like a mask. Not to mention the itchy cotton breasts and old-lady, too-big bra were uncomfortable as all get-out. *I really should have put a sock in there instead of this freaking cotton.* And then, at precisely 10:55 p.m., just as they were beginning to think it wouldn't happen: a knock at the door.

"Showtime!" whispered Mary. The officer knocked again, this time a bit louder. "Okay, guys, make yourselves scarce while I get rid of some turkey."

"Remember, they can't come in without a warrant," said Johnny. *At least I don't think they can.*

Mary rolled her eyes, "Thanks for the tip."

"You're welcome," he said, and then, just as Mary turned to head for the door, Johnny reached out and grabbed her arm. "Hey, get me their names and badge numbers if you can, okay?"

"No problem."

"Be careful," whispered Susan. The poor kid looked as if she was on her way to the guillotine.

Mary smiled and nodded reassuringly. On her way to the door, she plucked a large wad of pre-chewed gum off the table and started chewing it with her mouth open, making loud sucking and smacking noises. Feigning a giant yawn as she pulled the door open, Mary acted surprised when she saw the two officers. "Gee," smack, smack, smack, "is something wrong?"

"Are your parents home?" the younger officer asked.

"Nope."

"Is there anyone else here?"

"You're lookin' at her."

"You mind telling us where you parents are?"

"Nope."

The younger officer, exasperated, motioned something with his eyes and hands indicating a desire to yield the rest of the questioning to his partner, who nodded.

While the officers exchanged looks with one another, Mary blew a bubble half the size of her head then popped it and pulled it back in her mouth.

"Young lady, could you please tell us where your parents are?"

"Sure."

"Where are they?"

"At home."

"But you just said they weren't."

"I said they weren't here."

"So isn't this your parents' house?"

"Nope."

"But you live here?"

"Nope."

"Where do you live, then?"

"With my parents."

"And where is that?"

"Across town."

The officer gave Mary a stern look, and she figured he'd also had about enough; so when he asked her, "Then what are you doing here?"

She answered, "I'm, like, house-sitting for the Abels."

"I see," said the older officer, though he didn't seem entirely convinced. "And you're the only one here right now, is that right?"

"Yep, that's right."

"And when do you suppose the Abels will be back?"

"They went to Chicago with Johnny, their kid. He's about my age. We're friends." Mary smiled, faux bashful, and blinked her lashes several times. "They'll be back in a couple days."

"Well, there's been some dangerous activity tonight in this general area," said the younger officer, and he showed her some pictures. "Do you know these kids? Have you seen them tonight?"

How in the hell did you get those? There was a recent picture of Susan in her school uniform and pigtails along with a pair of sketches, one of Mary and one of Johnny. They were spot-on. Mary nearly lost it right there, then gathered herself and managed to stay on course. "Nope, never seen 'em."

The officer nodded. "All the same, we'd like to come in and look around, just to make sure everything is okay."

Mary, now over her little hiccup and back in full form, said, "Oh, that's alright. I'm sure everything in here is just fine."

"Well," the older officer now, "we still think it would be best if we just came in and had a look around. It won't take long."

Think fast, girl. She did. "Well," she huffed, "like, how am I supposed to know . . . like, maybe those police uniforms are really disguises? Everything is okay in here, and I don't let no strangers in. No way. I don't care what uniform they got on. No strangers. That's straight from my mom."

The officers were not happy. The younger one was about to say something but the older one gave him a look that quieted him. "Okay then. Here's my card," said the senior Partner. "You be sure to call if you see anything suspicious or if you have any questions or problems. Thanks for your help."

The two police officers left. Mary shut the door, turned around, and slid all the way down to the floor with her back against the door. She had no resemblance to the person who had just sent the officers packing. She looked exhausted and frazzled.

Susan flew over to her. "You did it. You were awesome. Everything is okay now." Mary looked at her and tried to smile but couldn't. "What's the matter, Mary? You did it. What's wrong?"

"They didn't believe a word I said. I don't know what they're going to do now, but they'll probably go get a warrant or the SWAT team or National Guard or some other bullshit." The two girls walked over and sat on the couch. Johnny had already plopped down in the leather recliner. "We don't have much time, Moonbrain. You have to think of something."

"Why me?"

"Because I'm used up." And she was. As soon as Mary closed the door, exhaustion had overwhelmed her as if she'd been hit by a freight train. "I'm going to bed," she said, and was off.

"You can't," said Johnny.

"What do you mean, I can't?"

"I mean, wait a second. I don't know if they believed you or not, but I nearly did—and I knew better. But you're right that it's not over. We need to come up with a new plan, find a new place to live."

"It won't be easy," said Mary. "I don't know where they got them, but the cops had three good pictures of us. We're probably on the freaking news already. There probably isn't anyone in the whole state that doesn't know what we look like by now."

"We'll manage," said Johnny, but his voice trailed off.

Susan's euphoria was replaced, once again, by despair. "Where can we go? What will we do? Oh God, oh God, I knew it. It's hopeless, isn't it? Hopeless? I'm sorry." She sniffled and a single tear fell from her left eye and started slowly down her cheek. "It's all my fault."

"No, it isn't," said Johnny wearily, "and we're not hopeless." He wanted to say something a little more reassuring but couldn't come up with anything . . . until he heard a small, but familiar voice from somewhere deep within, speak to him. He listened and realized it was his mother. She was saying, You're too tired to do anything productive right now. The best thing you can do is to get a good night's sleep. Everything will look different in the morning. What seems impossible now will be doable. She had been right, too, and not just once but several times. "We all just need some sleep. Everything will look better in the morning, and we'll be able to figure it out then. It'll probably be so easy we'll wonder what we were so worried about." Johnny got up and started to make his way to bed. "Everything will be alright," he said to Susan. "You'll see." Even Johnny was surprised at the confidence with which he said this, and it seemed to reassure her.

"We'll figure it out," said Mary, once again sounding optimistic. "I'm not going to have gone through all of this shit for nothing."

Johnny and Mary plopped down in their respective beds without 'passing Go' and were both sound asleep five minutes later. Susan, still brushing her teeth, was appalled. If *they don't shower and brush their teeth first thing tomorrow morning, I'm out of here. I don't care what happens.*

Chapter 35: Play it Again, Joe

At four o'clock, the next morning, Johnny was already in sleuth mode. He wanted to have a plan by the time the girls awoke. After a ceremonial spin or two, he settled himself in front of the computer monitor screen, rubbed his hands together, and got down to do what cybersleuths do best: combine their innate and quite advanced hacking skills with a Pentium 4 processor, two full gigabytes of RAM, and a high-speed Internet connection, and started searching for answers.

Three hours later . . .

Bingo! Johnny shot out of his chair, loaded the printer with paper, and relished his good fortune by letting the printed pages fall right into his greedy paws, savoring each one as he imagined Neil Armstrong might have savored those first steps on the moon. He had everything he needed, save for one detail. *How early does Henry get up in the morning?*

Downstairs, Johnny grabbed the OJ container out of the fridge and, after making sure no one was watching, chugged half a quart straight from the container. Not knowing when or if anything was going to happen that morning, he thought it best to get the girls out of bed. *But first, I'd better make security rounds.* He checked to see that all the doors and windows were locked, and all the shades and curtains were drawn. *Can't be too careful.*

By the time Johnny finished, Susan was awake, dressed, and sitting at the kitchen table furiously writing in what looked like a journal of some sort.

"Hey, Susan," he said, "what's up?"

Susan looked like a cartoon figure as she nearly came straight up out of the chair. Then, recovering, she inhaled sharply, and placed a hand over her heart. "You scared the bejesus out of me."

"Ah, I didn't mean to. Anyway, how you doing?"

"Well, let me see. I just ran away from home because my parents are worse than worthless, my brother killed himself, and some jerk shot me in the foot yesterday. Otherwise I'm fine."

Johnny cringed, "Sorry about the foot."

"Actually, all things considered, I feel pretty good. How long have you been up?"

He shrugged, "A while."

"Had breakfast yet?"

Johnny pointed upstairs. "I'm waiting for Mary's waffles. Come on, let's go get her up."

"Mary makes waffles?"

"The best."

"Okay, the bus probably won't be in this Neighborhood until about seven-forty-five, so I guess that's enough time. By the way, where is the bus stop over here?"

"Bus?"

"Yeah, those ugly yellow things that take us to school every day."

"School?"

Susan rolled her eyes. "Of course school. I haven't missed a day in over five years, and I don't intend to start now."

Johnny thought about this for a minute. *She can't be serious, can she?* "Ah, well . . . let's go get Mary up and ah, talk about it, okay?"

They went upstairs, and Susan opened the door. "You stay here," Susan said. "I'll go in first and let you know when it's okay." Mary was sound asleep and completely covered up with blankets. Susan waved Johnny in and gently rolled back the covers, taking care not to expose anything risqué. Then they both burst out laughing.

Mary's eyes flew open. "What," she said, looking back and forth between the two hysterical visitors, "is so funny?"

"It's hard to describe," Johnny said between laughs, "how silly you look."

"No," said Mary, examining herself, "I think I can picture it fairly well."

Mary was so exhausted the night before that, without as much as a bathroom stop and without passing go, she fell into bed, softly snoring before her head even hit the pillow. The blue marker from her hair, however, apparently not so sleepy, appeared to have been partying all night. It was everywhere. The sheets were decorated with big blue spots and long wavy blue lines. The pillowcase was almost completely saturated.

She had blue hands and blue streaks down her face and neck, not to mention her clothes.

"Susan," said Johnny, suddenly excited, "don't let her move." Then he took off down the hall saying, "I'll be right back." Thirty seconds later, he returned with his digital camera. Johnny managed to take half a dozen pictures before Mary made him stop and hand over the camera, so she could flip through the images on the LED screen.

"This is trick photography," said Mary. "That's not me," but then she was laughing right along with them. The blue ink had seemingly multiplied and spread out over her whole body. It looked like she'd been dumped into a vat of blue ink, which actually wasn't too far from the truth. Her hair resembled a bad attempt at a spiky hairdo. Her shirt was covered with big, blue, clown-like spots, and the oversized bra she'd enlisted as part of her disguise, one that used to belong to Johnny's mother, had slid down to bellybutton level and more closely resembled a pair of blue udders than anything else.

Mary handed the camera back to Johnny. "If you don't erase these pictures, permanently, I'll paint you blue," she said, and was off to the shower.

"I think she's going to be awhile," said Susan. She blew out a sigh and then added, "I guess school is kind of out of the question, isn't it?"

"Yeah," answered Johnny.

"I'll go ahead and get the waffles started."

"Great. I'll get these pictures printed before she gets out."

Susan gave him the evil eye, "I don't think that's such a good idea."

"Okay," he said. "I won't." But he did anyway.

*****

About an hour later, Mary came downstairs looking like a runway model on the catwalk. A strapless, lightly patterned, cotton sundress with ruffles on the sweetheart-neckline and hi-low hem, accented her figure perfectly, and the creamy yellow color set her auburn hair ablaze. It was the first-time Johnny had seen her in a dress of any kind, and he most certainly took notice. Finishing off the outfit were a pair of summer sandals, platform with six-inch heels and open toes to display her perfectly manicured, expertly drawn, flower-painted toenails. Her face was made up so 'naturally' perfect, she could have walked off the cover of Cosmopolitan. Her lips looked bigger and pinker than usual, and her eyes, which Johnny always found spellbinding even without any help, had been framed in such a way as to give them superpowers. Johnny could only stand there, open-mouthed, ogling her.

Mary wondered if he might need CPR soon and was about to say something when Susan came in from the kitchen and hit him square in the face with a cup full of ice-cold water. After he finished gasping and coughing, Johnny shook the water from his head, and, with his now long and still curly light brown hair swishing back and forth, he looked like a golden retriever throwing off water. "What'd you do that for?"

"You were starting to drool," said Susan disgustedly.

Mary broke into a raucous laughter and dropped her model-like gait. Amazingly, she looked even prettier to Johnny, because she looked like herself again.

"You're lucky my glass is empty," said Susan, shooting a glare at Mary.

"Oh, lighten up! You didn't have to dress up like the ugly blue witch of the Midwest. A girl has to do something to make herself feel better. And by the way," she added, looking in Johnny's direction, "I found the pictures in your room and tore them up into four thousand pieces. You have exactly thirty seconds to do whatever you need to do to get the evidence off of your computer's software or hard modem or whatever thingy it's on."

"I'm on it," he said, and took off for his bedroom. *What she doesn't know, he thought, is that I can hide pictures on my hard drive so that even the cops couldn't find them, let alone to her.*

Johnny was at the top of the stairs when Mary called out, "Don't try anything tricky. I may not be a computer whiz, but I know when you're lying."

"I . . . I," he coughed, "I know that. Besides, what kind of person do you think I am anyway?"

"One with a Y-chromosome," said Susan.

"A guy," said Mary at the same time, and they giggled.

He knew Mary was right, that somehow she would know,

but just as he entered his room and was about to sit down and erase every last byte of evidence concerning the blue witch of the Midwest, there was a knock at the door. Johnny flew off his chair and checked the driveway. A black-and-white unit was parked in the there, with the same two cops from the night before standing at the door. Holding a piece of paper and looking smug. Johnny turned around to get the girls, but Mary and Susan were already there, running through his door.

"Who's there?" asked Mary.

"Same cops as last night."

"What are we going to do?" Susan.

Mary and Susan looked at Johnny, lips dry and slightly parted and eyes wide, and he noticed, staring at him, boring into him in a way that would have made him most uncomfortable had he not been able to offer them the comfort and hope they seemed to be so desperately seeking. I will not let them down. The plan had holes. He understood that. There are always a hundred variables that are unpredictable, and a hundred more you can't even see. And yet, Johnny instinctively knew the girls could not deal with that right then, and so he chose to present what he had as if it were foolproof and hope with all his heart that it worked. "Don't worry," he said with such confidence that he nearly believed it himself, "I have a plan."

The girls' faces relaxed and they each exhaled a large sigh of relief. Then another knock at the door, this time louder.

"Police. Open up!"

"Well," said Mary, "don't keep us waiting."

Johnny started shuffling through the hundreds of pages he printed out earlier that morning. "I think they have a warrant," he said, and then, as he pulled about twenty pages from the middle of the stack and handed them to Mary. "These will buy us some time."

"How?" Susan.

"What?" Mary.

More knocking, faster and louder than before. "You have thirty seconds to open this door before we do it for you."

"No time to explain," said Johnny. He put one arm

around Mary and started leading her out of the room while at the same time signaling for Susan to stay put. As they were walking down the stairs, Johnny said, "You told me to make a plan, and so I did. It's a good one, trust me. Just do what I say, and I think we'll be okay." Mary started to say something, but he shushed her. "I'll explain later," he said, and they were at the bottom of the stairs, a dozen paces from the front door. The knocking grew louder.

"Twenty seconds!"

The noise distracted Mary, and she turned her head to the door. With his free hand, Johnny grabbed her jaw and pulled her back so she was looking at him. "Listen," he said, "I found out some things about the young cop, things that could get him in big trouble, make him lose his job, probably even get him arrested." He paused for a split second to make sure Mary comprehended what he was saying. She nodded affirmatively, and Johnny knew that he had her full attention. "Give this stack of papers to the older guy and tell him and his partner to get in the cruiser and drive well out of the neighborhood."

"TEN seconds."

"Mary," Johnny snapped, and she was back with him. "If they don't do what you want them to do, tell them the documents will be immediately e-mailed to all the local newspapers, the police station, and the attorney general's office. It's all set. All I have to do is press a button."

"FIVE..."

"Got it?" Johnny.

"FOUR..."

Mary nodded. Johnny pushed her towards the door and then disappeared upstairs.

"THREE..."

Mary put a hand on the doorknob and paused to compose herself.

"TWO..."

She took a deep breath and opened the door.

"ONE!" She could see it was the younger cop that'd been doing all the yelling. "Well," he said, "it's nice to see you again. We have a present for you."

"Aren't you just the sweetest little thing," she said, and

took the present, a folded piece of paper. She opened it. A search warrant. "Here," she said, handing the stack of documents to the older cop, "I'm kind of a slow reader, so why don't you take a look at these while I'm reading through this here thingy."

The older police officer gave no indication that he was about to read what Mary had given him. "Young lady," he said, his tone grave but polite, "whatever game it is you're playing at is over. Now step aside so that we can search the premises."

The older officer started to push her aside, but at the same time he glanced at his partner and stopped cold. "What's the matter with you?"

The younger cop, white-faced and shaky, pointed to the papers. The older officer started to read. "Holy shit! Where did you dig up this bullshit? Did you make it up? You're going to be in big trouble now, girl! Big trouble!"

"No, I don't think so," said Mary, calmly. "One look at your partner should tell you that these are no lies. Even a cop should be able to recognize that." The older man said nothing, just looked at his partner and shook his head, disgusted. When he looked back up, Mary knew he was ready to bargain. "So," she said as if talking about the weather or some other innocuous subject, "here's what's going to happen. You and your friend are going to take this nice present back," she handed over the warrant, "and get into your cruiser. Then, you're going to drive into downtown Indy, or farther if you want, but well out of this neighborhood, and you're going to stay there for one hour. When one hour is up, you can come back, and I will fully cooperate with everything you want me to do."

"And if not?"

"If you guys aren't gone in about one minute, these," she tapped on the stack of papers, "will automatically be e-mailed to all the major newspapers, the police department, and the Attorney General's office."

The younger officer grabbed his partner's arm, pleading, "Please, Joe, I can explain, really. Give me a break, man. Don't throw me to the slaughter. My wife ... my kids ... for God's sake, have some mercy."

"How do I know you won't send out these reports regardless," asked Joe, his voice hostile.

"Oh my! We do have a temper now, don't we? Well, the answer to your question is, of course, you can't be sure, but the truth is I have no desire to cause any problems. I just want my hour. That's it. One hour and all the stuff gets deleted, and no one is the wiser. It's like, what do you call it, oh yes, one of those win-win situations, don't you think?"

The older officer grabbed the younger one and shoved him towards the cruiser. "It's blackmailing, is what it is," he said, and then he and his partner got in the cruiser and drove off.

Mary closed the door, locked it, and threw herself on the couch. "Moonbrain!" she yelled. "What the hell was in those papers?"

Johnny smiled, and motioned for them to follow him into the kitchen, which they did, and they all sat down at the table. "Well," he said, mostly to Susan, "I asked Mary to get the badge numbers and names of the officers last night." Mary nodded agreement and Johnny continued, now talking to both. "I thought it might be a good idea to see if I could learn something about them, and so—remember how I found out about Ralph through the police database on the Internet?" Mary nodded again. "Well, the bad guys have the same thing, only it's a lot harder to hack into."

"What's harder to get into? What are you talking about?" asked Susan.

Johnny briefly explained what he had done with Ralph's picture, and then he continued. "Like I said, it's hard to get into, but once you do it's like a gold mine. The crooks are really well organized, tons better than the police. I just entered a city and a badge number and boom! There it was. I was surprised. Maybe I shouldn't have been, but I was, at how many of the police have dealings with crooks of one sort or another. Anyway, the younger officer apparently has a drug problem, and the crooks just about own him, is what it said. So I printed out all the stuff about him and gave it to you, and that's about it."

"But how did you know the older guy wouldn't just turn him in? That's what I would think he should do," said Susan.

Mary answered that one. "Cops don't usually rat each other out." Mary started to say something more, but Johnny interrupted, slapping the palm of his hand down hard on the table. "Jesus Christ, Moonbrain! What is it?"

"Sorry, but I just remembered something. The clock is ticking. We only have about 50 minutes to get packed and out of here."

"Where we going?" asked Susan.

"I don't know," Johnny answered, "but I'm about to find out."

"I thought you had a plan," said Mary.

"I do. I'm going to go get my neighbor, Henry. He owes me a favor, and he knows everyone. I'm sure he'll know where we can hide out for a while." Johnny looked at Mary. "You and Susan get packing. Whatever you think we need, just start loading it into the blue pickup in the garage. I'll be back with Henry in a few minutes."

Chapter 36: A Favor Returned

WELL, I'LL BE DAD-GUMMED, BARNEY. Look who's here," said Henry, kneeling down to scratch the hound behind his ears. "It's the young man who done pulled your ass outta that pile o' junk and like as not saved your life as well as my own." Barney, however, did not seem the least bit festive. He just growled and barked. "What in tarnation is that all about?" Henry asked, then turned his gaze from the hound and saw the grim look on Johnny's face. "Heavens to Betsy, boy, what is the matter? You looks like you just lost your Ma and Pa both."

Even though Johnny realized it was just an expression, that Henry couldn't possibly know anything, the boy still couldn't help but take it literally and replied, "Yes sir, Mr. Mayfield, actually I have. Remember when I brought your dog back to you, and you said that if I ever needed a favor, you'd be there for me? Well, I need your help now."

"My God, you poor child! Come on inside and tell me what you need."

"Actually, sir, it might be better if you came over to my house."

"Over there in Broad Ripple, isn't it? Well, that's fine too. You need me to drive?"

"Well, actually," Johnny hesitated, trying to figure out what to say that wouldn't unduly upset the old man. But he couldn't think of anything. "Actually, I lied to you before. I live in Jack Abel's house, just down the street. My name is Johnny. I'm his son."

"Whoa now. Slow down. Jack don't have no kids."

"Please, Coach, just come. I know it's confusing, but it'll make sense in a few minutes. I promise." Henry didn't seem to know what to say, and so when he didn't say anything, Johnny added, "You said you'd do anything I needed, and I need you to come with me right now. It will be okay. I promise. But time is of the essence. Please."

Barney shot through the open door, down to the sidewalk, and started barking.

"Well, I guess that answers that," said Henry, and he followed the hound down the block to Johnny's house with the boy beside him.

*****

Things did not go well at first. Convincing the Coach that Johnny was who he said proved more difficult than the boy figured. He thought it would be as easy as showing Henry pictures of the three of them, Jack, Jill, and Johnny, but after looking frantically around the house and not finding one, it dawned on Johnny that such a picture might not exist. Crap. *What do I do now?* As Johnny stammered away trying to explain about himself, he could see that Henry wasn't buying it. The old man seemed to be getting more and more uncomfortable but then, just when it looked as though he were about to get up and leave, Barney took over. The hound jumped into Johnny's lap and put his paws on the boy's shoulders, wagging his tail, and licking the boy's face.

"Well, I'll be gall-darned," said Henry. "Barney here looks like he knows you damn near as well as he knows me. Knows his way 'round the place, too."

"Yes, sir. Sometimes Barney would come around back while you were talking to my dad, I'd be there and I'd play with him a while."

"Well, son, I believe you're telling the truth, but it's about enough to give this old man a heart attack. You got a drink of water back there I could have 'fore I go and pass out?"

Mary, who was in the kitchen, came right out with a tall tumbler of water. She gave it to Henry and sat down on the couch with Susan, who had been trailing right behind her. When Johnny started explaining about his parents, especially Jack, and how they treated him, and what happened when he woke up the day after the tornado, Henry seemed to be getting a bit overwhelmed.

Mary could see that Johnny was losing this man, who, though she wasn't exactly sure why yet, she knew was important to their getting out of Dodge, and so she figured she could give it a try. "Why don't I try to explain, Johnny?" she said, and steered Johnny to the couch next to Susan. Johnny nodded. Mary knelt next to Henry and put a hand on his knee. "I know it's confusing Mr. Mayfield, but Johnny is telling the truth."

"I don't know what to think. I just gots to get out of here, though. I know that much. I just gots to get out of here. That's all," said Henry, and he started to get out of the chair. But Mary pressed down on his leg and pushed him back into his seat. He looked at her, incredulous, and was about to say something, but she beat him to the punch.

"It's like this: you were a high school coach and teacher for about a million years, right?"

"Yeah, but-"

"And I'll bet during that time you saw more than one kid whose parents looked as upright and respectable as anyone on this planet, and yet you knew for a fact they were beating the crap out of their kids. Am I right?"

Henry looked dumbfounded as he started to put things together. "Yeah, you're right about that . . . but Jack?" All three of the kids nodded. "I guess it's possible." And then he recognized Susan—he'd seen her picture on the news—and gasped. "You're, you're that girl who was kidnapped, the one whose brother died. And that means . . . " Henry pointed an accusing finger at Johnny and Mary, and was about to say something else when, once again, he was cut off. This time by Susan.

"They didn't kidnap me. I asked them to help me run away because my dad was keeping me locked up in my bedroom with a guard."

Henry looked between the three of them, slack-jawed and eyes wide, as Susan told her side of the story. She filled him in on some of the details her father conveniently left out of his statements to the police and news, such as the fact Susan had warned him about Stephen, even begged him to talk to her brother, among other prize examples of how messed up her home life was. In the end, Susan's story reeled Henry over to their side.

Johnny gave the old man some more refreshments and a few minutes to get himself together and then, not able to afford any more time, got to the point. "So you see Coach, we need a place to go, and I was hoping you might know somewhere, or someone who could help us."

"Let me get this straight. I'm supposed to help three fugitives of the law-"

"Innocent fugitives," chimed Susan.

"All right, innocent fugitives; but fugitives nonetheless. And I'm supposed to hide them, which means that I'll be aiding and abetting criminals; and, innocent though they may be, I'm liable to get into some deep doo-doo m'self."

"That's about right," said Mary. "One of those really shitty times when doing the right thing can get you in trouble. But you've probably never been faced with that either, have you?"

"Oh, horse-hockey, girl! And where in the Sam Hill did you get such a mouth, anyway? Let me just think for a minute, would ya'll?"

"I hope you have a backup plan, Johnny," said Mary. "Come on, Susan, let's keep packing. We have to go somewhere."

Henry watched the two girls filing out of the room, heads down and walking slow. "Shoot," he said, "how did I get myself into this situation, anyway?" Then he took a deep breath and said, "Wait here just a dad-blamed minute. This ain't exactly like asking someone for five bucks. I'm going to help ya'll alright, but you gots to be patient. I'll come up with somethin'."

Susan ran up to the man and kissed him on the cheek. "Thanks, Mr. Mayfield, we really appreciate your help. Mary and I, we still have a lot to pack though, and we only have-" Susan looked at her watch, "-about thirty minutes until those police come back." She kissed him again and ran off. "Come on, Mary, we've got work to do."

On her way upstairs, Mary stopped and turned around. "Thanks, Mr. Mayfield. I know I can be bitchy sometimes, but you have to, like, understand it's been a bit stressful this morning. Thanks a lot, though. It's really cool, I mean like great, of you to help."

Once the girls were out of the room, Henry turned to Johnny and said, "Why didn't you tell me all this before, son? I mean like, years ago."

Johnny looked at the floor and then back up. "I guess I was afraid you wouldn't believe me. My mom even told the police and social workers about the situation a couple of times, but Jack, I mean my dad, always wrangled his way out of it." Johnny stopped and shook his head then looked right into the old man's eyes. "And then, after the police or whoever left, well . . . trust me, you don't want to know."

Henry nodded. "Yes, I suspect you're right. Anyway, I figured out a place I think you can go fer awhile. My brother-in-law is what people refer to as a reclusive type of fella. You know what that is?"

"I'm not sure, sir."

"Well, it generally means folks who don't like to deal with people other than themselves, and they usually lives off alone somewhere. I haven't seen him in a coon's age, but I do know he's still alive." Henry stopped for a few seconds, shaking his head. Johnny thought he might be fighting back tears. "Reason he's reclusive is on account of life having dealt him a bum hand. He didn't do nothin' wrong and he ain't no criminal. But if he seems a bit gruff, just try to remember he's a good man. Lives up in Madison County, 'bout forty miles northeast of here. Hardly no one knows he's out there 'ceptin for me. You guys would be safe there, and I'm purdy sure yous is just the type of folk he wouldn't mind a-helpin'."

"Great," said Johnny. "So . . . how do we get there?"

"Fetch me a-"

And Johnny was already off the couch. "I'll be back in a flash with some paper and a pencil."

Left in what felt like a vacuum, Henry's voice trailed off, "and I'll draw you a . . . ." Then Johnny returned with a pencil and pad of paper.

"You can draw a map here, okay?"

"Right," said Henry and he did. Then he and Barney excused themselves.

Chapter 37: A Bumpy Ride

"Well guys, it's time to go," said Mary. Susan was still scuffling around gathering up things. "Come on, girl. Whatever we've got is what we're taking; we have to get outta' here."

Susan looked at her watch. "We've still got ten minutes."

"Exactly," said Mary. "That's cutting it plenty close enough. Let's go."

Susan looked at her two friends—her only friends—sympathetic, yet, at the same time, resolute. Not only would it be futile to argue with them, it would be just plain wrong. "Okay, I'm coming," she sighed, then scooped a few more books into her backpack on her way to the garage.

The three teens performed like a pit crew at the Indianapolis 500, with Mary, of course, the crew chief. In the space of fifty minutes, they had managed to open a bank account with over fifty thousand dollars, pack, and disguise themselves as the Abel family—despite the bitter protests, Susan made a fine looking young boy.

Johnny finished snapping the canvas cover over the bed of the pickup, and they were ready to go. The truck, a custom, four-wheel-drive, extended-cab pickup painted blue and white with tires so humongous the sideboards were at Susan's eye level, had only five thousand miles on it. "Is there a ladder or something I'm missing? Or maybe an elevator?" she asked as she struggled to pull herself into the cab.

"Oh dear, Jack, our little boy is having trouble getting into his daddy's big truck," said Mary.

"Here, son, let me help," said Johnny in a deep, cowboy voice, and he proceeded to help Susan into the back of the cab.

Susan glared at her 'parents.' "If you expect me to be a good little boy, you better be real nice."

"Well, let's do it," Mary said, closing the door behind her. She took in the plush interior, the stereo, and a multitude of other gadgets, most of them a mystery to her. "Wow! This is an awesome truck, Johnny." And then something occurred to her that she hadn't thought of before. "Johnny," she said in a serious tone, "you do know how to drive, don't you?"

"Of course I do," he answered, a*t least with the simula-*

tor on my Indianapolis 500 video game. And yet, even as he said the words, the left side mirror was being peeled off the truck by the side of the garage, and he was quick to add, "I'm, ah, better going forward."

After overcompensating for the mirror, the truck was soon riding half on grass and half on the driveway. "Oops, a bit too much," he said, "but no problem," and turned back the other way.

"What driving school did you go to, anyway?" asked Mary. "Wrecks-R-Us?"

The truck angled toward the sidewalk where Henry and his arthritic Bassett hound struggled to get out of the way. Susan put her hands over her ears and tucked her head between her legs, moaning something Johnny could not understand. Mary laughed.

The truck bounced over the curb and managed to find the street, but only after sacrificing the mailbox in the process. A week's worth of mail spilled out over the yard and street. At last, Johnny could put the truck into drive and started making his way between the parked cars on either side of him and towards the main road. "Nice job, Moonbrain," said Mary after her laughter had quieted down enough for her to talk.

"Well," said Johnny, "it's not my fault. I'm not the one who parked the truck backwards in the garage." Mary was trying to say something but was laughing too hard again. Johnny smiled and added, "Well, anyway, we should be okay now that I can see where I'm going."

"Let's hope so," said Susan.

*****

One hour and forty-two miles later, the two-lane, barely adequate country road turned gravel. "Oh," squeaked Susan as Johnny bounced the truck through the biggest pothole yet, "do you guys know what you're doing up there? I'm getting bounced to death back here."

"I have no idea," answered Johnny, cool as frost on a pumpkin.

"I do," answered Mary. *That is, assuming that this map isn't just some wild goose chase.*

"Geez, that was a big one," said Johnny after yet another record-setting crater. The only thing keeping them from going right through the roof was their seatbelts (it never occurred to Johnny that slowing down for these road hazards might be a good idea).

"Isn't there a better way than this?" asked Mary.

"Probably."

"You mean Henry did this on purpose?"

"He thought it would be better if we stayed off the main roads as much as possible," explained Johnny as the truck bounced its way forward, likely covering more distance vertically than horizontally.

"I think he succeeded," said Susan.

"Be quiet!" Mary said and adjusted the volume of the radio.

"What?" asked Susan.

"Just listen."

> *Police are looking for a late model Blue and White, four-wheel-drive, extended cab pickup with Indiana license plate MYC 476. The driver is described as a slender, young, Caucasian male in his late teens or early 20s, about 6 feet tall. He is suspected of kidnapping a twelve-year-old girl and then murdering a Mystic, Indiana couple and stealing their truck. He is considered to be extremely dangerous. Anyone who thinks they may have seen a truck matching this description should call the authorities immediately. Stay tuned to your local station for further updates.*

"Oh," said Susan softly. The reports had started coming at five-minute intervals about an hour after they'd taken off. "So," asked Susan, "you really do know where we are, don't you? We are going to be okay, aren't we?"

"Of course we will," said Mary. "Shit, Johnny, slow down. Hang a right, quick!" Johnny yanked the steering wheel hard, bringing the two driver's side wheels temporarily off the ground. "Whew, that's a relief."

"What do you mean. That's a relief?" asked Susan, suspiciously.

Mary turned and looked back at her friend. "To tell the truth, I was getting a little bit worried. I've been looking for this damn road forever. I thought we might never find it. But we're cool now. We've got, like, only one more turn to make."

"All I can see is corn fields," said Susan.

"Exactly. All we have to do is make the first right after the corn turns into soybeans and, wha-la, we're there."

"But don't know what soybeans look like," said Johnny.

"Neither do I," said Mary, shrugging her shoulders, "but it doesn't matter. All we need to know is that they don't look like corn."

After a brief pause, Johnny got it. "Right," he said, and not long after that, fields of short, leafy green plants replaced the corn. "Them there is soybeans, ladies."

"Like, thanks for pointing that out, Mr. Green Jeans. But I think you missed the turn," said Mary.

Johnny stopped the truck and backed up, this time uneventfully, and headed down a narrow dirt road. "I think I see it up on the left," said Mary, but the closer they got the more her excitement dwindled. Johnny stopped the truck at the end of the road next to an old burned-out John Deere tractor. Two hundred yards in front of them a huge old barn looked about ready to fall down. To their right was the foundation of a house or what they supposed used to be a house.

"Well, Mary," said Susan, "Coach was right about one thing. Nobody's going to look for us here."

Chapter 38: Ben

OH, JOHNNY," SAID MARY, "I think you can turn the truck off now."

"Right," he said, fumbling about for the ignition because, just like the girls, he could not take his gaze away from the spectacle of the old farmer.

A tall, lanky man, bare-chested, wearing a pair of tattered blue overalls fastened only on one side, emerged from the barn. His kilted work boots were unlaced, kicking up clouds of dirt as he strode towards them with the gait of a man half his age, and the self-assured toughness of a Clint Eastwood cowboy. Even so, his years were evident in skin bronze and leathery from too much sun, and in the thin, white head of hair sitting atop a face so worn and deeply furrowed it could only be explained by worry and sorrow and the passage of time. A long, tasseled piece of field grass stuck between his teeth bounced every which way but in sync with his steps on account of the wad he had packed into his right cheek. The old man's eyes were alive, and focused on the visitors in such a way that made them feel like he was the light, and they were the deer caught in it. About thirty feet from the truck he came to an abrupt halt, and turned his head. A thick, brown oyster shot out of the man's mouth like a torpedo, landing in the tall grass some thirty feet to his left.

"Oo-uuu," said Susan, "That was gross."

"Yeah, what was it?" echoed Johnny.

"You guys have, like, never seen chewing tobacco?" asked Mary. They shook their heads in unison, like two marionettes on the same string. "Jesus," she exclaimed, and then jumped out of the truck. "Well, let's go, dudes. It's not going to kill you." They hustled after her.

When Susan and Johnny caught up with Mary, she was locked in some sort of a staring contest with the old man. His piercing, blue eyes bearing down on her in a way that made Johnny more than a little uncomfortable, like the old man had x-ray vision and was examining her. Mary, however, was holding her own just fine. *I should have known.* Johnny relaxed. Then the man's eyes shifted, and he gave Johnny and Susan each the once-over. Johnny was about to say something, but before he had a chance, the old man surveyed the three of them one more time, top to bottom, spat out another oyster, and frowned. Johnny gulped. *I guess we didn't pass the test.*

"Well, if it ain't the three juvenile dee-linquents," he said, drawing it out in his low, raspy voice. He waited, watching as their anxiety escalated, then grinned and introduced himself. "Name's Ben." He held out a hand to Johnny. "Ben Waller. Pleased to meet ya."

"Very funny," said Mary, but gave Johnny a nudge.

"Oh, right," he said, taking the man's hand, "ah, and my name is Johnny Moonbeam."

"And I'm Mary Valentine."

"And I am not a delinquent," huffed Susan, stomping her foot for emphasis.

Ben considered the obstreperous young lady for a while then turned his head and expelled the entire wad of chew. "Excuse me," he said, wiping his mouth on the back of his arm and squatting down in front of her. "Well, young lady, that may be what Coach Henry believes, but I always like to make up my own mind." All the time he was looking into her eyes, not once did Susan flinch or back off. After a while Ben nodded and smiled. "It's too early to tell for sure, but I'm inclined to think I'll be in agreement with my brother-in-law. And that, I can tell you, is a rare circumstance." He stood up, took Susan's hand, and started walking. Johnny and Mary looked at each other, shrugged, and followed.

Without bothering to turn around, Ben pointed to the barn. "Boy," he said, raising his voice enough so that Johnny could hear, "you best get back in that truck and foller us over to the barn. We'll park it in there, with Bessie, for the time being."

"Who's Bessie?" asked Susan.

"Best damn cow in Indiana. Who the hell are you?"

Susan stuck her chest out, added a bit of swagger to her gait, and tucked her thumbs into her dress as if there were suspenders there instead. "My name is Susan Goodenough, and I'm the best damn thirteen-year-old in Indiana."

Ben chuckled and nodded, "I suspect you are."

Ben was moving along at such a brisk pace that Mary

had to jog a few steps to catch up. She fell in place beside the old farmer, opposite Susan, and looked up at him. "Henry said you were almost unreachable, that we'd probably be a surprise and have to explain ourselves."

"Yep," answered the old man, continuing to walk and looking straight ahead.

"What do you mean, yep?" she retorted, indignant, then jumped out in front of him, hands-on hips, and stopped. "You called us the three delinquents," and then, pointing to Susan, "and agreed with your brother-in-law that Susan was alright, or whatever it was you said. So, you had to have talked to Henry. See, I gotcha!"

Ben stopped and let go of Susan's hand. "What I said was maybe that's what Henry believes, not that I knew fer sure. It was an educated guess based on what I do know, which is that, aside from a few neighbors, Henry is the only one who knows I'm out here. And he wouldn't have sent you if he didn't think you was alright. So you see, Henry was right after all."

Mary crossed her arms over her chest and, not budging, said, "Okay, but even if you didn't talk to Henry, you still knew something about us before we got here. Right?"

The farmer held his arms up in surrender for a moment then plucked a cell phone from his pocket and dangled it in front of the teens. "Just got me this thing a few days ago. It's one of them wise-ass phones—"

"Smart phones," corrected Susan.

"That's what I said."

Susan rolled her eyes. "You actually get reception out here?"

"You bet. This here ranch is strictly big-time, young lady," and with that Ben nodded contentedly and surveyed his version of The Ponderosa, paint peeling off the barn, fields of wild grass, a rusty but still functional 1927 John Deere, and the dilapidated foundation of what was once a beautiful farm house. Then he nodded some more, and as he started out on his way again, this time, mostly to himself, added, "Yes-sir-re, strictly big-time."

Mary, still in front of him but moving backwards now so as not to be run over, rolled her eyes. "You never answered my question."

"Well, you see, this here contraption's got a little bit of everything, telephone, camera, Internet, and a bunch of other stuff that I'll prob'ly never use." He could see that the girl's question had not been satisfactorily answered, so he continued. "I especially like the Internet, so's I can keep up with the news. Don't you guys know that your pictures is plastered all over the place from here to Kalamazoo?"

"Well, we didn't know we were *that* famous," said Mary.

"Infamous, you mean," Ben said with a smile. "You guys did good just makin' it out here. There's one hell of a manhunt going on."

"Oh no!" said Susan. "Now I'm really in trouble."

"I'm glad Henry gave us the back roads," said Johnny.

"If you can even call them roads, that is," added Mary.

"Well, they're not called back roads for nothing, and I suspect that's the only thing that saved the three of yous."

Ben guided Johnny into the barn. "Careful now . . . okay . . . whoa now. Where the hell did you learn to back that thing up, anyhow?"

"He didn't," Susan said flatly.

"I guess that explains it. Okay now, turn the wheel a little bit to the right. THE RIGHT, damn it. That's better." Then, at last, when the truck was where Ben wanted it, well, at least close enough, "Okay, that's good." Johnny turned the truck off and engaged the parking brake. Ben waited a few seconds, and when the boy did not move, said, "Son, you kin get out now."

"Oh, sorry," Johnny said, and shook himself out of a trance. "Ah, should I leave the keys in here?"

"I don't care where you leave 'em. Come on, now, I ain't got all day." Johnny left the keys in the ignition and jumped out of the truck while Ben rounded up a bunch of empty crates. "Here," he said to Johnny, "take these and set them down by the back of the truck. Then you and your friends unload all the gear and pack it into 'em."

From the bed of the truck Johnny handed out its contents to the girls. Mary worked fast and efficiently, indiscriminately packing the items into one crate until it was full then starting another. Susan, on the other hand, made no progress, rummaging through the packages as if she would never see them again and having to decide which few items to save.

Ben saw the frustration mounting inside of her. “Hey, Miss Susan,” he said, getting her attention, “we don’t have time to be sortin’ that stuff out right now. We’ll come back later and get whacha need. For now just load it up like Mary’s doing.”

“But-”

“No buts. Just do it.” Still, even though Susan understood what he meant, she couldn’t seem to comply.

Mary saw what was going on and looked up for a second. “Don’t worry about it, Susan, just have a seat over there.” She pointed to an empty crate well away from the truck. “We’re about done here, anyway.” After a bit of urging, Susan sat down and watched.

Ben sat down next to the frustrated young girl. “Why don’t you just tell me what’s a- bothering you, girl, and we’ll try to work somethin’ out, okay?”

Susan wiped her eyes and looked up at Ben. “I don’t know why,” she said, sniffling, “I just seem to get stuck sometimes. I don’t mean to. I know it makes me look like an idiot, but I can’t seem to help it.”

Ben put an arm around her and pulled her head to his chest. “Now, don’t you be a-beatin’ yourself up about it, girl. It’s just the way your brain works. Seems to me like, overall, you’ve got one helluva good brain. But it’s a package deal and part of it likes to be a tad over obsessive about things. There ain’t no shame in that and, anyways, the main thing to remember is that no one here thinks you’s an idiot.” She didn’t say anything, but Ben could see that she’d taken it in and appeared to be feeling better. “Okay now, you stay right here. I’ll go help them finish up and then we’ll all go to the house together.” She nodded.

Ben grabbed some tarps and went to where the other two had finished loading the crates, and they covered them. He then signaled for them to follow him over to where Susan was. When they were just a few steps away from the truck, he reached up and yanked on a rope. A trap door above the truck opened and unleashed a huge pile of hay from above, burring the truck.

Geez, thought Johnny, *I wish he'd tell me when he's going to do something like that.* "What did you do that for?"

"Gotta hide the evidence."

"Good idea," said Mary, impressed. Then, as she was sizing him up with those eyes of hers, his expression suddenly changed. "What?"

"Haven't I seen you somewhere before?" He closed his eyes and started grabbing at his chin, searching, but then gave up. "What the hell's your name again?"

"Mary," she said.

"No, that's not it."

"Excuse me, but it most certainly is."

"No, I mean, not that one. There was something else they called you, long time ago, but for the life-o-me I can't remember what it was."

Susan looked at Mary. "What is he talking about?"

"I have no flipping idea." She turned back to the farmer. "You must be mistaking me for someone else, Mr. Wall-"

"Call me Ben."

"Ben."

He looked at her again, long and hard. "You could be right, little girly, but there's somethin' strange familiar about you. Oh well, we got business to do." Then, placing a thumb and forefinger in his mouth, Ben blew out a whistle loud enough to be heard halfway to Ft. Wayne. "Okay now, little lambkins, follow me."

"I am not a lamb," Susan huffed, though not loud enough for Ben to hear, as she fell in beside her friend.

"Baaa, baaa," bleated Mary, earning herself a jab to the shoulder.

"Where are we going?" asked Johnny.

"Right there," said Ben, pointing to the naked foundation. "There's a bit more to it than might be apparent at first glance."

"Or, like, even at second glance." Mary.

After they'd trekked across the fifty yards or so to the foundation, Ben kicked away some branches and revealed a set of storm doors painted a dirty brownish green and opened them up.

"You, like, live underground?"

"Now you're catchin' on."

"It looks really . . . really . . . dark down there," said Johnny, trying his best not to sound frightened.

"Don't worry 'bout that, son," said Ben. He reached in and flipped a switch on the inside of the door. "See there? I got 'lectricity and light bulbs and all that good stuff." Relief spread through Johnny at once. "Go on, now, it won't bite."

A deep stairwell, about six feet wide, simple but well constructed and made of smooth concrete descended almost sixteen feet below the surface. Johnny counted the steps on his way down. Number twenty-five opened onto a fifteen-foot square slab of concrete, bare save for a small watering trough and a neatly stacked pile of hay at the far end. The sides of the slab were sloped towards the middle where they gave way to a large drain. There was a door to his right and a switch on the wall next to it.

"Excuse me," said Ben, as he reached across the boy and pushed the door open. The light did not penetrate past the entrance way, and so whatever was beyond the door remained in the dark. Ben waited a couple seconds for the girls to make it down to the foyer and then flipped the switch.

The girls gasped in amazement. Johnny managed to say, "Wow," as his mouth opened, but then, like his friends, all he could do was stand there, slack-jawed at the view. A huge room measuring about a hundred feet deep by fifty feet wide opened up before them. An array of track lights and white-washed, maple-hardwood flooring amply illuminated the room. Instead of walls, Ben used large Persian rugs and groupings of furniture to divide the room into different functional areas. A semi-circular couch opened up to a big-screen TV. Leather couches and leather chairs, along with a coffee table, were in what was, apparently, a more formal living room or den. At the end of the long room was a tall bar with bar stools, and, behind that, the kitchen.

As Ben was waved the three comrades into his underground fortress, Susan looked up. "What's that?" she asked.

Ben turned around. "What's what?"

"I hear it too," said Mary. "Sounds almost . . . like helicopters."

"My old ears ain't pickin' 'em up yet, but if you say it sounds like helicopters, then that's for damn sure what they are. Okay now, come on, there's no time to lose."

Chapter 39: Hidin' Out

"Remember, I told y'all there's a man hunt a-goin' on?" They nodded as he waved them back behind the bar and into the kitchen. "Every time there's a manhunt, they get them choppers out. And, when them choppers see this patch of land in the middle of all that corn, it makes 'em suspicious. I go through this drill three or four times a year, seems like, but haven't had the excitement of actually hiding anyone here for a while." Like everything else the kitchen was high end, including a nice stainless-steel, double-oven set up. Except one of them wasn't an oven. Ben pulled off the phony oven's door, took out the racks, and pointed. "Okay now, in you go."

"It looks awfully dark down there. What is it?" asked Johnny.

Ben handed each of them a flashlight. "Somewhere safe to hide. You'll see when you get down there. It's comfortable enough even though it ain't been used for a while. All the same, I still like to make sure it's ready, 'cause you just never know what's gonna happen."

Susan was the first to come forward. Ben helped her in. "Are you sure it's safe down here?" she asked.

"Oh, it's safe, all right. You ain't the first notorious Hoosiers to hide out down there neither." Ben helped Johnny through, and then it was Mary's turn.

Before turning around so she could step into it backwards, which is how one had to do it, she could see her friends' flashlights scanning the premises below and heard Susan call out, "Come on down, Mary, it's really neat."

Mary started her decent, and just as she was about to disappear, looked back up at Ben. "What notorious Hoosiers?"

Ben grinned. "You ever heard of a man by the name of John Dillinger?"

"Of course I have," she said. "Wow, like, that's so cool." Then, after a short pause, "John Dillinger was from Indiana?"

"Damn sure was," said Ben. "You ask Miss Susan down there. I bet she can tell you all about him." Then he put the oven back together, closed it up, and headed outside to greet whatever representatives had been sent by the local Sheriff's

Department.

*****

"Well Abigail," said Ben, making his way up the long set of stairs leading outside. He often sought counsel with his long-dead wife when something unusual was going on, and this was about as unusual as it ever got. "You prob'ly think I'm crazy as a damn loon agreein' to hide them kids out here." He pushed open the huge storm doors and stepped outside. "What's that, darlin'? . . . No I can't hear nothin' except that damn whirlybird . . .Okay then, we'll talk later."

*****

The County Sheriff's Department helicopter landed about 50 yards away in the open field. As usual, there were two men. The pilot, a slender young man Ben had never seen before, turned off the chopper and waited inside. The other, Deputy Sheriff Amos Laughton, Ben knew well. Amos stood about five feet seven, wore his white hair in a flattop, was always clean-shaven and well-dressed, and sported a healthy paunch that, year to year, continued to gain momentum. He had jumped out of the chopper when it was still a foot or two off the ground and walked over to Ben.

"Dammit all," said Ben as he approached his longtime acquaintance, "when you guys gonna start using the heliport? I must-a done asked y'all 'bout 100 times by now, and still every time you come land down here a-messing up my weeds. Ain't y'all got no respect for an upstanding, taxpaying citizen no more?"

"Ben Waller, you wouldn't know what a tax return looked like to save your life," said Amos. And then he pointed up at the roof of the barn. "Is that what you're calling a heliport?"

"Damn right. You can't see it very well from here, but it's right on top. Don't see how in the hell you could miss it when you're flying in."

"And how the hell am I supposed to get down? Tell you what. I'll start landing there as soon as you put in a goddamned elevator."

"Well, I'll get right on it." Ben reached out his hand and shook Amos'. "What can I do for ya?"

"Why, Ben, this here is just a social visit."

"Right, 'cause we all know how sociable I am."

"What?" Amos threw his arms open in a gesture of bewilderment. "Do you really think the only reason I come out here is just to give you a hard time?"

"Yep, that's exactly what I think."

"Well it just so happens there was one thing I was hoping you could help me with."

"That's what I thought."

Amos put an arm around Ben's shoulder. "I suppose you've heard about them three kids who ran off earlier today?"

"You must be talkin' 'bout them kids that iced that couple down there in Mystic then took a little girl and have managed to elude the po-lice since last night?"

"That's right. Here's a picture of the girl, her name is Susan Goodenough, and a sketch of the other two. We still don't have an ID on them." Ben studied the pictures. "Seen any of them?"

"Can't say that I have. Fact is, you're the first person I seen in a few days."

The Sheriff looked into Ben's eyes. "Well, if you do see them, are you going to give me a call?"

"I might have to shoot 'em first, but I'll give you a call all right."

"Well, all right then. We'll be moving on."

"You don't want to poke around the premises a bit, mess up all my stuff?"

"Wouldn't find anything, would I?"

"Other than a sleeping cow, not much."

"Okay then, you let me know if you see anything, all right?"

"You got it, Sheriff."

*****

"What's taking so long, anyway?" asked Mary. "This place is driving me nuts. It's hot and it's boring. Not to mention Moonbrain's farting." A few minutes later they heard some noise coming from above.

"That must be Ben now," said Johnny.

"Okay, kids, coast is clear. You can come out now."

"Hallelujah," said Mary, and she jumped on the ladder before the other two could even stand up. "Last one in, first one out."

Before he could even see the top of her head, Mary was firing salvos at Ben as fast as she could. “It’s too small. TV wouldn’t hurt the situation at all, not to mention a bathroom. Oh, and you really should have some better ventilation down there.”

“Excuse me, young lady,” said Ben as he helped Mary out of the oven/tunnel. “Next time I save your ass from the sheriff, I’ll try to have those things worked out.

“Sorry.”

*****

It was past six o’clock that evening when everything finally settled down. “I don’t know about you kids, but I’m hungrier than a toady-frog in winter. Why don’t y’all grab a movie to watch and make yourselves comfortable whiles old Ben conjures up some grub?” After dinner they sat up and talked until they were too exhausted to carry on. The kids filled Ben in on the particulars of each of their situations and explained what had really happened the night before. Ben said he believed them, which he did, but that this was just a temporary situation until he could figure out “What in the Sam Hill we’re going to do.”

“Well I’m plum tuckered out. Foller me,” and he and he showed them to their quarters, a large bedroom for the girls to share, and a small room that looked more like a den or a library but had a pullout sofa in for Johnny.

The first one was quite large and set up with fine furniture and a pair of twin beds. This would be Susan and Mary’s room. Seeing that the beds were unmade, Susan asked where she could find some sheets and pillows. “You’ll find plenty of sheets and towels and bedspreads and pillows in that closet right there.” he looked at the three of them, “Ya’all set?” They nodded. “Good, I’ll see you in the mornin’.” Ben was just about to close his door when Susan’s meek voice stopped him.

“Mr. Waller?”

“Call me Ben.”

“Okay, then, Ben, what if something bad happens during the night, like we get scared or something?”

Ben sighed at the question. He was exhausted, looking forward to seven or eight hours of uninterrupted sleep. But when he saw the needy, frightened look in Susan’s bright blue eyes, he regretted having put her off. Shifting his gaze to Mary, he saw the same disconcerting look reflected in her eyes, eyes so big and so brown they reminded him of Bessie's, and he realized, underneath all their teenage show of toughness and independence, how frightened and lonely they really were. He smiled a big, warm, reassuring smile, and nodded. "Anything at all bothers you or goes haywire whiles I'm asleep, no matter how trivial it may seem, you just charge into this here room and wake me up, okay?" The girls smiled, and, though he didn't see it, so did Johnny. "Alright then, I'll see y'all in the mornin'."

*****

Ben sat down heavy on the bed. *I sure hope them kids don't have to wake me up tonight.* Even so, he was glad to have made himself available. He reached for the night lamp.

You're not going go to sleep without talking to me, are you old man? I've been waiting all day.

Ben looked around for a second then relaxed. "Is that you Abigail?"

Of course it's me. I know you're exhausted but it's been a big day and I'd like to talk to you about it for a couple minutes, if you're up to it.

"I am tired, but I've always got time for you, Abigail. Whad'ya think of them kids?"

Well, they're cute as the dickens, but they're going to need a lot of help.

"That's what I'm-a-plannin' to do."

They're going to need more than you can give them, honey.

"I know, I know."

Do you? Because I know you too, Ben Waller, and, as much as I love you, sometimes you try to do too much by yourself.

Ben chuckled. "Don't you worry about that, sweetheart. I feel the burden good and heavy right now and I'll be glad at havin' help. They're gonna' need a good lawyer and some money, I can do that for them."

That sounds good, I'm proud of you. Just don't lose your head now, and stay in touch, all right?

"I'm good on both counts, don't you worry."

Well then, good night.
"Good night."

Chapter 40: Life on the Farm

Ben whistled. "Hey, girly girl, time to get your pretty buns in here an' keep this old man comp'ny whilst he cooks up somethin' for y'all vultures to chew on."

"I'm coming, ya ole coot," said Mary. "Do I need to bring some mints so you don't knock me out with that Red Man Tobacco-breath, or you got some in there already?"

"I done took care of that, sweetheart. Heck, even as much as I know you loves a-kissin' me, I realize there's a limit to what a girl'll put up with."

"Don't you wish, old man," she said as she walked into the kitchen. Then she was smiling and gave him a hug.

"I reckon that'll do," he said and resumed smashing his pot full of tomatoes.

If anyone else had tried talking to her like that, she would've given him the what for and a slap across the face. However, after ten days of living with Ben, Mary had learned much, including this: when you're eighty-two-years old and sweeter than a double whipped hot cocoa with two sugars, you can get away with things like that.

How long the children were going to be staying with Gentle Ben, as they now called him among themselves, they had no idea. He didn't ask, and they didn't say. They all felt the same: the kids didn't want to leave, and neither did Ben. Any discussion seemed destined to jinx the future. So they didn't talk about it. For the first time in over forty years, Ben had a renewed interest in life. He felt like a young man again. Well, a young man of sixty maybe. But still, for the three desperadoes, life had never been better. In Ben they found someone who not only knew how to love them, but knew how to guide them and help them grow as individuals. Of course, they only noticed the first part of the equation because, like any good parent, Ben made sure the second part was of a more cryptic nature. He didn't need any help and could have just let them wallow around all day and do whatever, but he put them to work.

He taught Johnny how to drive the tractor and work the fields and put him in charge of tending the gardens of tomatoes and cucumbers and lettuce and sweet corn and beans that were scattered in patches throughout the acres of field corn. Academics, he knew, is what Susan craved and needed. She was already too advanced for him to be of any assistance other than to guide her into subject areas and keep her from getting frustrated when she got in far over her head, which she was prone to do.

Mary, he was surprised to learn, was interested in domestic activities. So he dug-out Abigail's old sewing machine and the reams of material she'd left behind and put Mary on an independent study program. She'd wanted him to teach her but explained, "Girl, I ain't gotta clue what to do with that shit. Besides, you're smart enough to figure it out yourself." She realized she was on her own. Not really though, because Ben had Susan download patterns and lesson plans on how to sew, and she even put some videos on CD for Mary to watch. And then he monitored her like a hawk. He needn't have bothered. Mary took to it and was soon on her way to becoming, as he liked to say, "One hell of a seamstress."

The other subject for Mary was cooking, which she liked even more than the sewing. For this Ben was the perfect teacher. He enjoyed cooking and had taken it on with a passion after Abigail had passed, and all on his own, had developed into quite a chef. "Hell, with forty years of practice I should to be able to put some decent food on the table." He took her under his wing every afternoon, instructing her as she helped him prepare the evening meal. Because he had a penchant for good eating, and had always been embarrassed to serve guests anything but the best, the meals were generally quite extraordinary.

*****

"Alright now, young lady, you ready for your cookin' lesson?"

"You bet, what is it tonight, teach?"

"Ben Waller's world-famous spaghetti and meatballs."

Johnny's voice drifted in from the other room. "Did someone say spaghetti?"

"You just keep your seat belt on out there, boy. It's gonna take an hour or more for me and Miss fancy pants to get this here feast on the table just so you can whip it down in about thirty seconds. You think you can make it that long?"

"I'll try."

"When I make my spaghetti sauce," Ben said to Mary, "I usually make a big batch and freeze it. Usually lasts me about ten months, but the way that boy can pack it in, we'll be lucky to have any left over at all tonight."

"I know! It's amazing how much he can eat. It's like he just inhales it."

Ben laughed at that. "You just ain't been around a growing teenage boy before. They're all that way, natural-born eatin' machines, like sharks. Now, let's get on with it." He picked a tomato out of a two-gallon bucket of them that Johnny had harvested for the occasion. "See this?" She nodded. "This here is what's known as a plum, or I-talian tomata." She nodded again. "The first thing we've got to do is peel all these little buggers. How would you suggest we go about that?"

"Ah, like, do they have something for tomatoes, like one of those carrot peeler thingies?"

"Well, they do, but that'd still take us until about a week from Tuesday, and I don't believe Johnny can wait that long."

Mary shrugged. "Then what?"

Ben winked and picked up a handful of the tomatoes and placed them in a pot of boiling water waiting on the stove. "We cheat," he said, and Mary laughed. "I thought you'd like that. Anyways, put 'em in here for about thirty or forty seconds is all." They waited. "Then you take 'em out like this," which he did. He then picked one up and held it by the fat end. "Give her a little squeeze and," the inside of the tomato shot out into another pan and the skin was left dangling from his fingers, "there ya go."

"Wow, that's cool," she said, then picked one up and did the same. "I did it," she said, jumping up and down a couple of times for emphasis.

"I knew you could," he said. "You's a natural-born cheater if ever there was one."

Mary did not argue the point.

*****

That night Ben sat down on heavy on his bed, exhausted yet happier and more content than he'd been in a long time.

He reached for the string of his night lamp and started to pull.

Ben Waller, you've been avoiding me.

"Why Abigail," he said, looking around as if she might actually be there. "I wa—"

You was nothing. Don't lie to me.

He hung his head. "I'm sorry, dear. It's just that—"

I know what it is. I've been watching you and those kids. I'm proud of the help you've given them, and I can't tell you how much it thrills me to see you happy for the first time in forever. But you're damn near eighty-three years old, and they're going to have to live in the real world long after you're up here with me. With your heart, the way it is, that's likely to be sooner rather than later. She paused for a minute, and he blushed. You didn't tell them about your heart, did you?

"Ah, I forgot."

You did not forget.

"Well, I didn't want to worry them."

Think how worried they're going to be when you keel over one day, and all of a sudden they got no one again.

"I know. I know."

I hate to say it, Ben Waller, but I believe helping those children has crossed over into pure selfishness on your part. You're so damn happy you don't want to give them up. But if you don't get them some help now, while you're able, who else is going to do it?

"You're right. I'll get around to it soon. I promise."

Well now, that's better. You keep me updated. You hear?

"I will," he said then paused for a minute. "Abigail, you still there?"

I'm still here.

"Thanks."

For what?

"For straightening me out. I needed it."

You're welcome.

Ben pulled the lamp string and was out with the light.

Chapter 41: The Storyteller

AT FOUR O'CLOCK, THE NEXT AFTERNOON Ben had just finished cleaning and restocking Bessie's stall and was about to call it quits. He was stroking her on the forehead and down the bridge of her nose, whispering sweet nothings into her big brown cow ears, when Susan came running toward the barn holding a blue ribbon up over her head and waving at him. Mary was hot on her heels and when they were about twenty feet or so from him, Susan pointed the ribbon at him and screeched, "What's this all about?"

"Yeah," said Mary. "You've been holding out on us, old man."

"What in the Sam Hill are you talkin' about?" he said, but then he saw the ribbon. It was too far away for him to read, but he knew what it said: First Prize Storytelling, Indiana State Fair, 1968.

The girls were giggling, jumping up and down and acting about half their age, and chanting, "We want a story. We want a story."

Ben's face was grim like they'd never seen it before. "You've been snooping around my stuff," he said, trying to keep his voice level. "I thought you two were above that sort of thing. Guess I was wrong." He spat his wad of tobacco out of the barn floor. "Where in tarnation did you dig that thing out from, anyway?"

Susan couldn't speak. Mary, however, had no such problem. "And I thought you were above accusing people before you knew the facts," was all she said and then crossed her arms over chest and nodded defiantly.

"What the hell other facts could there be?"

"I don't think I'll tell you," said Mary.

Susan, desperate for him to know the truth and to not be under suspicion of performing illegal activities, found the words. "I . . . I was just doing my . . . my homework. Remember, you told me to read Huck Finn?" He nodded but was still scowling. "Well . . . when I pulled it off the bookshelf, this was right in the middle of it, sticking out like a bookmark. I, I, I wouldn't have even looked at it if I knew it would've bothered you. I, I would have just put it back in another book. I'm sorry."

Ben sighed and shook his head. Mary started to say something, but he held up his hand to stop her. "No, no, no, you ain't the one needs to apologize. That would be me. I'm sorry I jumped all over y'all before I knew what the hell was going on." Then he looked up at Mary and added, "You're right. I shouldn't a-done that."

Ben looked so solemn the girls ran up and gave him a hug. "It's all right. We didn't know it would upset to you," said Susan.

"You gonna be okay?" asked Mary.

Ben sat down, and they noticed he had started to cry.

"What's the matter?" asked Susan. Mary gave her an elbow.

"It's all right," he said and held his hand out, gesturing for them to give him the ribbon, which they did.

He looked at it, fingering the gold lettering and shaking his head. He sighed and looked down at the girls kneeling in front of him. "I remember now. It was about twenty years ago, and I was plumb wore out by all the memories around the house a-starin' at me and a-hauntin' me. So one day I just packed 'em all up in a chest and put it up there," he said, pointing up to the loft. Except this one. I just couldn't part with it. So I stuffed it in my favorite book and put it on the shelf. Never thought about it once since then. Mostly there're pictures in the trunk. Pictures of me and her before we was married—before World War II, if you can believe that. There's even a picture of Abigail a-meetin' me as I stepped off the ramp from the boat that brung me back from France after the war. That was 1945."

He stopped, shaking his head at the memory and trying to hold back the tears. "Can you believe that? Twenty-year-old Abigail a-talkin' her daddy into drivin' all the way to New York City, so she could meet me right at the damn docks! What a girl she was. We held on to each other so tight I don't even know how we managed to keep a-breathing. But we must have, 'cause, we stayed that way for a long time. We might never a-let go 'cept for her daddy, who had to come and get us a-moving. It was him that took the picture."

Ben wiped his brow. "Of course, there were the pictures

of our wedding and our honeymoon down in Tennessee. You see, we didn't have much money back then." He started like he was going to explain something but then stopped and smiled. "Shoot, not that it mattered. I don't think it would've been possible for two people to be any happier than we were then." He took a breath. "Then there's pictures of us buying our first car, lookin' at and finally buyin' this here property and puttin' up the barn. We lived out here for a year 'til we got the house built."

"Were there animals in here then?" asked Mary.

"Nope, just me and the missus."

"What did the house look like when it was done?" asked Susan.

"It was beautiful. A two-story, brick farm house with four dormers off the attic—so it was more like three stories. Abigail insisted on a wraparound porch, and she was right. We used the hell out of that porch. She used to." And then, all at once, he stopped talking. He looked weary and wrung out.

"You . . . want something to drink or maybe go inside or something?" asked Mary.

He shook his head but then, a few seconds later said, "Actually, a tall glass of iced tea might be nice. There's some in the fridge, if you wouldn't mind running in and gettin' me some. When you get back I'll tell you the rest of the story." Mary took off running.

"You don't have to, you know," said Susan.

He smiled and touched her on the cheek. "I know, darlin', and I appreciate that. But, the truth is, I've done gone too far forgettin' about things. It's good for me to get 'em out once in a while. Specially since y'all's like family now, I suspect you got a right to know."

Mary came back with the tea and handed it to Ben. He gulped the entire glass in one shot then smacked his lips. "Thank you, that done hit the spot," he said, and set the glass down.

"You really loved Abigail, didn't you?" asked Susan.

"Oh, you bet I did, girl. I sure did." He looked at the ribbon one more time, ran his hand over it, and handed it back to Susan. "You can hang on to this for me if you want to –just put it back in there with Huck when you're done."

She nodded. “You see, it wasn’t because of the first prize that I had trouble packin’ this one up. I’ve got a whole mess of blue ribbons just like it. Won the competition five years runnin’ at one stretch, and all of them is up there in the trunk. It’s on account of Abigail what makes this one special.” Ben collected himself and the girls waited patiently, knowing that the next part was going to be especially difficult.

“We was at the state fair, just like the ribbon says. It was the last day and the Storytelling contest was just after lunch, about one o’clock. We got the blue ribbon and walked around the fair a-lookin’ at the livestock an’ other exhibits and so on, having us a good time. Then at about 4:30 it was time for the midget car race.” Neither Susan nor Mary had any idea what a midget car was, but knew better than to ask right then. “So anyway, ’bout the same time as the race, they was moving about 100 heifers across the grounds for the night when there was this big explosion. Turns out there was one hell of a wreck at the race. That’s what caused the explosion, you see. One man even died-first time in over thirty years.

“Problem for us was that when the heifers heard the blast they went crazy, got loose and started a-runnin’. And we was right there in the way. I still don’t know how all them heifers missed me, but they sure didn’t miss Abigail. It was a sight I still can’t imagine even though it’s right up there in my brain, clear as a goddamned photograph. Abigail was a mess.” He shook his head. “But she was still a-holdin’ on to that ribbon, clutchin’ it in her fist.” He picked up the glass and swirled it around a couple of times to break up the ice cubes. Then he tilted his head back and siphoned off the liquid that had melted and collected at the bottom, and set the glass back down. “That’s the last damn fair I ever went to. Last storytellin’ competition too.”

Mary was shaking her head, tears running down her cheeks. “That’s terrible, Ben,” she sniffled. “I don’t even know what-” and then she stopped. Susan had placed a firm hand on Mary’s thigh and given her a look that, in no uncertain terms, said to shut up. She looked back at Ben and understood why. *Oh my God, there’s more.*

He took a deep breath. “There’s one more memory in the trunk, too, and it’s the worst kind I reckon anyone can have." By now, Ben's speech was so soft the girls had to strain to hear him. "You see. Most of the pictures was of Bruce. He was our only child. We'd wanted more, but it just didn't work out." He smiled and his voice picked up a bit. "Abigail, bless her heart, always liked havin' pictures of her boy out around the house, but when he left for Vietnam in '66, she like near went crazy with 'im. Then..." Ben seemed to lose his breath. The girls were about to intervene when he finally inhaled a huge load of air and continued. "He come back in a body bag in '67 and we both thought that it was the end of the world. They didn't want to let me look at the body. But I had the right to do it, so I did. My beautiful boy. He didn't even look human anymore. I don't take to losin' my stomach very often, but I did then. I thought I'd never stop vomitin'. 'Course, just like every other parent who's ever lost a child I suppose, I would-a given anything to jump in that bag and take his place if that meant he could come out and be with his mama. But it don't work that way, do it?" He stopped there for a while and sucked on some ice.

When Ben started talking again, his voice was clear and animated, almost fresh. He even smiled. "When Abigail fin'ly finished hangin' pictures of that boy after he left for Nam, I would-a sworn there wasn't enough wall space left to hang even one wallet-sized picture. Mind you, it was a purdy good-sized house too–three stories high. But when she found out that he weren't never comin' home, well, that woman done found room for a whole 'nother boxful." He took out another piece of ice and started laughing. "You should-a seen that woman a-runnin' around the house hangin' picture upon picture. It was ridiculous, really, but I knew it was just her way a grievin'. I will tell you this much, though, it sure enough was rough on this old boy having all those pictures of Bruce a-lookin' back at me all day. But when a mama loses her only son, everything, and I mean the whole rest of the world loses its meaning and there ain't no such thing as normal behavior. So there wasn't nothin' for me to do 'cept to get out of her way and let her keep 'em up as long as she needed to. Turned out about six months later she fin'ly admitted she couldn't stand lookin' at 'em no more neither. So we took down the most of 'em. Left just a few of our favorites out so we could look at him when we wanted to, without havin' to look at 'em all the damn time. He bit down on a piece of ice and then, after a minute, stood up and put an arm around each one of the girls and started walking back towards the house. "And that's about it. We had to let him go, had to get on with our lives. You never get over losing a child, but you do have to carry on, and that we did.

"We was just startin' to enjoy life again, able to put Bruce out of our minds for a few hours at a time, gettin' back into our routine of square dancing on Saturday and playing bridge on Wednesday nights. We'd been to every state fair from 1945 up through 1965. But after Bruce left, we just didn't feel like it. So we ended up skippin' the ones in '66 and '67. But when the 1968 fair rolled around, it'd been a little over a year, and we felt like we should go back. We thought it would be good for us – 'healing' was the word Abigail used – and so we did." He moaned an almost inaudible but disgusted sounding "Shit" before taking another breath and continuing. "We was havin' a nice time, too, until . . . " Ben lost his balance and nearly fell, but the girls caught him, and he recovered. "Well, y'all know the rest."

*****

By the time they got inside, Ben looked quite haggard. Mary took care of dinner while Susan put him to bed. They checked on him every hour or so.

By the time Johnny got back from the fields, Mary had dinner on the table. "Where's Ben?" The girls filled him in. "Jeepers, I hope he has some pictures of those tornadoes packed away in that chest. I'd love to see those." The girls glared at him, incredulous. "Sorry," he said, but they just continued to glare. It took a second, but then he got it. "Okay, okay I won't say anything to him." And then he stabbed a meatball and muttered something under his breath.

"What was that?" snapped Mary.

"Nothing," said Johnny.

After a fitful couple of hours, Ben drifted off and slept soundly through until morning.

Chapter 42: Holiday

MARY WOKE UP EARLY THE NEXT morning and found a recipe for cinnamon rolls on the Internet. Then she printed it out. And, she did it all by myself. *Techno-chick*. Three hours later, both Mary and the kitchen were dusted with flour, white from top to bottom. The rolls, however, were ready to be put into the oven. She brushed herself off as best she could. *I'll clean up the rest later*.

The rolls were regulation size, as big as softballs, and came out perfect. Mary frosted them and put them on the table still warm. Twenty minutes later, Johnny snatched up the last one—his fifth—devoured it in three bites, then downed his third glass of whole milk and burped as politely as possible. "Gee, Mary, those were awesome. Are there any more?"

"Anymore? I thought there'd be plenty left over for later. Next time I'll have to triple the recipe. Where do you put all that stuff, anyway?"

"I don't know," he said, then shrugged his shoulders and smiled. "Just hungry, I guess."

Ben laughed. "Like I keep tryin' to tell you, Mary, them teenage boys is eatin' machines." Ben gave his belly a satisfied pat. "In the boy's defense, though, those rolls were so damn good that I'd likely still be-a-eatin 'em myself if'in there was any left. Not that I need any more mind you." Mary rolled her eyes. "It's the truth girlie, you gonna' have to start giving me lessons soon," and even through her white-powdered face, Ben thought he saw a little blush come into her cheeks. He smiled and said nothing.

"Well," said Susan, "It's getting late. I better start studying."

"No studying today, girlie, it's a national holiday."

"No it's not."

Ben rose up from the table. "It is on this farm," he said, and then planted himself on a couch in the next room.

Mary laughed, "So, like, what's this national holiday called?"

"It's called national provisions day for juvenile deelinquents."

"What does that mean?" asked Mary.

"I think it means we're going shopping," said Susan. Mary turned to Ben, her wide eyes asking for conformation.

He nodded.

"Really? Shopping? Does that, like, mean clothes?"

"Yes it does. And toothpaste and toothbrushes and personal hy-giene products that I don't even want to know about and anything else y'all might be a-needin'"

"All right!"

"I thought you might like that."

"But what if someone recognizes us," asked Susan.

"Don't you be worryin' 'bout that. It's been a few days, and people forget pretty damn quick. Prob'ly be alright if we just went to one of the local malls. But as an extra pre-caution we'll drive on up to Fort Wayne where you guys ain't likely to be so popular."

"Are you sure it'll be okay?"

Ben nodded and smiled, "Besides. My guess is that miss fancy-pants here can alter your looks a tad 'fore we head out as a bit of extra in-surance. Am I right?" he said, looking at Mary.

"Deception is my middle name, sir."

"That's what I thought. Well all right then, we got a couple hours drive ahead of us and then shoppin' and gettin' back home, so we best get started." The kids evaporated from the table. Ben waited. Abigail didn't say anything, but he knew she was listening. *Don't you worry none, girl. I'm gonna' be at the bookstore a-buying' 'em out of whatever legal resources they gots so I can start-a-figurin' out what to do with these three young'uns.*

After the three delinquents had been made-over by Mary, Ben led them out about 300 yards into the cornfields where there was a hidden garage. They piled into his vintage-orange-1970 Chevy Nova. "Ain't drove this thing in a coon's age, but I bet she'll start right up." He grinned and turned the ignition on the classic Chevy 350 engine. The car roared to life, and they were off.

*****

At five thirty that evening they returned, undetected, from a successful shopping adventure. The kids were flush with clothes and whatever else they needed that he didn't want to know about. As for Ben, true to his promise, he'd come home with a stack of books on various aspects of the law; criminal, family, children's rights, adoption, wills, and a directory listing the best lawyers. And he'd been careful to keep it all under the radar because he didn't want to spook the kids.

"Y'all go on inside. I got to take care of Bessie." While Ben provided husbandry for his high maintenance Guernsey, the children went inside, unpacked, and put away their plunder.

The kids finished before Ben and decided to go out and see if he needed any help or, more likely, just to bother him. Walking towards the barn, Johnny patted his stomach a couple of times and looked at Mary. "You sure were right about those White Castle burgers, they were good." He paused a second for effect then added, "By the way, what are we having for dinner?"

"Jesus, Moonbrain, you just had ten Sliders, three fries, and a couple of milkshakes not an hour and a half ago."

Johnny grinned. "I was just kidding," and this time, he was.

"Nice one, Moonbrain," she said then went up on her tip toes and gave him a kiss on the cheek. Johnny blushed. She laughed.

How does she always manage to get the last laugh?

Ben watched the three of them as they slowly made their way to the barn, joking and jostling one another playfully, and turned to Bessie, "I reckon I feel about like that old Grinch must've felt the time his heart done growed," he paused, "how much was that, anyhow?"

"Moo moo moo."

"I think that's right, girl," he said, stroking her neck, "His heart done growed 'bout three times its size that day."

"Mooooo."

Johnny felt something in the air and stopped just short of the barn. The girls went on in, oblivious.

"So, Ben," said Susan, giving Bessie a friendly pat on the back, "how's your national provisions day for juvenile dee-linquents going?"

"Just fine, smarty-pants," he said, grinning, "I reckon

it's about the best holiday of any sort I've had in a long time." Susan smiled.

Mary wore a new sundress, light cotton, yellow with lacy trim and delicate flowers embroidered throughout tied off in front with a big yellow bow. She twirled around twice and it parachuted out like a big yellow parasol. She looked young and innocent, like a kid. All the sharp edges turned to melted butter. "Thanks for taking us shopping today," she said and twirled again. "How do you like it?"

"I like it a lot," said Ben, smiling and nodding. "Looks real nice on you."

"It's a bit different than your usual attire," said Susan, her voice dripping with sarcasm.

"I know. I'm not sure what got into me. It just, like, caught my eye, and I couldn't resist." She shrugged her shoulders, "Anyway, I kind of like it."

Ben finally noticed Johnny was missing. "Where's that boy anyway, I thought he was with ya'all."

"I thought he was too," said Mary.

"There he is," said Susan, pointing.

And there he was.

Chapter 43: More Strormy Weather

JOHNNY WAS STANDING OUTSIDE THE barn with his arms spread wide, spinning slowly, and staring up at the sky.

"I'll be dogged and flogged if'in he don't look like a damned human radar device."

Mary nodded agreement, "That's probably about right."

Johnny dropped his arms and made a bee line for the barn.

"Whoa now, slow down, boy, what's the matter?"

"Storm front moving in fast. A big one."

Ben stood up and sniffed the air. "Well," he said, "you might be right, but I don't feel nothin' yet."

"You will. I've never felt it change this fast before. When we got out of the car, there was nothing. I would've noticed if there was. But all of a sudden, the pressure is dropping fast. I can tell."

"Could be," said Ben, "I reckon we'll find out soon enough."

"I'm sure he's right," said Mary. "Johnny knows storms. He's like a living barmo . . . barato . . . "

"Barometer," said Susan.

"Right, barometer. Anyway, Johnny predicts storms better than the freaking National Weather Service. He's, like, totally awesome."

Ben cut his eyes to the boy, "Is that right?" Johnny nodded. "Well then, I guess we best be getting' us inside and let her rip. The nice thing about livin' underground is you're always safe from inclement weather." Then, looking back at Johnny, "As long as you're not doing something stupid."

"Like playing chicken with a tornado," Susan finished, and they all laughed.

Mary was looking up at the loft, pointing. "Do you think we could."

"You're a-wantin' to look at them pictures up there in the trunk, right?" Mary nodded. "Well, I reckon we'll be-a-needin' somethin' to do while we's a-waitin' for the storm to blow over."

"All right!"

"Suzie Q, why don't you help miss fancy pants bring

some of them photo albums out of the trunk so we can have us a look at 'em." The girls took off. Ben turned to Johnny. "You gonna' come inside with the rest of us sane folks?"

"Ah, well, I think I'll just stay out here for a while."

Ben looked at him hard. "Alright, but no cuttin' it close. If I have to come out here and fetch ya', you're gonna' find out just how mean I can be."

Inside, Ben took advantage of the facilities while the girls got a pitcher of tea and some cookies and set up at the kitchen table. "Let's do this one first," said Mary. It was the wedding album. Ben nodded. She opened it up and was surprised at how young they looked. The date was June 16, 1945. Ben wore his dress uniform from the Army: a perfectly pressed pair of olive-drab pants, brass-buttoned jacket, khaki shirt, and tie, with a Garrison cap atop his head.

"Wow," said Mary. "What a hunk you were."

"Handsome as the devil, ain't I?"

"And so young," noted Susan.

"I wasn't born old, you know," and he laughed. "I'd already been to war and back by then but I's still just 21 at the time. Always did look kind-a-young for my age, though," he said. "'Til recent, anyway."

"And that's Abigail?"

"Yep," said Ben, grinning. "She's a beauty, ain't she?"

"I'll say," said Mary, gawking at young Abigail. She had a petite girlish figure flattered even more so by the lily-white wedding gown trailing some twenty feet behind. Wavy, auburn hair flowed over both sides of her shoulders to mid torso and shimmered in the sun. And yet, with all of that, it was Abigail's face that captivated Mary. It wasn't a model's face—the cheeks were too full and there was the small, pointy nose—but she had an alluring smile and the biggest, brightest eyes Mary had ever seen—except maybe for hers.

The girls took turns picking out which books to look at. Ben gave a short vignette about each picture, including relevant historical context, and recounted each situation as if it were yesterday. Without intending to, he fell into his prize-winning storytelling voice, a beguiling mixture of highbrowed sophistication that, instead of trying to deny its country roots, embraced them, and by doing so was elevated to an even higher level. Its deep, resonating tones oozed out like honey and suffused the surroundings with a grace and nobility that transformed each image into a slice of history so vivid and real his listeners felt as if they'd had stepped into the picture and back in time. The girls were mesmerized, walking with a young, swashbuckling Ben Waller through the glorious early years of his life on the farm with his vexing bride, Abigail. Even Susan couldn't help but relax and enjoyed the process as much as Mary. "It's my turn," she said, batting Mary's hand out of the way and blowing the dust off another album, "This one."

"World War II memories, y'all come up with the damnedest choices." He handed it back to Susan, and she flipped it open to the first page. "These here is a bunch of clippings and pictures that Abigail put together for me. She was great at scrap booking." He sighed. "Got in touch with all my Army buddies' parents, had them send clippings out of every newspaper from Warshington DC to Warshington State. Ended up with a book that'd make Life Magazine proud."

"What's that?" asked Mary, pointing to a picture on the first page.

"That there is none other than Buckingham palace."

"Cool, what were you doing there?"

"They run out of regular barracks, so they had to house us there."

"Did not," said Mary, though she looked anything but certain.

"'Course they did," he said, and winked at Susan. "I'll bet Susan's done read all about it in her history books. Ain't that right, girl?"

"Liar," said Susan.

"I knew it," said Mary.

"So what were you doing in England?" asked Susan.

"It was 1943 and I'd just been there a couple of weeks. On that particular day, of course, I was just a-sightseein', but the reason they had us there was to start a-trainin' for some big mission. We didn't know at the time what the mission was but most of us figured it out before long. We was a-getting'-ready for the Normandy invasion."

"You mean D-Day?" asked Susan, her eyes widening.

"You bet your sweet life. Seemed like about a million of us over there getting ready for the big event. General Eisenhower didn't want to leave no room for doubt that, when the time come, we was gonna' take that ole' beach and get France back for the French. And we sure as hell did."

"Did you come out of one of those little boats like in Saving Private Ryan?" asked Mary.

"Yep, sure did."

"Wow, like, I guess you're lucky to be alive. Were the Germans shooting at you like in the movie?"

Ben closed his eyes and didn't say anything right away. The girls waited. "Yes, I'd say the movie was pert near right on target." He shook his head. "Let's move on, if'in you don't mind." Though Mary was dying for details, she knew better than to push. She turned the page, and Johnny burst into the room.

"Hey everybody, come quick, you gotta see this."

"What?" asked Susan.

"Storm clouds," answered Mary, rolling her eyes and sounding bored.

"How close?" asked Ben.

"It's fine, at least twenty or thirty minutes away. Come on!"

Ben shrugged his shoulders, "Well, I reckon it wouldn't hurt to have a quick peek. You girls coming'?"

"I am," said Susan.

"I'll pass," said Mary and she pulled another album from the pile and opened it.

"Suit yourself," said Ben and he and Susan joined Johnny and went outside.

Johnny was so excited he could hardly stand it. "See that over there?" He didn't wait for acknowledgement. "That's what you call a giant storm cell. It's so huge it's almost certain to spin off several tornadoes. Isn't it awsome?"

It was. Enormous swirls of dirty-cotton clouds hung over an orange sun-streaked horizon.

"How do you know how far away it is?" asked Susan.

"It's easy. I have a formula based on the visibility before everything turns black, the time of day, and the average speed of these fronts. I just plug in the numbers and do the arithmetic."

"You're worse than I am."

Ben laughed, "I don't know if I'd go that far." To which Susan gave him a playful backhand to the belly. They watched for about ten more minutes and the wind started to blow, and the first raindrops fell. "Okay, Suzy Q, you'd best getting' on back inside. Johnny and I got something to do here and then we'll be right behind you." He turned to Johnny, "Come on boy," he said and headed for the barn.

"Where are we going?"

"You don't think I'd leave Bessie out there all by herself do you?"

"You mean we're going to take her inside?"

"That's right."

"How are we going to do that?"

"Depends on what mood she's in, but it usually does take a bit of persuasion. Let's go."

*****

By the time Ben and Johnny coaxed and pushed and pulled Bessie down the stairs and into the safety of her indoor stall, the wind was blowing with purpose, and the sky was black. That was no surprise. It was Susan who shocked them, running from the living room and screaming, "She's gone."

"What in the Sam Hill are you talkin' about?"

"Mary, she's not here."

Johnny ran through the house yelling her name, looking under beds, in closets, and everywhere he could think of; he even checked in the hidden room behind the stove. While he was busy, Susan explained to Ben. "She was still at the table, sorting through the scrapbooks, you know, when we all went outside. I came back in expecting to see her there, but she wasn't. I figured she might be in the bathroom or something. But she's just not here." Susan looked up at Ben with pleading, wet eyes, "Where is she?"

"I don't know, darlin'," he said, and took her in his arms.

Ben made his way over to the table to see what Mary had been looking at. There was a picture of a young girl from an old newspaper clipping. The old man's heart missed a beat as his mind instantly made the connection. "I knew there was something familiar about that girl," he mumbled. He tried to hide his reaction, but Susan was too sharp.

"What is it?" she asked, and ran up to see.

He turned the book to the front. It was titled *The Wandering Girl*. "This was a gift from Abigail's older sister, who was also Henry's wife. She made it for me because it was something Abigail might have done. I never really understood, but thanked her for it anyways. Never even looked inside it until just now.

"I still don't get it." screamed Susan "What's it got to do with Mary."

Ben flipped back to the picture and gently tapped it with his finger. "That's Mary."

Susan scanned the article enough to get the general gist of what happened. The girl, Mary, eight-years-old at the time, had lost her entire family in some bizarre accident when a car, speeding through Mystic's quaint shopping district, jumped a curb and plowed into a small open-air cafe. The only reason the girl survived, it said, was because she'd been in the bathroom. The trauma of seeing her family wiped out had given her a rare and severe form of amnesia. No one noticed the girl when she emerged from the dust-cloud of bricks, and she'd just wandered off—walking the streets of Indianapolis for ten hours until collapsing on a bench where Michael Quackenbush, a Metro bus driver, found her and took her to the hospital.

Susan was stunned and horrified. Finallly she looked at Ben and said, "So you think she just wandered off again?"

"That would seem to be the case."

"Come on," said Johnny, who'd finished searching the house, "let's go. We don't have much time." Ben seemed to come alive and took off with Johnny, but Susan just stood there, paralyzed. "Come on Susan, we've got to find her."

"I know but I'm scared."

"We're all scared darlin', but you've been brave before, and you can do it again. Come on now, there's no time for discussion." It didn't look like she was going to move, but Johnny took her hand and pulled her along. When they got outside the wind had turned fierce, and the first rain droplets, big, fat, and cold, were coming down. Visibility was still fair, about a couple hundred feet, but wouldn't last long. "Damn."

Susan looked at the cornfields stretching out in all directions. "It's worse than a needle in a haystack. She could have gone anywhere."

"Look," said Johnny, "if I came out walking around in a stupor I think I would go with the wind. She's probably out there somewhere." He pointed off to their right, where rows and rows of harvest-ready corn were bending in the wind.

"It's still so big. We'll never find her."

"I think Johnny's right," said Ben. He looked around and his eyes lighted on something. "We've still got a chance if we can get us a good line-o-sight down between the rows, but we have to hurry. Johnny, you go get the tractor and meet us behind the barn. I got an idea."

Ben grabbed Susan by the arm a jerked her along with him. "Come on Suzie-Q, this is no time to be a-fretting."

"Ouch," she said, snapping out of her own little funk. She ran with Ben to the barn.

Ben pointed to the side wall of the barn, where some coils of rope were hanging. "While I'm getting the trailer out, you grab us two of them coils, at least ten foot long each, and meet me out back." Susan did as she was told then helped him pull the trailer around. It was a rickety old flatbed, and Ben could see what she was thinking. "It don't look like much," he was shouting now, in order to be heard over the wind. "But it'll hold up for what we need it to do. Don't you worry."

About a minute later, though it seemed interminable, Johnny arrived with the tractor. Ben hitched the trailer up to the back then motioned for Johnny to jump down and for Susan to hand him the ropes, which they did. Ben climbed up into the driver's seat and looped the ropes around a pair of long braces that stabilized the steering column on each side. "Okay," he said, handing one of the loose ends to Johnny and one to Susan. "Now hang on to the rope and stand right here," and pointed to a plate about 12 inches wide that covered the rear axle on each side. Johnny stepped up onto the plate, "Good," said Ben. "Now reel in your rope in a bit and let your feet rest on the edge of the plate so you's leaning back 'bout thirty degrees." Johnny did. "Perfect, now hang on." Ben indicated for Susan to do the same, but she couldn't seem to move.

"Come on Susan," said Johnny, "you can do it."

"I can't."

Johnny jumped off his mount. In one motion, he lifted Susan up, set her down on the plate already tilted back at the right angle, and handed her the reins. He saw how scared she was but that didn't matter. He'd figured out what Ben had in mind, and they needed two sets of eyes to do it. The words were simple but spoken with the ferocity of a roaring lion, right in the girl's face. "Do...not...let...go." Susan became one with the tractor and her rope. Johnny remounted his side. The tractor lurched, and they were off.

"I'm going to drive perpendicular through the rows of corn. Johnny, you look down the rows to the left, Susan to the right. It's the only way we can cover any ground." Just then it started to pour, huge drops of rain coming down so hard they stung. The front end of the tractor breached the first row of corn, "Hang on tight now, 'cause it'-a going to get rough."

"What do we do if we see her," yelled Susan.

"Scream," said Ben. The fields were bumpy, and it was all Johnny could do to hang on. He glanced over at Susan, to see how she was faring: solid as steel, as if he'd literally riveted her in place. The tractor slowly bounced through row after row, knocking down a four-foot swath through the corn as it went. Occasionally, one of the stalks sprang back up and slapped Johnny or Susan in the face, but with everything else going on, they hardly noticed. Meanwhile, the wind picked up to near gale-force. The rain began pouring down in buckets, and visibility went from bad to worse.

Damnitall to hell, thought Ben, *I'm gonna get us all kilt if we don't get back purdy soon.* "I'm afraid we's-a gonna to have to give this thing up directly," he yelled.

"Not until we find her," the two teens shouted back in unison.

"Five more minutes, that's all," he said. Then Susan screamed. Ben whipped his head around thinking she'd fallen off the tractor. She hadn't. She was pointing down a row of corn.

"There she is, stop, stop!" The tractor stopped abruptly, and all three of them jumped off at once. Mary was splayed out in the mud like a rag doll. No one said it, but they all wondered the same thing: *is she alive?*

Johnny got there first. "She's alive, she's breathing," he said and then Ben and Susan were right beside him. "But she's not talking, or doing anything." Her eyes were open but glassy and unfocused. Johnny picked her up as if she were light as air.

"You gonna be okay with her?" asked Ben.

"I'm fine," yelled Johnny, "you go get the tractor turned around." He knew that would be a difficult and time-consuming job. Ben was off like an eighty-two-year-old rabbit.

Susan stayed with Johnny."Are you okay? You need any help?"

"I'm fine," he groaned, "just stay behind me."

Trudging through the broken corn was harder than Johnny thought it would be, like walking through thigh deep water against a strong undertow. It didn't matter. He would keep on going no matter what. But then Susan screamed again and jumped on his back, and he nearly did drop Mary. "For crying out loud, what are you doing?"

Susan just pointed. Johnny turned his head to look. Not one, but two funnel clouds were dancing in the sky, trying to decide whether or not to touch down. This time when Johnny saw them, his only wish was that they would disappear. With Susan on his back and Mary still in his arms, he started running like a deer.

Ben had the tractor turned around and ready when they got there. Susan jumped up on the flatbed and helped lift Mary up. She cradled her friend's head tightly in her lap while Johnny held Mary's limp body down as best he could. "Okay," yelled Ben, "here we go," and they were off.

Johnny watched the twin twisters as they bounced out of the cornfield. It was hard for him to keep to his own body on from flying off the flatbed, let alone Mary, but he managed. One of the funnels decided to go back where it belonged, but the other touched down about half way to the barn and was chasing them. A big, surly, elephant's trunk of a twister close enough so that Johnny could see the individual ears of corn flying around its base like they were in a blender. He daren't tell Ben for fear the old man might have a heart attack if he saw what was chasing them. Heck, anyone might have a heart attack. He looked at Susan. One hand was gripped tightly to a little hole in the flatbed; her other arm wrapped around Mary's head like a vice. Johnny smiled then looked back a tornado and almost went into cardiac arrest himself. He watched as it broke out of the cornfield and into the open about 500 yards behind them. *What am I, some kind of tornado magnet? Go away!* The tractor lurched to a stop. "Susan, you get the doors. I've got Mary. Go!"

This time Susan did not hesitate. She jumped off the flatbed and had the doors open before Johnny was done telling her to. "Here, hand me the girl," said Ben, "then jump out and don't look behind you. He did and Ben handed Mary back to him. Johnny did not need to look. He could hear the barn breaking apart less than 50 yards behind them. Ben and Johnny ran down the stairs while Susan held the door open then let it slam shut when everyone was in. It was pitch black and Bessie's mournful mooing ricocheted off the walls of the concrete stairwell like a wailing Super Ball. For a moment, the roar above them rose to a deafening level, and the ground shook. It was like a freight train ran right over the top of them, which, as it turned out, was not far from the truth. But they were inside.

They were safe.

Chapter 44: A Bedtime Story

Susan guided Johnny through the dark to a couch where he laid Mary down. Ben found some candles, lit them, and then he and Susan rounded up a bunch of pillows and comforters and blankets and brought them out to the great room. "I think we should all stay here, together, tonight," said Ben and, even on the dimly candlelit faces of the children, the relief was obvious.

Johnny saw Mary's lids flutter. He spoke softly. "Mary? Mary, are you awake?" She looked at him, and though he couldn't hear her voice, he was able read her lips, "Is that you, dad?" She said.

Johnny didn't know whether to go along with her or not so he stayed neutral. "Everything is going to be okay." He knew at once it was the wrong thing to do. Mary's eyes grew wide and scared, darting around the room.

Ben and Susan kneeled with Johnny, in front of Mary. "Daddy?" said Mary, this time looking at Ben.

Ben looked at Johnny, who nodded and motioned for Ben to go along with it. "Daddy's right here. Everything is going to be okay. I promise."

"Are mommy and Sarah okay?"

"This is Sarah," said Susan, "I'm fine. Mommy's here too." She nudged Johnny.

"That's right," he said, in a rather bizarre falsetto, "we're all here with you. Everything is going to be all right."

"You sound funny, mommy."

Susan piped up, "Don't you remember, silly? Mommy has a cold. That's why she sounds funny."

"Oh, I forgot. Daddy, could you tell me a story?"

"What kind of story would you like, darlin'?"

"Do a pretend story."

Ben took in a breath. "Once upon a time," he started. He told her a story about three beautiful children who were very brave. All they had was each other. One day they ran into a grumpy old farmer and asked if he would help them. At first, he wasn't sure, but then he took them in. The reason the farmer was so grumpy was that he'd lost his family, too, and was lonely. Soon he found that he loved the children, and the four of them became a new kind of family. But there was a problem. The farmer was very, very old and knew that he couldn't take care of the children forever. So guess what he did?"

"He made sure that, before he died, the children would always be okay."

"That's exactly right."

Mary smiled, and her body relaxed. "Okay, I love you daddy," she said then closed her eyes and though she was snoring soundly, Ben continued.

"This is how he did it. He found the best lawyer in the world and she helped get the children through all of their legal mess." He looked at Johnny, "And let me tell you, it was a big mess. But, in the end, she found the children a good place to stay where they would always be together."

"What happened to the old farmer?" asked Susan.

"As for the old farmer, he was never a grumpy again. Soon after the children were settled he died a happy old man and joined his beautiful wife, Abigail, in heaven, and they watched over the children as they grew up to live happy, healthy, productive lives. The end."

Susan and Ben soon joined Mary in a sonorous slumber. They looked content and peaceful. Johnny, however, who no longer believed in fairytales, could not sleep.